The Sin Eater's Daughter

Melinda Salisbury

SCHOLASTIC

First published in the UK in 2015 by Scholastic Children's Books
An imprint of Scholastic Ltd
Euston House, 24 Eversholt Street,
London, NW1 1DB, UK
Registered office: Westfield Road, Southam, Warwickshire, CV47 0RA
SCHOLASTIC and associated logos are trademarks
and/or registered trademarks of Scholastic Inc.

ISBN 978 1407 147635

A CIP catalogue record for this book is available from the British Library.

Printed and bound by CPI Group (UK) Ltd, Croydon, CR0 4YY
Papers used by Scholastic Children's Books are made
from wood grown in sustainable forests.

1 3 5 7 9 10 8 6 4 2

This is a work of fiction. Names, characters, places, incidents
and dialogues are products of the author's imagination or are
used fictitiously. Any resemblance to actual people, living
or dead, events or locales is entirely coincidental.

www.scholastic.co.uk

The Sin Eater's Daughter

For my Nana,
Florence May Kiernan

Chapter 1

Even when there are no prisoners, I can still hear the screams. They live in the walls like ghosts and echo in between footsteps. If you travel down deep into the belly of the castle, beneath the barracks where the guards sleep, beneath the Telling Room, that is where they linger behind the quiet moments.

The first time I was brought down here I asked my guards what they did to make them scream so. One of them, Dorin, had looked at me and shook his head, his lips pressed together so tightly they turned white, his pace quickening towards the Telling Room. I remember at the time feeling a thrill of fear, the idea of something so terrible, so horrifying that even my calm, strong guard couldn't say it aloud. I promised myself that I'd find out, that I'd discover this dark secret hidden underground. In my thirteenth harvest year I was naïve. Hopelessly, blindly naïve.

When I first came to the castle, many, many moons ago, I was awed by it, by the decor and the beauty and the richness of it all. There are no rushes on the floor here, no straw embedded with lavender and basil to keep it sweet-smelling. The queen demanded carpets, rugs, runners woven especially for her to tread upon and so our footsteps are muted as we walk.

The walls behind the rich red and blue tapestries are grey stone, flecked with mica that flashes when the servants pull the hangings aside to wash the walls. Gilt and gold adorn the antlered candelabras above my head; cushions are velvet and tasselled and replaced as soon as the pile is rubbed the wrong way. Everything is faultless and pristine; everything is kept ordered and beautiful. The roses in the tall crystal vases are all cut to the same length, all the exact same colour and arranged the same way. There is no room in this castle for things that are not perfect.

My guards walk carefully at my sides, holding their bodies rigid and keeping a good distance between me and them. If I raised an arm to reach for one of them they would recoil in horror. If I tripped, or fainted, if reflex sabotaged them and they tried to help me, it would be a death sentence for them. They would find themselves with their throats slit where they stood as an act of mercy. Compared to a slow death by my poisonous skin, a slit throat would be lucky.

Tyrek was not lucky.

*

2

In the Telling Room my guards move to stand against the door and the queen's apothecary, Rulf, nods curtly towards the stool I am to take, before turning his back on me and checking his equipment. The walls are lined with shelves containing jars of murky substances, strange powders and unnamed leaves, all jumbled together with no obvious order to them. Nothing is labelled, at least not that I can see in the dim light the candles cast, for there are no windows this deep under the castle. At first I thought it strange that something like the Telling would be performed here, hidden away in warren-like passages carved underground, but now I understand it. If I were to fail. . . Best for that not to happen where the court, the kingdom, could witness it. Better for it to happen in this secret little room, halfway between the underworld of the dungeons and the relative paradise of the Great Hall.

As I arrange my skirts around me on the stool, one of my guards, the younger one, scuffs the floor with his feet, the sound too loud in the stone chamber. Rulf turns, dealing him a sharp glance and as he looks away he catches my eye. His gaze is blank when it skims over me, his face a mask, and I suspect even if he weren't mute he'd have nothing to say to me now.

Once he would have smiled and shaken his head as Tyrek told me about the trees he'd climbed and the pastries he'd filched from the kitchen. He'd have waved a hand at Tyrek to tell him to stop showing off, even as his eyes shone with affection for his only son. Though the Telling itself only

3

takes a few moments, I used to stay down there for an hour, sometimes two, sitting opposite Tyrek, two arms' lengths between us as we exchanged stories. My guards would hover close by, keeping one curious eye on Rulf as he went about his experiments and the other on Tyrek and me as we chatted. Back then I had nowhere to be after the Telling, save my temple or my room, and there was nothing to stop me having those few stolen hours down in the Telling Room under my guards' careful watch. But things are different now; these days I have other demands on my time.

I keep my eyes down as Rulf performs the Telling, cutting my arm and catching a few drops of my blood in the bowl held beneath it before he carries it across the room. He'll add a single drop of blood to the Morningsbane, deadly poison with no earthly antidote, before bringing the mixture to me. I wait silently, my head bent as he mixes the blood and poison together, as he decants it into a vial. I hold still as he approaches me and drops the vial into my lap. I lift it, the oily liquid crystal clear in the candlelight, no sign my blood is even in there. I remove the stopper and drink.

We all pause, watching and waiting to see if the poison will take me this time. It doesn't; I play my part to the letter. I place the vial on the table beside my stool, smoothing my skirts down and looking to my guard.

"Are you ready, my lady?" Dorin, the elder of my guards, asks, his face eerily pale in the torchlight. The Telling is over, but I have another duty to perform and I feel Rulf's baleful glance on my back as I leave the Telling Room.

I nod and we walk to the stairwell, Dorin at my right and the second guard, Rivak, to my left. And then we descend to the dungeons where the prisoners wait. For me.

As we arrive outside the Morning Room we startle the servants removing the last of the captive's final meal. They press themselves against the wall when they see me, their heads bowed and their knuckles whitening on the dirty plates and goblets as they scurry past. Dorin nods at Rivak and he enters the small chamber. A mere moment later he appears in the doorway and nods the all-clear.

Two men sit at a small wooden table, both clad from neck to ankle in full-sleeved black shifts, their arms bound to those of the chairs. Their eyes rise slowly to meet mine as my guards take up their stations by the door, both with their swords drawn, though I'm as safe here as I am anywhere, even with criminals, traitors to the crown and realm.

"As Daunen Embodied I offer you blessing." I try to sound regal and strong, righteous in contrast to the churning in my stomach. "Your sins won't be eaten when you are gone, but I can offer you the blessings of the Gods. They will forgive you, in time."

Neither man looks grateful for my words and I can't blame them for it; the words are hollow and we all know it. Without the Eating they're damned, regardless of my blessing. I wait to see if they will speak. Others have cursed me, or pleaded for my intervention, pleaded for clemency. I've been begged to let them die by the sword or the rope – one desperate soul even asked for the dogs – but these men say nothing, keeping their flat eyes on me. One man has a tic above his left eye, making the eyebrow twitch, but that's the only sign that either of them cares that I am here.

When they say nothing, do nothing, I bow my head. I thank the Gods for blessing me and then I take my place behind the condemned, standing between them. I reach out, resting the palm of each hand on the back of the men's necks, curling my fingers around to cup them, seeking out the hollow in their throats where I can feel the blood pulsing through the veins beneath their skin. Their heartbeats are almost synchronized as I close my eyes and wait. When their pulses begin to quicken – again in near-perfect harmony – I step away, bunching my hands under my sleeves, the itch to wash them immediate.

It doesn't take long.

Moments after I've touched them they are slumped against the top of the table, blood streaming from their noses and pooling on the already-stained wood. I watch as a thin red river flows over the edge, spattering the bolts that pin the chairs to the floor. If it wasn't for those bolts, and the ropes binding the legs of the dead to those of the chairs, their bodies would be at my feet now. Morningsbane is a violent poison. The eyes of the man whose eyebrow had twitched are open and staring and it is only when my own start to burn that I realize I'm staring too. It doesn't matter how many men, women and children I execute, it still tears at me inside. But then I suppose it would, because every time I perform an execution it's as though I'm killing Tyrek all over again.

Tyrek was my only friend, one of the two people at the castle who were always pleased to see me. My position in the court meant we could never be in each other's company outside of the short time I spent in the Telling Room. But in the Telling Room I would see him and we could talk about everything we'd seen and, in his case, done. I'd never met anyone like him; he was fearless and opinionated and, back then, the days between each Telling lasted for ever. They dragged by until my guards escorted me down and there he would be, waiting in the doorway, grinning at me and pushing his blond hair out of his face impatiently.

"There you are," he'd say. "Hurry up. I've got something to show you."

He'd wanted to be one of my guards when he was old enough and he'd taken great delight in challenging them to fights, him with his wooden training sword and them with their steel. I would sit on my stool, grinning at their antics while his father took my blood for the Telling.

"And then thrust." He'd jabbed his sword towards Dorin, who'd parried it easily. "Obviously I wasn't trying to hurt you then."

"Obviously," Dorin agreed, and I laughed.

"And then sweep, and then thrust, and then sweep back and then – ha!" he'd crowed when he managed to prod Dorin in the arm.

I had clapped as Dorin held his sword out. "I yield."

7

"See, my lady," Tyrek turned to me. "I'll be able to keep you safe."

On the day my world caved in, he didn't call for me to hurry up, or tell me how hard he'd been practising; he didn't look at me at all. For the first time during the two harvests I'd been at the castle he didn't grin at me; he bowed. I should have known then that there was danger ahead but I didn't see it. I thought it was part of a new game; that we were playing at chivalry. I'd bowed back to him, acting the lady, excited in a way I couldn't explain. Even Rulf's silence was different and he'd pulled Tyrek away from me before he took my blood, handing the bowl to Tyrek to carry to the Telling table.

When the door flew open and the Queensguard rushed in, my first thought was that we were under attack and I'd raised my hands to defend myself. Something smashed as the guards rushed past me and I'd twisted in my seat in time to watch them seize Tyrek, his face grey with fear, his father motionless beside him.

"What is this?" I'd cried but the soldiers ignored me, dragging my friend to the door.

I'd darted between them – my presence was enough to stop them in their tracks. "Unhand him and explain yourselves," I'd demanded, but they'd shaken their heads.

"The queen has ordered that he should be arrested," one had said.

I'd laughed. The idea of Tyrek having done wrong was too much, too ridiculous.

"On what charge?"

"Treason."

There was a choking sound from behind them and I'd moved involuntarily towards where Rulf stood clutching his chest, one hand braced against the wooden counter. When I'd turned back the soldiers were moving again, Tyrek gripped between them like a straw doll, shaking his head from side to side.

I'd moved to follow but Dorin had stepped between me and the door, holding out his sword.

"My lady," he'd said, a warning in his eyes and I'd stopped.

"Take me to the queen," I'd said and he'd nodded.

But there was no need, for as we left the Telling Room she had appeared in the corridor, alone, as if my demand had summoned her. Her face was beatific and still above a gown of white-and-gold silk. She'd looked like a May Fire bride, innocent and angelic, and I'd been relieved to see her; she must have realized this was all a mistake and come to pardon Tyrek herself.

As I'd opened my mouth to thank her for coming she'd thrown up a hand; the motion sliced through the air and silenced me. "Follow me," she'd commanded, sweeping past us, and we had to, hurrying to keep up with her. When we'd reached the bottom of the stairwell she'd stopped abruptly. I'd nearly stumbled into her and I'd heard my guard's sharp gasp behind me as he came to a sudden halt too.

"Leave us," she'd ordered my guards and they'd turned immediately and left, climbing the stairs we'd just descended.

I'd looked at her, waiting, a creeping feeling stroking my spine, warning me of danger.

"For two harvests I have held back part of your role, Twylla. I wanted to be sure you understood the gift you've been given and could bear the burden of it." She'd paused, her eyes searching mine before she continued. "Because that gift comes with a cost. The price, if you will, of what it means to be special, to be chosen. But womanhood is fast approaching and I can protect you from it no longer. Now you must truly act as Daunen Embodied."

I had kept my eyes on her, not understanding what she meant about costs and prices. I took the poison as she willed; I did everything she wanted. What more was there?

"The boy in the room at the end of this hall has committed treason," she'd said, raising a hand to stop me from interrupting her, "though I know you won't want to believe it, trust me when I tell you that I have been thorough in my investigations and there can be no doubt of it. What is more, you have been party to it." She allowed her words to sink in.

"He has probed you for your secrets – our secrets – courted your friendship and all the while he has been trading your words to our enemies."

"He wouldn't! He can't have! I've told him nothing. . . I know no secrets."

"You have been his cloak and his informer, Twylla. Fortunately you are right: you know little of consequence. But it remains that you have told him of your life and duties

10

here – secret, sacred rites that concern us deeply. And so you must be the one to mete out the punishment. Being Daunen Embodied means more than singing, more than praying. There is more to proving yourself than merely taking the Morningsbane. Both it, and you, have another purpose.

I had stared at her, trying to understand. What more? What punishment could I give out? Then with clear, cold horror I realized she meant for me to touch my friend.

Ever since I'd arrived at the castle I had taken the Morningsbane once every moon to prove to the kingdom I was Daunen Embodied, truly the Gods' choice. It was the mixing of my blood, the drinking of the poison and surviving it that showed I was divine, something more than a girl.

I'd thought the price I paid for my new life at the castle was that I could never touch anyone, because the poison I took willingly stayed in my skin and would kill anyone who came into contact with it, save for those also blessed by divine right: the queen, the king and the prince. It didn't seem such a terrible price, to not touch and not be touched; after all I'd left behind the only person who'd ever shown me love and affection. But that wasn't the price at all.

The price was that I *would* touch and I would do it deliberately. I would touch on command, knowing full well that it would kill. There is no antidote for Morningsbane, even the lightest brush against my skin is enough to kill a grown man in seconds. And that was the extent of my role, the price I paid for being favoured by the Gods; I was to become an executioner. A killer. A weapon.

"I can't," I'd said finally.

"You must, Twylla. Because I cannot vouch for your safety from the poison in your veins if you deny your duty to the Gods. It is their will that keeps you immune to it. It is their will that you do this for them."

"But surely they—"

"Enough, Twylla," the queen had snapped. "To be Daunen means to do this. Every incarnation of Daunen since we began has been both hope and justice. You are here to show the kingdom we live in a blessed age. And you are here to strike down those who would hurt us. You will go and do your duty. You don't want to anger the Gods, do you?"

"No."

The queen had nodded. "Your dedication does you credit, Twylla."

"No, I mean I can't," I heard myself say. "I can't kill someone."

"I beg your pardon?"

"I don't think I can be Daunen Embodied if that is what it means. I'm not right for this."

The queen had laughed: a brittle, crooked sound. "Do you believe the Gods have chosen wrong? Do you believe it a mistake that you survive the Morningsbane at the Telling? And what of your family, your little sister? Will you truly sacrifice the food and coin I send them because you don't like the Gods' path for you?" She'd shaken her head at me. "You know you can't go back," she'd said softly. "The Gods would never allow it. They gave you to me, to Lormere, and I

12

accepted you. You came here with no dowry, no alliances for us to make. And yet I accepted you because this is what you were born for, Twylla. We obey the Gods. As must you."

"But—"

Her eyes had stolen the words from my mouth.

"I'm going to forget you attempted to question me," she'd said quietly. "I'm going to forget you spurned my generosity and patronage. I'm going to forget that you were ungrateful. I am going to be merciful. Pray the Gods will be too."

I did as she asked. I entered the barren room where my best friend was tied to a chair, his mouth cruelly gagged with dark cloth that cut into his cheeks, his eyes streaming with tears. His wrists were already red where he'd pulled against the ropes that bound him. He'd wet himself; the front of his breeches were stained dark with urine and I had blushed, ashamed for him. His head shook wildly from side to side as I approached. He was fifteen, the same age as me. The queen stood in the doorway and watched as I placed my hands on his neck, the only exposed skin I could see. When nothing happened I thought the Gods had intervened, proving him innocent. Then he had shuddered, his body convulsing and jerking, and I'd pulled my hands away but it was too late. Blood trickled from his nose and his mouth, and he was dead before me. It had taken less than a minute for my touch to kill him.

I was still staring at him with wide, unseeing eyes when the queen cleared her throat.

"You needed to be the one to do it. To see what it meant to be chosen. You cannot take it back, not now. This is your destiny."

Two harvests have passed since I executed my best friend. Twenty-four Tellings. Twenty-four times I've had to walk into the room Tyrek was dragged from and take the poison that made it possible for my touch to kill him. I've killed thirteen traitors, including the men today and Tyrek, in those twenty-four moons. For Lormere. For my people. For my Gods.

Because I am Daunen Embodied, the reborn daughter of the Gods. The world has always been ruled by two Gods, Dæg, Lord of the Sun, who rules in the day and his wife, Næht, Empress of Darkness, who rules the nights. And once, millennia and millennia ago, when Lormere was nothing more than a collection of feuding villages, greedy Næht decided that ruling the night was not enough for her. She hatched a plan and seduced her husband, tiring him so much he couldn't rise. Then she took the skies for her own and ruled alone, plunging all of the world into darkness. Nothing lived, nothing thrived and death was everywhere without the Lord of the Sun to light the world and give warmth and joy to the people.

But as Næht seduced Dæg she conceived a daughter, Daunen. And when Daunen was born her song as she entered the world woke Dæg from his slumber and he rose back to his place in the sky. Dæg's return brought light and life back to Lormere and in his gratitude he vowed that whenever

14

Lormere needed her most, he would return the spirit of his daughter to the world as a symbol of hope. They would know her by her red hair – hair the colour of sunrise – and by her voice – a voice so beautiful it could waken a God. They would call her Daunen Embodied in her returned form and she would be a blessing to the land.

However, Daunen was the child of two Gods, light and dark, life and death. When Dæg vowed to return his daughter to the world, Næht insisted Daunen Embodied must represent her too. So Daunen exists as the balance between both God and Goddess; she must be death on behalf of her mother, as she is life on behalf of her father. Each moon, Daunen Embodied must prove herself chosen by taking the Morningsbane and living despite it. And she must keep the poison in her skin so that that her touch would mean death to traitors, as her mother's touch is death.

Of the two guards with me on the day the queen had me kill Tyrek, one chose to leave his role almost immediately. But before he did he told me why the prisoners screamed so loudly. He'd waited until Dorin had gone to fetch my supper and then he'd leant in, as close as he dared, smiling viciously.

"You want to know why they scream?" He hadn't waited for my response. "The queen's men cut them. They take the bluntest knife they can find and they cut them, wherever they please." He'd grinned. "And in those cuts they pour brandy. And it stings. By the Gods, how it stings. Brandy burns, little girl. It's liquid fire in the throat; in a cut, a deep, messy cut it's hotter than Dæg himself. Not nice. Not nice at all. Sometimes they have to do it again and again, for the especially bad ones."

He'd paused, licking his lips as he watched my face to see how deep his words cut me.

"But that's not why they scream. They scream because of you. Because no matter what the torturers do to them, it's nothing compared to what you'll do. So tell me, little girl, does that explain to you why they scream?"

I never told anyone what he told me. I'd seen enough death on my account. Sometimes I can show mercy. Like the queen.

Chapter 2

I'm standing in my solar, scrubbing my hands, rinsing, repeating it again and again in the small basin when there's a knock on the door.

"Enter." I reach for a cloth to dry them, though they still don't feel clean, as I turn to greet my visitor.

Dorin stands before me, bending into a small bow.

"Forgive the interruption. A hunt has been called, my lady."

"Now?" I look at him. I can't think of anything I want to do less than chase an innocent creature through the woods. I continue rubbing the cloth over my hands, hoping his next words will be to tell me that I don't have to go, that he's merely letting me know the queen's plans for the day.

"The queen has insisted you attend, my lady."

I turn away, closing my eyes and then opening them again when the eyes of the dead men stare back at me. Why is

there a hunt today? We rarely hold them at all, but today. . .?
I want to go to my temple. I want to close the doors and think
of nothing. I want my hands to feel clean.

"I'll leave you to prepare, my lady," Dorin says and retreats.

I stare after him, a knot forming in my stomach. There's
no point trying to send a message to plead my absence, to
beg to be allowed to go to my temple. She knows I'll come.
I could have sent one man or a hundred to their deaths this
morning and still I'll go because she has ordered me to. My
family can't afford to lose the coin and food she sends to
them each moon and she'd withhold it if I displeased her –
she has before. She knows I won't risk my sister suffering any
more than she has to on my behalf; she knows the guilt I feel
for leaving Maryl behind. She knows *me* and I'm a good little
puppet, easy to control if you know which strings to pull –
and the string attached to my sister is the one to tug for my
obedience. But even if that weren't the case, she speaks with
the Gods' authority. It is their will that I take life. If this is
what they will I can't challenge it.

When I leave the room, my cloak around my shoulders,
only Dorin waits for me.

"Where's Rivak?" I ask, looking for my other guard.

Dorin purses his lips. "Reassigned, my lady."

Today keeps getting better and better, I think to myself,
though I'm not surprised. Almost all of my guards have left
within a few moons of taking on their duty. Though the men
the queen chooses are trained to kill, quickly and without
mercy, only one man I know is strong enough to stay in the

18

company of a girl who could kill him with a single touch. . .
The rest petition for reassignment and it's always granted. It's
my belief that the queen prefers it that way. After all, a guard
that stayed with me might stop fearing me, might even grow
fond of me and switch his allegiance to me. She could never
allow that.

Save for once; once she allowed it – though I doubt she
realizes.

Dorin has been with me from the beginning. He's older
than the king, grizzled, streaks of grey in his neatly trimmed
beard and at his temples. He has kept his hair long, wearing
it tied at the nape of his neck, and his eyes are hazel and
watchful. He is the consummate guard, gruff and professional,
and I know we're not friends, but we are something. I live in
fear of the day he'll be taken from me too. We know each
other's movements now; it would be hard to wrong-foot him.
Like a long-married couple we know how the other dances
and I don't have to fear him making a mistake.

"So it's just you and I then?" I say.

"Temporarily, my lady. Trials were held yesterday and I
believe the new guard will join us later today. I'm to take him
through the role while you are at the hunt. The Queensguard
will be your escort there, as always."

"Was Rivak reassigned after the Telling?" I say, trying to
keep my voice level.

"He requested to be moved some time ago, my lady, but
the queen had not yet approved a new guard. I understand
she has now."

"How long do you think this one will last?" I smile ruefully.

"Not as long as you deserve, my lady. Come, we don't want to keep Their Majesties waiting." He smiles quickly, kindly, and I feel the knot inside my stomach tighten.

He walks ahead of me down the stairs and I keep back, my hands by my sides as I follow carefully, praying to the Gods that I can keep him.

The party is assembled, the ladies clad in green and silver, the men in hunting blue and gold, and me in my scarlet cloak. The queen likes me in red; she believes it emphasizes my role, and so most of my gowns and cloaks are red. The dogs lope around the king, snapping their jaws, their eyes trained on him, waiting for his word. I hate those dogs, more than almost anything.

They are different from the dogs in the village near where I grew up; they won't cower at a cross word, or show their bellies for a kind one. These dogs have long, heavily muscled legs; their large heads are flat and broad. Part Alaunt, part mastiff, part something wilder and deadlier, their fur is coarse, speckled and mottled with brown and gold. I'd get no pleasure from stroking them, even if they allowed it. Their mouths grin and leer and there's nothing behind their eyes – looking into them feels the same as looking into the eyes of the men I executed this morning. They are blank, without conscience, without soul.

I know all about souls. Before I became Daunen Embodied, I was the Sin Eater's daughter.

The smell of the dogs fills the hall, musky and rancid with meat and death, and I see the queen cover her face with a delicate shawl. The dogs dislike dead flesh. They prefer to eat the life from their victims as they pull them down, and they are always eager to hunt. They know what it means to be gathered here and their excitement, their pacing and circling, leaves a bitter taste in my mouth. I hope today they aren't hunting for a man, or a woman. I hope today they are hunting for an animal.

When I first saw the queen set the dogs after a prisoner – a thief who'd plundered one of the lord's manors – I nearly vomited my breakfast on to the floor of the hall. I knew she did it, the whole realm knew the queen's punishments were unusually cruel, but to see them, smell them, hear them as they ripped the man apart was too much. Even for someone like me, it was too much. Dorin had covered for me, telling the queen I had complained of being unwell all morning. I was sent back to bed to rest; a healer was dispatched to poke at me with a glass rod and feed me tea brewed with rank-smelling herbs. Since then I've been haunted by nightmares of the dogs coming after me, after my sister, after Tyrek, after Dorin. I wake bathed in my own sweat and shaking, convinced I can smell them in the room. No crime deserves that fate, no matter what the queen says. But then I'm sure the people would say the same about what I do, even if it is traitors to the realm that I execute.

"Twylla," the cold, clipped voice of the queen calls and I

dip into a low bow, a reaction born of the same instinct that makes a mouse cleave to the ground when it hears the hoot of an owl. "Blessed Telling," she says and the court murmurs it after her. "You may go to the temple after the hunt."

I lower my head further in acknowledgement. "Thank you, Your Majesty."

Two of her guards walk to my side, keeping an embarrassing amount of space between us. When the great wooden doors open we descend the stairs to the horses that are saddled and waiting, the queen and her guard, me and mine, and then the rest of the court.

I climb on to the broad back of my mount without help; the Queensguard stand dumbly watching me struggle, then urge my horse forward to join the queen's train. Horses are immune to Morningsbane and I run my fingers through the tips of her mane where it falls on to my skirts. It's pleasant to touch something warm, something living, and know she won't suffer under my touch.

Blank eyes staring, blood dripping on to stained wood.

I shudder and my fingers tighten on the mare's mane, but the action draws the queen's gaze and I flick the hair away and wind the reins around my fingers instead.

She leads us off ahead of the king and the hounds and I breathe a soft sigh of relief. I'm glad today we ride out separately and don't follow the men as they hunt, and I suspect I'm not the only one. The laughter of the dogs unsettles the horses even more than it does their riders. And there have been times when they've tired of their quarry and take down a horse and rider.

As we ride I gaze up at the mountains. We are bordered on three sides by them; they cradle the realm like a new mother would her child. The town of Lortune and Lormere castle sit at the most easterly point of Lormere, and parts of the castle are built into the rocks, so it seems as though the sprawling outbuildings are born of the mountain itself and trying to escape it.

"A natural fortress," my mother once said. "Lormere will never fall because of the mountains."

We're lucky with the geography of the kingdom, or so I'm told. The mountains make it impossible for anyone to invade us and we have the vast and dense West Woods to shield us too. We always have the high ground, the West Woods grow on an incline to the plateau where Lormere thrives, so we have the vantage point over our enemies.

Beyond the West Woods lies the realm of Tregellan, our sworn enemy for a time. A hundred harvests ago we were locked in a bloody war with them, a war they started, but Lormere prevailed and a treaty of peace was signed by our royal family and the Tregellian council.

Over the mountains at their most northerly, where the rock gives way to the outskirts of Tregellan, and stretching north and west until it meets the sea, lies the lost kingdom of Tallith, virtually abandoned for half a millennium. All that's left of it now are small hamlets locked into perpetual fights for land with their neighbours. Tallith was once the richest of all the kingdoms, back when Lormere was nothing more than a few feudal villages in the mountains, governed by the queen's ancestors. But after the royal dynasty died out Tallith fell into ruin and the people left, at first in trickles and then in droves. Some settled in Tregellan and others travelled on, braving the woods and the height, and came to Lormere. It's said that a quarter of Lormerians have Tallithi blood in them, and you can see the quirks sometimes, when a child is born with the Godseye or with the grey-blond hair the Tallithi were famed for.

We ride in silence and the forest around us hushes as we make our pageant through the trees. Lormere is fertile, but the altitude means a lot of the land is best used for livestock. We can grow our own potatoes, turnips, parsnips, rye and beans, but grain doesn't thrive here. We have to import it from the north of Tregellan, where they have abundant farmland next to the river that separates Tregellan from Tallith. All of the fish and seafood for our table comes from Tregellan too, fished from the river or brought upstream by the fishermen who brave the Tallithi Sea. It puts those foods at a premium. Before I came to the castle I'd never eaten white bread.

There is a rustling in the trees to our left and we all turn, the Queensguard draw their swords. A moment later a pine marten bursts from a bush, chattering angrily as it shoots up into an old spruce. One of the ladies laughs softly and the guards re-sheath their swords, looking embarrassed. The queen rides before me, our guards forming a ring around us. Her long chestnut hair gleams in the dappled sunlight that falls through the gaps between the oak and linden and spruce trees.

24

She is beautiful, her profile proud when she turns to check her convoy is in order. Her skin is pale and unblemished, her cheekbones high and her eyes dark, as are those of all her family. The royal line breeds dark good looks; their blood stays true. It's become the fashion at court for the ladies to mimic the royal colouring; those with pale hair try to colour it using dyes made from bark and berries, with varying results, and more than one lady has nearly blinded herself adding atropa to her eyes in an attempt to obscure a blue or hazel iris. Next to them, with my red hair and green eyes and freckled skin, I look like a being from another world. Which I suppose I am.

Deep in the woodland to the north of the castle a golden pavilion waits for us, pennants at each crest snapping when the breeze rushes past. Beneath the peaks a long table is buckling under the weight of more food than the company could possibly consume: roast boar, candied duck, gingerbread dumplings and thick goulash, breads and puddings. Silken carpets imported from strange, exotic places cover the forest floor and slippers for us line the edges. When the queen dismounts we do the same, exchanging our riding boots for slippers and taking our seats. As I take my seat on the right of the queen's elaborate chair, pulling it as far from hers as I reasonably can, two of the serving girls glance at me, furiously exchanging whispers before the larger one pushes the other towards me. I look away, but not before I see the victorious friend smirk with satisfaction.

"Some wine, my lady?" The girl forced to serve me hovers at a safe distance, holding a carafe in her hands.

"No," I say. "I'd like some water."

The girl bobs a dainty curtsy, hurrying off and returning with my water. As she approaches I stiffen, holding my body stock-still. She leans so far to pour it that she spills some on to the table and I watch as it soaks into the golden tablecloth, ruining the silk. She ignores the dark stain, instead scuttling back to her friend where she resumes her whispering.

When I first came to the castle and I was told what would happen if I was touched, it made me feel special, powerful like the queen. No one could ever hit me, or pinch me, or take things from me again. It also made me spiteful. When I didn't get what I wanted I would waggle my fingers at the servants, delighted when they blanched and tripped over themselves to grant my requests. But back then I'd thought the purpose of the Morningsbane was to prove my worthiness. The servants realized though, that I was a weapon. I can't blame them for their hatred now; if I hadn't been so naïve I might not have been so cruel to them. But it's better for them if they do stay away, lest Tyrek's fate befall them too.

The queen idles with a fan, opening and closing it as she scans the forest for a glimpse of blue, her head tilted for the sounds of the horns that will herald her husband's arrival. It's unusual for her to be so attentive to the king's whereabouts and it puts the company on edge. We are all sitting perfectly straight and still, breathing as lightly as we can. I look subtly back and forth, watching the queen as she

26

fidgets, then scouring the forest for movement.

We never know when the hunters will join us; they won't break before the hounds have made a kill and if they are hunting wild stock there's no telling when it will happen. Our task is to wait here, looking delightful and picturesque for when they do. When the scribes record the days of this court the queen wants to be sure they'll write of elegance and beauty and tradition. She is determined to reign during her own Golden Age of Lormere, so everything must be perfect.

"Twylla, what will you sing today?" The queen turns to me and gestures for a page.

"Would 'The Ballad of Lormere', 'The Blue Hind' and 'Carac and Cedany' suit Your Majesty?"

"Very good," she says.

Though she presented it as if I might choose the songs, it's an illusion. Had I said "Fair and Far" or "A Laughing Maid", she would have fixed me with cold, dark eyes.

"And what makes you think they are suitable?" she would say in a treacherously soft voice. "For a hunt, Twylla? Those songs?"

The ones I have chosen are sung by rote at a hunting party; I know that now. "The Ballad of Lormere" tells how the queen's great-great-great-great-great-grandfather founded the kingdom. "The Blue Hind" is a more recent song, recalling how the queen's mother in her kirtle of blue was mistaken for a magical doe and hunted by the then king, only to be saved by him before the slavering hounds could take her.

"Carac and Cedany" is a battle song, written for the

27

queen's grandparents. It was their reign that we now call the Golden Age of Lormere, when the last Daunen Embodied was amongst us, and the song is the queen's favourite. She loves to hear the tale of how we Lormerians beat back the invading Tregellians, decimated their people even after they'd surrendered and temporarily emptied their vaults of gold.

King Carac and Queen Cedany wanted Tregellan to give us their alchemists so we could make our own gold, as they do, but Tregellan refused and threatened to put the alchemists to death to protect their secrets. Rather than lose the gold completely, Carac and Cedany settled for having huge sums of alchemic gold sent to us, hence "the Golden Age". It's said the alchemists of Tregellan now live in hiding so they cannot be kidnapped and forced to work for us.

Before I came to the castle, I would sing whatever I wanted, making up songs about the sky and the river and the kingfishers. When I first sang for the king and queen as Daunen Embodied, I sang one of these made-up songs. The queen was not impressed.

"Who taught you that?"

"I made it up, Your Majesty. It's my own."

"Then I suggest you forget it. While I'm sure it was suitable for the Sin Eater's daughter to sing such nonsense, Daunen Embodied will not. The Gods would not like it."

I had nodded. Back then I was still desperate to impress her, still desperate to prove myself to her. Before I knew all of what it meant.

*

There is a terrible scream from the forest and we all turn as one. I try not to imagine the violence of the hounds taking down their prey. I hope it was fast.

"They are coming." The queen rises to her feet and claps her hands. "Ready the feast."

It is a needless command; the pages ensured everything was prepared well before we arrived, but at her word they move a little faster, topping up carafes of wine, bringing more pies and birds to the already groaning table. We relax our posture, forcing smiles to our faces, eyebrows raised as we turn attentively towards the queen as if she has uttered a jest.

The horn sounds and the men arrive, sweaty but jubilant as they swing down from their horses, the dogs dragging the remains of the carcass in behind them. The four largest fight over it, snapping teeth and snarling fill the peaceful clearing and I turn away. There will be no spoils from the hunt; no trophies will remain. The dogs will devour it all, even the bones. The thrill for the men is in the chase and they look satisfied with their work.

We stand as the king approaches and then my stomach swoops. The prince is with him.

Chapter 3

My jaw falls open; I'm stunned that he's here, that he's grown so tall, that he looks like a prince, not the gangly, sullen-seeming boy I used to glimpse on my way to and from my temple. His shoulders are broad, his dark curls brushing the top of his tunic as he inclines his head to his mother. He's truly handsome, I realize with shock. My betrothed is handsome, despite the same cruel edge to his features his mother has, the same watchful brown eyes.

Then anger floods me; no one told me he'd returned, or even that he'd been planning to.

When the queen first brought me to the castle she said Næht had come to her in a dream and offered the embodiment of her own daughter – me – in place of the lost princess, for her son to marry. Only my marriage to the prince will be enough to sever my role as Daunen

Embodied and that is only because Næht willed it that way. Once I'm married I won't be pure enough to be Daunen any more. But one day I'll be the queen of Lormere, sitting on the throne where the queen sits now.

As one the court bows, first to the king and then to Prince Merek. For two harvests he's been away on progress, visiting cantons and spending time with minor lords, learning the way the kingdom works and its history, and making friends and alliances. I know he's spent some time in Tregellan as an honoured guest and I thought I heard two of the maids once say he was in Tallith. No one told me directly where he went or when he'd be back and I was too proud to ask.

Prince Merek takes the seat opposite mine and I wait for him to acknowledge me, my heart thrumming rapidly under my gown. When he doesn't, my stomach twists and I look down at the table, hurt, but, in truth, not surprised. At a ceremony four harvests ago the prince had placed his hand on top of mine, and a red ribbon had been placed over them, meaning we were betrothed. It was the last time anyone touched me. I'd hoped that afterwards we'd spend time together, become friends before our wedding, but it never came to pass. He never spoke to me and then he went away and has never so much as sent a note to ask after me. I can't blame him for it though; if parts of my role sicken me, imagine how they must look to a prince. Imagine taking a bride to bed who would kill you, but for the grace of the Gods.

"Good sport?" the queen asks the king as we take our seats, the king and queen at the head of the long table, me at

31

her right, the prince opposite me to the king's left and then the others, seated according to how much land they hold or how highly favoured they are at present.

"Indeed, indeed," says the king. "We were led a pretty chase by a devil of a beast – his antlers must have been twice the height of Merek." He nods at his stepson. "But we brought him down and the dogs had their day." As he finishes a distinct crack echoes from where the dogs feast and I wince.

The queen nods. "I am glad to hear it." She turns from her husband, her expression softening as she looks at her son. "Merek, how did you find it?"

"Very well, Mother," he replies, though with none of her warmth. His voice is deep and soft, pleasing to the ear. I watch him furtively as he talks, seeing the curl of his lip as he answers her, the way he lounges in his chair. "It was a pleasant distraction. I would do it again. While we were in Tregellan we hunted boar on occasion. Though not a court they still enjoy some of the old sports and courtly pastimes."

"I'm surprised they find time," the queen says drily. "I was under the impression it took them the best part of a moon to agree to any decision."

Merek raises an eyebrow. "True. But that's the price of democracy, I expect. Each voice needs to be heard. Whilst it could be more efficient, I can't deny the system works. For them, at least."

"For them," the queen says with a tone of finality and Merek looks down at his plate, reminding me of the awkward boy I pledged my hand to. "The Hall of Glass will be complete soon," she says in a soothing tone, missing the twitch of irritation at his mouth. "We've modelled it on the original in Tallith. There are pastimes enough to be found here too."

"I saw the remains of the original whilst I was there. I'm sure it was quite something. In its day."

"I think you'll find our version will supersede it. Whilst modelled on the Tallithi design, I've made some modifications to it myself," the queen says. "It's no relic."

"It won't be the same as a tourney or a sport though, will it?" Merek says.

"It's a more refined entertainment." The queen's voice is honeyed. "We're not savages like the Tregellians. We can take our pleasure from more gentle things." When Merek doesn't reply she turns to us all. "My son, the traveller. I only hope Lormere has enough to occupy him now." She smiles fondly at Merek and moves to take his hand. But he jerks it away, raising his eyebrows at her before lifting his knife and thrusting it into a pheasant breast. He watches her as he brings it to his mouth and tears into it. The queen turns aside and I also look away, pretending I didn't see his small act of rebellion but glad that I did.

The queen glares down the table at the court and we all become occupied with our food. After a moment she pulls a small metal disc on a chain from inside the bodice of her dress and begins to toy with it. Merek puts down his knife and looks at her.

"You made it into a necklace," he says quietly, nodding at the medallion pendant the queen holds between her fingers.

"I could hardly add it to the treasury." She smiles, showing it to him.

He frowns. "Where did the design go? The piper and the stars that were on the front?" He narrows his eyes at the pendant. "Did you have them filed away?"

"Of course I did. What reason would I have for wanting to wear an old coin with a Tallithi musician on? This is much better. See, now the centre is unmarked and it looks like Næht's moon. And the gold around the edge is Dæg's sun. I've made it Lormerian."

Merek shakes his head. "That was possibly the last alchemy-made Tallithi coin in the world. Over five hundred harvests old, a priceless piece of history."

"But not our history, Merek. I'm only concerned with our history. Besides, it's not as if it will tell us the secrets of alchemy, is it? It's merely a useless coin from an obsolete currency."

As she tucks it away Lord Bennel, calls from further down the table. "Did you find the Sleeping Prince, Your Highness?"

Some of the courtiers laugh, though it takes me a moment to recall what the Sleeping Prince is. I've half remembered a legend about a prince trapped in an enchanted sleep, when I realize the company has fallen deadly, treacherously silent. Prince Merek is frozen, his mouth comically open in abandoned reply, but the queen. . . The queen is staring down the table at Lord Bennel with wild, vicious eyes. The air around her is heavy with malice, as though Lord Bennel has grievously insulted Merek with his question about an old

34

children's story and now she must defend him. In contrast everyone else at the table is frozen and pale; even the king looks nervous as we wait for something to break the tension.

"Forgive me, Your Majesties, and Your Highness," Lord Bennel says hurriedly. "I did not mean to interrupt you."

The queen says nothing and I can feel the anger rolling off her, can feel that she is still, poised to pounce. After a moment, she sits back in her seat and some of the tension leaves the court. People lift glasses to their lips, knives scrape across plates and the servants approach the table to remove or replenish platters. But from the corner of my eye I can see the queen's movements are stiff and deliberate; she pushes her plate away, her gaze still stormy.

"Twylla, you will sing now," she says.

Flanked by my temporary guards, I rise immediately, trying not to run as I make my way to the other end of the table where she and the king can see me best, the instinct to flee from the queen almost too much to ignore.

"You have been given a gift, little Twylla," the queen told me after I underwent the first Telling. "You have been chosen to represent Daunen here in the world and today we have dedicated your life to her. Lormere has waited a long time for you to come again. You are anointed now, a sacred vessel, like I am. It's your destiny. You're my daughter in the eyes of the Gods."

I am singing "Carac and Cedany", my voice soaring as I recount war and bloodshed and righteous glory, when I hear something else underneath it, a soft hissing, whispering sound. At the table I realize that Lord Bennel is whispering to Lady Lorelle under his breath. She sits white-faced and poker-straight as she desperately tries to ignore her neighbour's chattering, her husband Lord Lammos leaning as far from them as he can. I snap my gaze away, ignoring him as sweat breaks out across my shoulders. When I come to the chorus I sing louder, endeavouring to drown him out, throwing back my head so my hair catches the light.

Lord Bennel leans closer to her, continuing to mutter, even as she shakes her head violently and nods towards me. His cheeks are red, his gaze unfocused and my heart sinks as I realize he's drunk, too drunk to be cautious. Of course he is. When else would he be foolish enough to have interrupted the queen and the prince as they talked? I raise my voice again, thrusting my arms to the side and turning my face to the sky as I sing, desperately willing the party's attention to remain on me.

The sound of smashing glass silences us all. My voice dies abruptly in my throat. At the head of the table, the queen holds the stem of a goblet in her hand, all that remains of the glass that has shattered across the golden cloth.

"Does Twylla bore you, Lord Bennel?"

Nausea curdles in my stomach, my pulse racing, as all eyes turn to Lord Bennel.

"Does Daunen Embodied bore my lord?"

I watch Lord Bennel's thick neck become blotchy as he stammers his response, his words slurring. "Forgive me, Your Majesty, I was merely saying to Lady Lorelle how lucky we were to live in such times, to have Daunen Embodied amongst us once more. I meant it to be a compliment." He thrusts a hand out to point to me and knocks over his goblet, red wine feathering across the silk.

"Odd. Surely a better compliment would have been simply to listen to her and appreciate her, as the rest of us were managing to do. Lorelle didn't seem to have a problem appreciating the song without talking over it, did she?"

From where I stand I can see Lady Lorelle gripping the folds of her dress so tightly her knuckles have turned white and I realize I am doing the same thing, the sweat from my palms staining the silk of my gown.

"No, Your Majesty."

"Perhaps your compliments, as you say, were ill-timed then?"

"Yes, Your Majesty."

"Perhaps you'd do better to leave us to enjoy the gifts of the Gods without you?"

"Helewys—" the king begins but she waves a hand curtly to silence him. The king glares at her, a shadow passing over his face as his jaw clenches, but he says no more, turning away and staring into the trees.

"I – Your Majesty?" says Lord Bennel.

"Go. You interrupt Daunen Embodied with your chatter and you interrupted a private conversation between me and my son with nonsense. Do not aspire to be in my company until you have learned some manners." The queen drops the stem to the floor and turns to summon a new glass.

Some of the tension falls from me. For a horrible moment I had thought she would declare his actions treason and ask me to touch him. I look up again, waiting for my cue to continue and watching Lord Bennel gesture for a page to bring his horse.

"I think not, Lord Bennel. You may walk and use the time to reflect on your ignorance."

My heart slams against my ribs. We all watch as he stands stiffly then struggles to remove his slippers and replace them with his riding boots, his cheeks darkening to purple when one becomes stuck around his foot.

"Continue." She nods at me.

"*In the West Woods of Lormere, Fair Cedany stood tall. She cried. . .*" I falter as the queen beckons the Master of the Hounds.

"Twylla, continue," she snaps and what choice do I have but to try, my voice quavering as I sing to an audience that would give anything to be anywhere but here.

"*In the West Woods of Lormere, Fair Cedany stood tall. She cried, 'Onwards for Lormere! The heathens shall fall. . .'*" I can't watch as the Master of the Hounds pulls two of the smaller dogs from the meagre remains of their meal, leading them to Bennel's chair. Lorelle cowers as they move around her, their bristly fur rasping against her gown as they learn the scent of the man who sat there. Then they are gone and the world holds its breath.

"*Carac rode to battle, sword screaming for blood. Tregellan fell as his love said it would.*"

Less than a moment passes before the air is filled with shrieking and snarling.

"Start again, Twylla." The queen smiles. "I could hardly hear you over the wildlife. Though less of the theatrics this time, if you please. You're Daunen Embodied, not a village minstrel."

Lord Bennel wasn't a traitor. I only kill traitors. Though given that he died for insulting me I might as well have killed him. One glance at the court tells me they agree.

The applause at the end of my performance is painfully enthusiastic; the entire court is hell-bent on appreciating me lest the queen takes their lack of zeal to heart. It makes me sick.

"You may sit, Twylla," the queen says pleasantly.

I look at her as I bow and that's when I see the prince.

He is leaning towards me, his head tilted as if he is seeing me for the first time. His formerly inscrutable face is alive as he stares and my legs start to weaken, as though he were taking my strength to fuel the tempest in his eyes. Earlier I craved his attention; now I have it and it's paralysing me.

My cheeks burn as I walk back to my seat, and I can feel his gaze follow me along the length of the table. No one else would dare to look too long at me in case the queen decides their glance offends her. But the prince does not have to fear losing his life. He is the only person in the world the queen would not cut down to have her way and he must know it.

Dessert is served, but I can't stomach the rose pudding

before me. The petals atop it are red and I move the pudding to cover them. The mood is sombre now; the feast has the feeling of an Eating, as though we must all consume Bennel's sins and hope our actions are enough to appease the queen.

When I put my spoon down the prince is still staring at me and I get the impression he hasn't looked away from me once since I sang. Worse, the queen is staring at him as he does, her mouth pinched and sullen, and her fingers worrying at the medallion around her neck. The sun vanishes behind a cloud, the bright greens of the forest mute to grey. When the queen stands we all rise with her.

"Ready the horses," she commands. "We shall return now."

Within moments we are changing our slippers for our boots; the horses are led around so swiftly the grooms must have anticipated a hasty departure. We mount in silence and begin the procession back. I am grateful that I am behind the royal family, grateful I don't have to worry about them watching me as I ride, and I twine my fingers into my horse's hair, pressing against her and eking out the contact for as long as I can.

The queen and the royal party ride at speed for much of the journey, though I don't know how she manages it seated side-saddle, and I'm thankful that she doesn't demand I try to keep up with her. By the time I arrive back in the courtyard, bringing my mare to a halt amid the sweat-sheened flanks of the other horses, the queen has dismounted and is cutting a sharp path up the steps and into the castle, her husband and son jumping down from their own mounts and travelling in her wake.

At the last moment, before he crosses the threshold, the prince turns back and looks at me. Again his gaze holds me to the spot. For three suddenly violent heartbeats we stare at each other and then he turns into the castle, leaving me trembling inside.

Dorin approaches to escort me, a man I don't know at his side. I pull myself together, my fingernails making crescents in the palms of my hands where my fists clench tightly.

"Good day, my lady." Dorin bows. "May I introduce Lief, who joins your private guard from today?"

I glance briefly at the new guard. "Good day, Lief."

"My lady," he says. His voice is melodic and deep; there is something foreign about it, a slight upturn in tone at the end of his words that makes me look more closely at him. His eyes are green, darker green than my own, his light brown hair pulled back tightly in a ribbon against the trend of his peers; if loosened it would touch his shoulders. He doesn't look much older than me. I'm filled with the urge to tell him to leave, now, while he has the chance, but instead I nod at him and then turn to Dorin.

Dorin is staring past me and I turn to see what he's looking at. Lord Bennel's horse has been led in, rider-less, and Dorin turns to me, his mouth tight.

"To the temple, my lady?" he says, brushing away a bee that is buzzing around our heads.

I nod. "Yes. May I have a moment alone with you first?"

"Wait over there," he tells the new guard, who bows and then smiles widely at me, a flash of pink tongue just visible, resting impishly between his teeth. It's both disarming and infectious and I find myself smiling back before Dorin clears his throat and Lief leaves us.

When I am sure he is out of earshot I turn to my oldest companion. "He's not Lormerian," I say in a low voice.

Dorin shakes his head, looking at me with something similar to paternal pride. "Well discerned, my lady. He is Tregellian."

"The queen hired a Tregellian? To guard me?" I don't even try to keep the shock from my voice. Although Lormere won the war and is now at peace with Tregellan, the queen is known for her dislike of its people and I've heard her call them lazy, sly and feeble.

"She has. He's—" He slaps the bee away again and then it dives at him. He yelps as it stings him on the forearm and bites his lip to stop himself from cursing.

"Are you well?" I ask.

He shrugs, peering at the wound. "Don't worry, my lady."

"Is the sting out? You must get it out, and swiftly."

He examines the wound, the skin ringed red around the puncture, then tweezes the sting out with his fingernails, dropping it to the floor in disgust.

"You should get a poultice," I tell him.

"It will be fine, my lady. I'll keep an eye on it."

I'm about to protest when he continues speaking. "As I was saying, he's good," he says with stern deliberation.

"Despite his origins. He bested all of her own guards and –" he pauses "– and me, my lady. He's swift. And he claims to have no love for Tregellan. The queen says he's able to protect you and that she'll sleep better knowing that, Tregellian or not."

"I sleep well with you on my door," I say huffily and he smiles swiftly before assuming his standard professional frown.

"Thank you, my lady." He bows, absently rubbing at his arm. "Come, Lief," he calls and Lief trots over like an eager puppy. It makes me sad, because he reminds me of myself when I first came here.

Chapter 4

Once in my temple I close the doors, but instead of kneeling before the altar I pace the room back and forth, fuelled by anxiety. Lord Bennel, foolish Lord Bennel, why would he allow himself to get so drunk? Why couldn't he stay silent? What was he thinking, to make such a mistake when the queen was already riled from his stupid questions about fairy tales? And the prince, why does he notice me now? Why does he stare at me?

As the shadows move across the walls I light the incense and kneel before the altar to ask for Næht and Dæg's aid, to help me see what this means.

I don't mean to be ungrateful, I tell them. I truly don't. I know they have blessed me. And haven't they only given me what I wanted? I wanted to come here and here I am. I wanted to marry well and I'm going to marry a prince. They have granted my prayers and now I'm living the life of my dreams. I am lucky. I am privileged.

I'm a tool, a knife.

I look up at the Gods' totem, the vast metallic sculpture showing the sun eclipsing the moon, or the moon eclipsing the sun, depending on the light in the room. For half of the day the gold is cowing the silver, but as the light changes the silver takes over the gold.

"Will I help the villagers?" I had asked the queen when I'd first been anointed. I had visions of standing on a podium singing in front of the realm, flowers thrown at my feet as I blessed the crowd, my sister gazing up at me with proud, shining eyes. "Will I visit them and sing for them?"

"Why would you do that?" she had asked.

"So they know they are blessed."

"Twylla, as you are Daunen Embodied, so the king and I are the worldly representatives of Næht and Dæg. That is how the villagers know they are blessed, because we exist. Yours is a gift meant only for a chosen few to appreciate, because only a chosen few can understand it. Besides –" she'd paused, looking at me with pity "– we have to protect you. They will resent your good fortune, they will resent the fact that you've been chosen by the Gods to represent Daunen and to become our daughter one day. Better that you stay in the castle, where your guards and I can protect you from them."

Time passes and I rise, stiff-kneed from praying for so long. I light the candles, pacing now to keep warm as the light fades. It's colder in here than in the main castle, and the walls are whitewashed and clean. There are benches around the edges for people to sit on, though no one ever comes here but me. The walls are adorned with screens; though I'm a terrible seamstress every now and then I try, and so there are numerous scenes of suns and moons mounted on the painted stone. I'd like to stitch flowers, wild flowers, but the queen wouldn't approve. She might accept it if I embroidered cultivated, expensive blooms, but I've never found those as lovely as the flowers that grew near my old home and she won't tolerate those.

Two years past we were riding out on a picnic as part of the prince's seventeenth harvest celebrations, the last time I saw him before he left for his progress. It was a beautiful day in late spring, warm enough for us to leave our heavy cloaks behind and wear our light summer raiment. As we rode through the kitchen gardens we were suddenly caught in a wall of white fuzz; dandelion clocks, thousands of them, dislodged by the steps of the horses and swirling around us. It had been like magic; like snow falling when snow shouldn't fall, a storm in the sunshine, and I'd laughed aloud for what felt like the first time in for ever. To feel the softness of them against my face, to see nothing but white before and all around me. As the haze had cleared I'd seen the prince's face, glowing and upturned towards the sun. For a moment he'd caught my eye and we'd smiled at each other, happy to have been in such a place, to have seen such a thing.

Later, each gardener lost the index finger from his

dominant hand for allowing dandelions to grow in the kitchen gardens unchecked and in such high numbers; the cook lost both her little toes for suggesting the queen might eat the leaves and roots of weeds in her salad or drink them in tea. The queen had wanted her thumbs, but that would have left the cook unable to do her job. The queen called it mercy. Again.

Outside the temple I can hear murmuring through the open door as Dorin drills the new guard in his role.

"Who is my lady?"

"She is Daunen Embodied, embodiment of the daughter of the Gods."

"When is the Telling?" Dorin coughs wetly.

"Are you well?"

"Answer the question, Lief. When is the Telling?"

"On the last day of the full moon," Lief replies.

"What is the Telling?"

"An ancient ceremony to prove my lady's willingness to work for the Gods and that she is their chosen vessel. My lady gives a drop of blood to mix with the Morningsbane and then drinks the mixture as an act of faith to assure she has the Gods' favour."

"When may you touch my lady?"

"Never. It would kill me if I did."

"Who is permitted to touch my lady?"

"The queen, the king, the prince, by divine right."

"And who else?"

47

"No one. Only the anointed can receive my lady's touch without death coming for them."

"Good enough, for now," Dorin says grudgingly.

I smile, and then wrinkle my nose. The smoke from the incense snakes around me and it reeks of jasmine. I tip the incense out of the brazier, crushing it under my foot. Someone must have sent the wrong kind; I have frangipani in here, not jasmine, never jasmine.

"Twylla."

I turn sharply, stunned to find the prince on the threshold of my temple, watching as I viciously stamp on the incense. I dip into a bow, feeling light-headed as he enters and walks towards me.

"Do I disturb you?"

At first I'm too shocked that he is in my temple, speaking to me, to respond immediately. "No, Your Highness. Not at all," I manage after a moment.

"I haven't interrupted your prayers then?"

"No, Your Highness. I wasn't praying, as such. I was. . ." I trail off limply.

He nods, his lips suggesting a suppressed smirk, before he peers around the room. "Did you do all of those?" He nods at the screens.

"Yes, Your Highness."

"Do you not tire of always creating the same images?"

I look from him to the screens and he watches me, his dark eyes shrewd. Before I can decide how to reply, he speaks again.

"I enjoyed your performance yesterday."

"Thank you, Your Highness."

"I also wanted to say that I appreciated the . . . *theatrics*." He emphasizes the last word and my chest tightens. "Though it didn't end in the way I'd hoped, it was still heartening to see some things have changed since I've been gone. There aren't many here brave enough to be *theatrical* if the occasion calls for it. I'm glad you're one of the few."

Again I'm lost for words. He says *theatrics*, the same word the queen threw at me, but he says it approvingly. Why? He made no move to save Lord Bennel, so why would he be pleased that I'd tried? When I look at him his eyebrows are raised as he waits for a response but I have no idea what to say that isn't treasonous or accusatory.

"When will you sing again?" he says at last.

"Tomorrow, Your Highness. It is my fortnightly audience with the king."

"And when after that?"

"When I'm told to, Your Highness," I say, realizing too late how churlish I sound. Before I can add something more courtly, he speaks again.

"So Daunen Embodied sings only as the king wills it?"

I don't understand. "I sing at the king and queen's pleasure."

He nods, then looks at the walls again and frowns. "You should stitch flowers. I've always liked dandelions," he says, stunning me again, before he turns briskly and strides away. I don't have time to bow to him before he leaves the temple.

I stare after him, open-mouthed. He sought me out. He

49

came to my temple. But why? Because of Lord Bennel? And telling me to stitch dandelions. Does he remember? I look at the totem, hoping vainly to find my answer there but there is none.

Discontent and confused, I sit on one of the benches, trying to put my thoughts into some kind of order. When I see night has fallen, I give up, offering a swift murmur of thanks to the Gods before I summon my guards and return to my tower.

The moment I cross the threshold I know I'll find no sanctuary there either.

I pause in the doorway and gasp, a brief start, but enough for Dorin to notice.

"Step aside, my lady. Lief, secure the tower door."

Lief heads down the stairs and Dorin draws his blade and circuits the room, glancing behind the long golden curtains and under the bed, checking behind the screen of my bathing area and in my privy. My tiny wardrobe contains no threat. He can find no sign of what may have disturbed me.

That's because the intruder is long gone, having left their calling card on my bureau.

Dorin raises his eyebrows as I re-enter, a calm smile on my lips.

"Forgive me, I thought . . . I believed I saw a shadow at the window . . . perhaps a bird? An owl?" I say.

He isn't fooled and his expression is thoughtful as he moves to examine the glass. My solar takes up the second and topmost floor in a small tower in the west wing. It is mine alone and there is no possibility someone could climb to my room; the walls are bare and slippery outside.

"My lady –" Dorin looks from the window to me, a light sheen of sweat on his forehead "– are you well?"

I nod my head, smiling as much as I'm able, and a shadow passes over his face. He knows I'm lying, but he'd never press for the truth and so he nods in return.

"I'll be outside, my lady. Should you need anything. At all."

"Thank you," I say softly.

I wait for five heartbeats after the door has closed before I cross to the desk, lifting the folder and opening it, my pulse racing. There's no note included, nothing to indicate who my mysterious benefactor is. But I know.

You should stitch flowers, he'd said.

The folder is full of pictures of flowers, his mother's favoured blooms: roses, poppies, irises, all those that grow in the manicured gardens of the castle. But there at the back is one small, faint sketch of dandelion clocks, on a scrap of paper no bigger than the palm of my hand. I study it, smoothing the creases from the paper. It looks as though it's been folded and unfolded many, many times. I didn't know he could draw this well. But then I don't know much about my future husband at all. I wonder if it is an order, or a test, and I don't know what I am to do.

I take the sketches and lay them on my bed, marvelling at the detail. Does he mean for me to keep them, or are they a loan? I take them back to the desk, placing thin parchment over them and begin to trace them as best I can, taking extra care over the dandelion one. I will leave the folder on the bureau. He can collect them when he wants to.

Later that night, after I've dined, I pull out my silks and begin to sort them. I'll use pink for the roses, soft pink, the colour of my sister's fingernails when she was a day old. Rich indigo for the iris. A muted red for the poppies, not blood-red, not terror-red. And white – snow white – for the dandelion clocks. White so pale you'd have to hold it up to sun or candle light to see the flowers.

I lay the colours out, side by side, stroking them. I will make a screen of these flowers as if they had grown together in the wild, all entwined and unfettered, climbing together as their kind are rarely allowed to. And in between each stem I'll hide a dandelion clock. The queen would hate it and though I know she'll never see it the thought pleases me. By some miracle that night I sleep well, dreaming of flowers and dark eyes.

The following morning I ready myself for my visit to the king. The Telling happens on the last day of the waning moon, a time of natural endings and death. The day after it, the first of the new moon, the queen takes her closest courtiers on a brief pilgrimage to the sacred pool at the base of the East Mountains, where she spends the whole day, sunrise to sunset. The water pipes up hot from under the mountains into the mere, the same mere Lormere is named for, and it's reputed to help a woman make a child, though it's never spoken of so bluntly. The new moon is a time for new life. New beginnings.

For the day that she is away I go to the king and sing for him, just as I did the first time we met. The queen makes it clear that it's an indulgence, and she refuses to be part of it, claiming it's a frivolous use of my gifts. But the king asks for little from her and she has decided to allow him this, as far as I know the only boon she has ever offered her second husband.

Her first husband, the previous king, was the queen's own brother, a marriage forged in tradition. Lormere must be ruled by both king and queen; no one may rule alone; that is an edict that has never been broken. And for generations, in order to keep the royal bloodline pure, brothers have been married to sisters. There's no law saying the rulers must be siblings, but the desperation to keep the bloodline wholly royal means each set of parents must produce at least one son and one daughter to be considered successful.

In the villages we knew the dangers of this, we'd seen the kittens and piglets born of those kind of unions, some deformed and blind, some spoiled and out of their minds. Though there's a strength, of sorts, in preserving a bloodline, it comes at a cost and the cost is high. Blood should be mixed if you want to avoid death and madness.

The queen and the first king lost both their daughter, and the prince's future bride, when Princess Alianor died before her third birthday. And, as always happens, no matter how highborn or lowborn the deceased is, they called my mother, the Sin Eater of Lormere, to Eat the dead princess's sins.

My mother is a fat woman, made large from gobbling the sins of the dead, the meal prepared and served to her as if she were a queen for the day. For an Eating the mourners cover the surface of the coffin with breads and meats and ale and more, each morsel representing a sin known, or suspected, to have been committed by the deceased. She Eats it all; she has to – it's the only way to cleanse the soul so it can ascend to the Eternal Kingdom. To not finish the meal is to condemn the soul to walk the world for ever. We've all heard the tales of the wraiths that haunt the West Woods because people less dedicated than my mother could not finish the Eating.

She sat before the princess's tiny coffin and Ate her sins, sins flavoured with pomegranate and nutmeg and sugar, sins too rich and decadent to belong to a little girl. She Ate them and the first king and the queen mourned their lost child, even as they tried to make another to replace her, for the eight-year-old prince still needed a bride if he would ever be able to take his throne. But within two moons of Alianor's death the first king had sickened and died too.

With the queen now a widow and the prince both brideless and too young to hold the throne, the kingdom was thrown into chaos and uncertainty. I remember my mother hiring two local men, armed with scythes and short swords, to escort us to and from Eatings. Even she was scared of how quickly lawlessness had gripped the land, and for my mother to feel threatened is no small thing. But a solution of sorts was eventually found; the queen married her first cousin and he became king. Though unconventional, he is of the blood; his parents were the siblings of the queen's parents; the bloodline was still secure. But their union is not considered wholly pure. Although they grew up in the same nursery they did not share the same womb and therefore the blood is not true enough. They say that is why the queen has not been able to have another daughter for her son, despite many, many trips to the mere.

I had met the soon-to-be king at the dead king's Eating and I had taken to him instantly. As my mother's apprentice, my role was to observe her perform the Eating, to learn the order the sins must be consumed in, the time that must be spent ingesting each one according to severity. It hadn't taken long for me to grow tired of watching her consume the seemingly endless meal. So as she had entered the rapture that comes with a large Eating I had wandered off into the castle, singing to myself. I hadn't known the soon-to-be king had followed and was listening to me. When he'd clapped I'd tried to run back to my mother but he'd stopped me and asked me to sing another song. And I had basked in his attention, had sung my heart out for him, relishing his applause before he eventually took my hand and led me back to the Eating.

After we'd left the castle I'd asked my mother if he was my father. I'd never known my father, nor that of my brothers and sister, for I doubted they were the same man. When I learned how children were made, I couldn't attend a man's Eating without wondering if he were my father, whether one of the sins my mother Ate was because of me. I scanned the faces of the relatives for my eyes, my hair, but never found my likeness in them. I didn't find it in the face of the soon-to-be king either, but still I wanted him to be my father. I imagined him realizing I was his long-lost daughter, being taken to the castle and becoming a princess to replace the lost one, saw myself bringing a smile back to the queen's eyes. My mother hit me, hard enough to loosen one of my milk teeth, and told me never to say "my father" again.

Four harvests ago a great carriage had appeared outside our cottage, surrounded by tall guards mounted on jet-black horses. It was the queen herself, the queen of Lormere, dressed in blue, at our door, asking for *me*. I'd thought all of my dreams were coming true at once.

Because I didn't want to be the next Sin Eater; I wanted to grow up, to get married, and to be happy. I didn't want to be aloof and secretive and think only of my role. I didn't want to live alone, isolated from everyone around me because of what I was. I wanted a normal life.

For years after we'd attended the first king's Eating I couldn't stop thinking about the castle. So much light and beauty; nothing like the dark, dreary cottage that I'd grown up in. I imagined everyone had their own room and bed in the castle; not four children crammed in one bedroom while their mother sequestered herself in another. In the castle surely everyone spent their days laughing together before attending sumptuous feasts in jewelled gowns.

To be summoned there, by the queen herself, to become

a lady seemed impossible. And yet here she was, claiming me as her ward.

"And what of her duty as a Sin Eater?" my mother had said to the queen as I'd gazed in awe at the liveried guards, their armour polished so brightly I could see my reflection in it; could see my fingers twitching with the desire to stroke the rich velvet cloaks that flowed from their shoulders. "What of her responsibilities to the realm?"

"She has a bigger responsibility to the realm," the queen had said, resting a hand on my hair.

"She's needed here," my mother had replied. "She needs to learn her role and she needs to keep the others in line. She's to be the next Sin Eater. It's what she was born for."

"And I say she was born for another purpose," the queen retorted smoothly. "There is a duty her queen and her country needs from her. You'll be compensated for it, of course. But why don't we ask Twylla what she wants?"

I'd looked from the queen and the golden carriage to my mother. Behind her I saw Maryl's small face staring at the queen with round, shining eyes and I knew her expression must mirror my own. I'd looked at my sister, in her patched clothes, and then back at the fine lace of the queen's shawl.

The queen must have followed my gaze, because she shrugged the shawl off as though it were a forgotten thought and held it out to Maryl, not even flinching when she darted forward and snatched it like an animal. The image of my sister with her tangled hair, wrapped in gossamer fine lace, her face blissful, was all I needed.

"My duty is to the queen and my country," I'd said, earning myself a smile from the queen as my mother closed the door of my former home in my face.

I'd stared at it in shock before the queen took me by the hand and led me to the carriage.

"We'll have to have new dresses made for you." The queen's lip had curled as she examined my plain black smock. "You'll need something more fitting for what you're about to become. Do you like red, Twylla?"

I did like red, back then. Now I can't stand it. Since I've been at the castle the list of things I dislike has grown ever longer. Now I dislike things I never even knew existed four harvests ago.

But the only thing I hate is the queen.

Chapter 5

I dress and pin my hair up before Dorin and Lief come to escort me to my audience with the king. The queen and he have claimed the whole of the south tower as their private domain, much as the west tower is mine, though my tower can only be accessed by the corridor leading to it. The south solar can be reached through the royal doors in the Great Hall or, the way we walk today, down the long hall and along the walking gallery, where the courtiers spend their time gossiping and politicking. They fall silent as we pass; everyone knows today Daunen Embodied must attend her royal appointment, and they bow to me with much more vigour than usual. No one wants to be the next Lord Bennel.

I am announced as the king's men open the doors to the royal solar and the king rises from a damask-covered love seat to greet me.

"Twylla." He smiles as my guards melt away for the few hours of respite they are allowed, leaving me alone in the gilded room with the king. It's round, like the shape of the tower it sits in, and artfully arranged with cushioned love seats and broad oak benches, tasselled footstools and side tables holding crystal decanters and goblets. It has a dining table with four carved seats like those we take hunting; there are shelves full of jewelled boxes and books bound in leather dyed every colour imaginable. It's a room that shrieks of privilege and luxury, and above that, privacy. In a castle that has never felt like a home, this room more than most makes me feel like an outsider. This is the queen's inner sanctuary and portraits of her and the first king keep a severe watch over it. My feet sink ankle deep into the thick rugs under my feet as I walk over to the king.

"Your Majesty." I bow and smile back at him. I like the king; I always have and secretly I think he looks as out of place in this room as I must.

"And how does today find you? You look well."

"I am well, Sire, thank you. Might I ask after your own health?"

"You find me in good spirits, Twylla. I look forward to the delights of today. It is the highlight of my days, to hear you sing."

This exchange is a script for us; we play our roles by rote at each meeting. For someone who is revered in part for her voice I don't have much chance to use mine, so coming here is a pleasure – a chance to talk, as well as sing – and the king is gentle and happy company when it's just he and I.

I take my place before the window, my back to the stained glass, the heavy brocade of the curtains framing me as I begin "The Ballad of Lormere". My voice soars and fills the room and I'm not the vessel of Daunen any more. I am Twylla. The queen, the castle, the horror all falls away. It's the only part of my life that I love, when I can sing and forget. When I sing I could be anyone, anywhere. When I sing I am free.

I am about to begin "Fair and Far" when the door is thrown open and the prince enters unannounced. As the guards scramble to close the door behind him my heart leaps into my mouth. So this is why he was so keen to know when I would next sing. He meant to watch me.

"Merek, my boy. I am glad you could join us. Twylla was about to begin 'Fair and Far'."

Merek's eyes slide to me, narrowed as he frowns. "I do not know it."

"One of my tutors taught it to me when I was younger than you are now, and I in turn taught it to our Twylla."

"Indeed," Merek says, looking back at me. "Could you move from the window, Twylla? The light hides you."

I look to the king. He nods at me and I move, standing between the windows, my back to the small expanse of wall between the panes.

"Better," Merek says, lounging in one of the love seats, his long legs stretched before him and crossed at the ankle, his arms folded loosely across his chest. "Please continue."

I am afraid I will falter under his scrutiny. But my voice stays true and I don't look at either them, keeping my eyes on the wall above their heads, singing as though my life depended on it. As I finish a song the king calls the name of another, giving Merek no time to comment or applaud. When it's time to break for luncheon I am exhausted and when Merek stands and leaves the room without speaking to either of us it's as if the room fills with air. I hadn't realized I was holding my breath until the door closed behind him.

"It does not disturb you that he was here?" The king's voice is soft. "I had not thought he would join us."

"I'm happy for him to be here, Sire."

"I suppose we ought to be flattered that he thought our company was worthy of him, should we not?" He laughs, but the sound is hollow. "He is a good boy – or man – as he is now. Forgive my confession, but I fear the castle will be a cage for him, after his time in the realm. Perhaps it would be different if he had people his own age to spend time with. Children need siblings, do they not? You had brothers and sisters?"

"I did, Sire. Two brothers and a sister." There is a sharp pang under my ribs when I think of my sister. I would give almost anything to know how she is, whether she remembers me. I see her again in my mind's eye, wrapped in a delicate shawl that's surely fallen apart by now. To become Daunen meant to give up my old life completely, including my family, a choice I hadn't fully realized I was making at the time. I'd gathered from the door in my face that my mother was content to be rid of me and that our relationship was at an end, but Maryl . . . I'd thought I might keep her. I had thought we would still be part of each other's lives in some way at least; visits to one another, a few snatched hours spent together, even if rarely. But the queen said it would be unseemly for me to associate with my former family, that it would anger the Gods if I spurned my new life and clung to my old. There was also the obvious fact that the queen despises my mother as much as the rest of the kingdom does, but since the women in my former family have held their roles as Sin Eaters for much longer than this royal family has been in power, she tolerates her. After all, my mother holds the keys to the Eternal Kingdom in her meaty hands. For now. But one day Maryl will be the Sin Eater and I shall be the queen and no one will be able to stop us being sisters then.

My thoughts fly back and forth in time, with no regard to the present until I realize the king has asked me a question and is waiting for my reply. I turn red, embarrassed to have been so rude to one of the few people who is kind to me. "Forgive me, Your Majesty, I forgot myself for a moment."

The king looks at me with concern. "Are you well? Can I call for something to help you?"

"No, Your Majesty. I'm well. Merely lost in thought for a moment. Forgive me; it was rude of me to allow my concentration to lapse."

"Happens to the best of us," he smiles. "I asked if you remembered much of Prince Merek before he left for his progress."

"Not much, Your Majesty."

"I said as much to Helewys, you know. That you and he should be brought together a little more. She forgets that she and I, and Rohese as well, were brought up in the same nursery, and you and Merek were not. I—" He stops, remembering himself before continuing. "Still, he keeps himself occupied. He'll make a good king."

"Gods willing, you and the queen will serve the country for a good while yet," I say smoothly.

"Gods willing."

Merek returns as we are about to begin again. His expression is still impenetrable and I have to look away because I worry my own is not as closed. I don't understand this prince who barely speaks with words yet whose eyes speak a language I don't know. I don't know what he expects from me.

"Twylla will sing three more songs." The king's voice is firm and I know he's noticed how uncomfortable his stepson's scrutiny makes me.

"A pity," Merek says. "I had hoped to teach her some of the songs I heard on my progress."

"Another time," the king replies. "She has worked hard enough today."

Merek looks back and forth between me and the king. "Perhaps Twylla might like to decide for herself?"

The king looks at me expectantly and I hesitate. How do I choose between the man I'm going to marry and my sovereign king?

"I cannot learn new songs," I say softly. "I would not do them justice if rushed. But another time when I can give it my full attention, I'd be glad to. More than glad."

"A perfect solution," the king says.

Merek says nothing, not acknowledging his stepfather at all. His eyes remain on me. Finally he nods. "Another time," he says and I realize too late that both his words and my offer echoed the king's decision.

I take a deep breath and sing the remaining songs, keeping my eyes fixed on the wall above my audience's heads. When my concert is over Merek rises, nodding briskly at me.

"Very good, Twylla. Very nice. How pleasant to spend an afternoon without the need for theatrics, don't you think?"

He sweeps from the room as abruptly as he arrived, leaving the king staring at me in confusion. My hands are damp with sweat, the same sweat that cools on my back, and despite his words I cannot shake the feeling that I have been tested and found wanting.

I'm tempted to stay in my room the next day, ashamed to admit that I'm scared of going to my temple in case the prince comes there, asking more odd questions. But I am supposed to be his betrothed, so I pull myself together and attend, singing softly to the totem, dusting off the silk atop Næht's Well and rearranging the screens.

When it is time to return to my tower and take lunch, I tell Dorin and Lief that I want to walk back through the gardens. Where the sunlight manages to break through the clouds, the garden is bright, but there is an edge to it, delicate fingers of autumn stroking the edges of the shadows. It won't be long until all hands turn to the fields to begin the harvest, and I find myself wondering again what is happening at my old home, how my brothers and even my mother are. But as always it's Maryl I think of most. How can it be four years since I've seen her? She'll be eleven now; her hair may have darkened from white blond to the colour of corn. I imagine her grown out of her childish softness, taller; she could even be as tall as I am now, reed-slim and graceful, following my mother around the kingdom as I used to, learning to be the Sin Eater.

In Lormere only women become Sin Eaters, as it was a female who committed the first sin. Næht tempted Dæg and stole the sky but brought death to the land. To atone for Næht's folly, Dæg decreed a mortal woman must bear the burden of the sins of the dead, generation after generation of daughters loaded with the weight of more and more; sin is inherited in our family, as hereditary as the maladies of the royal line. So now Maryl will take up the mantle when my mother passes and her first task will be to consume the sins of my mother. I don't imagine it will be much of a meal.

It's peaceful in the garden and I'm lost in my thoughts until a thud on the dusty ground makes me turn. Dorin has fallen, clutching at his arm, and when he pulls off his gauntlet I see the skin beneath is red; an angry, large blister has formed in the centre of his forearm.

"Why did you not tell me?" I demand. "Why did you not say you ailed?"

"I'm fine, my lady," he says, but it's clear he isn't. Bright pinpricks of blood under the surface of his skin circle the wound and his face has taken on the pallor of sickness.

"Go and get a poultice," I tell him, but he shakes his head. "You must, lavender and oxymel. Come, I will take you now. Please," I say. There was a child in the village who reacted badly to a bee sting once, and it killed him in the end. "Dorin, we must go. You've already waited too long. I order you to go to the healers. Now." I look at Lief. "Help me."

As Lief steps forward to take Dorin's good arm, the older guard raises it. "No. I'll go, my lady. Lief can stay with you. You –" he turns to Lief "– you cut down anyone who tries to harm her. You stay close and you make sure she is safe." Lief nods solemnly. "My lady, I will be back as soon as I am able."

"I know you will." I try a smile. "Now go. Rest if they tell you to. I will see you soon."

He bows, grimacing, and then he is gone, leaving me alone with my new guard. We both watch Dorin until he passes through the doors into the castle. There is a moment when I yearn to run after him, to help him, to keep him by my side. Guilt eats at me – I should have noticed sooner; I should have made him go to the healers immediately. Is this the Gods' way of telling me not to make a screen of flowers? Is this somehow a warning to me?

I turn to go home but Lief doesn't follow. When I look back at him he's staring at a plume of opaque black smoke rising from behind the wall of the stables and I shudder. I know what that smoke means.

He looks at me searchingly before he bows slightly. "Forgive my impertinence, my lady. Is there a fire?"

"No. It's a funeral pyre. Lord Bennel . . . passed recently."

"Ah, forgive me, my lady. I did not know the dead were burned in Lormere."

I nod. "We used to bury them, but there was. . . Winters here are harsh – they make the ground hard and it's cruel to wait for spring so people can lay their loved ones to rest."

Lief nods and I wait, wondering if he'll press on. It wasn't a lie. In winter it is impossible to dig a grave; the ground freezes solid, as though the mountains are trying to take the land back by crawling underneath our feet as we sleep. The queen's mother died in winter, back when we still buried the dead. After the Eating her coffin was moved to an outbuilding to keep the corpse from stinking while they waited for the ground to soften so she could be interred.

But the dogs found her long before spring came. Despite the fact they prefer live prey they made an exception for their owner. It was only when King Kyras found his wife's wedding ring in the courtyard with her finger still inside that they realized what had happened. What remained was burned and all the dead have been since, regardless of season.

"I hope he didn't suffer, my lady."

I pause briefly, my stomach rolling before I speak. "He met with an accident. It was swift."

"I'm sorry for your loss, my lady."

I nod, turning away and continuing my path back to my tower, thinking of Dorin. *He will be fine; he will be fine. I will go to the temple and petition the Gods. I will beg forgiveness for my sins. I will be grateful and I will trust in them.* I'm repeating the mantra when Lief speaks to me again.

"My lady, forgive me. What kind of accident was it?"

Again I stop and look at him and he returns my gaze, his head held quizzically. "He disobeyed the queen," I say after a long moment.

He looks at me with his eyebrows raised and I wait for his next question. But it doesn't come; instead he looks thoughtfully at the smoke, before he bows his head and I begin walking again.

Later, I am sat at my screen, trying to sketch an outline of flowers. There has been no word about Dorin, so when the door flies open I expect it to be Lief with news. It *is* Lief, white-faced, but he is quickly obscured by the grave face and forest-green gown of the queen. The charcoal I have been drawing with falls to the floor and rolls away as I dip into a deep bow.

"You may rise, Twylla," she says as she closes the door herself, shutting Lief from the room and leaving us alone.

I do as she bids, the strength draining from my legs until I have to keep my knees bent under my gown so I don't fall. She has never visited me before. If she wants to see me I am summoned to her, never this; never her attending me. First the prince and now her.

I keep my neck bent as I watch her examine my quarters, her ivory fingers trailing across the golden counterpane of the bed, along the wooden posts that hold the canopy. She crosses to the bureau, looking down at the sketches scattered across it. She gazes at them, her lips pursed.

"What is this?"

"I plan to embroider a screen, Your Majesty."

"With flowers? Not the sun and moon?" she asks, her head tilted in question though her eyes remain hard.

"It . . . it was the prince's idea, Your Majesty."

She looks at me sharply. "And when did you speak to the prince?"

"Two days past, Your Majesty." I don't mention that he came to my audience with the king. "He came to the temple."

"Did he? Those are his drawings, are they not?"

"Yes, Your Majesty. He lent them to me to aid me."

The queen stares at me. "Good. It's about time you two began associating. It'll make your marriage easier if you're not total strangers." She smiles crookedly. "Let us sit, Twylla. I have come on account of your guard."

I wait for her to sit in my chair, my heart speeding again as I kneel before her and wait.

"I've been good to you, haven't I?" she says.

My stomach drops to the floor. "Your Majesty?"

"Haven't I always done what's best for you? Haven't I brought you here, guided you in fulfilling your role serving the Gods? Don't I take care of your former family? Haven't I invited you into my family and offered you my son?"

"Yes, Your Majesty. You've been too kind to me." I try not to shiver, though each word she says feels like someone is walking over my grave. It's dangerous when she's reminding me how much she cares for me.

"I can't allow you to wander the castle with one guard, Twylla. It wouldn't be safe."

"I understand, Your Majesty. I won't go anywhere in the castle, save for my temple," I say dutifully.

"No, Twylla, you misunderstand me. I don't want you leaving this room until the other is fit to return."

"But, Your Majesty – the Gods . . . the temple . . . my duties. . ."

"The Gods will understand. You don't need to worship them there to receive their blessing. You're Daunen Embodied. Wherever you are you can worship them. The king and I don't spend all our days in a temple, do we? I told you once before, you worship them by pleasing me, in the way their daughter pleases them."

"Your Majesty, forgive me, but is there no one else you can appoint to me while Dorin recovers? Is there no other guard who can be spared to protect me?"

The queen looks at me with pity. "Come, Twylla, you're not so naïve. You go through guards so quickly it's becoming harder and harder to find suitable men to fulfil the role. Why on earth do you think I allowed a Tregellian to become your guard? He was the only one willing to take on the position, though fortunately for you he is skilled enough to reassure me he's capable of protecting you. But I would trust no one man with that role. You know how much I value you, the lengths to which I go to ensure you are safe. You will remain here, at my pleasure, where you are safe. Let that be an end to it."

She says it so candidly it sends a shiver down my spine, and it strikes me how much at times she reminds me of my mother. Both of them favour manipulation as a means for control; with the queen it's the reminder that all she does is for me, how ungrateful I would be if I spurned it. My mother was the same, playing on guilt and gratitude to get her way. She might not have had the queen's absolute power, but she has a command of her own and she was always willing to wield it like a knife if she had to.

It is known that the soul will linger near the body for three days and nights after a death. During that time, the Eating must take place so the soul can ascend, otherwise it will drift to the West Woods to join its damned brothers and sisters in the trees. Though nowhere in Lormere is more than a whole day's ride away, dawn to dawn, sometimes my mother would deliberately delay to repay a slight she felt had been visited on her. Once, when a woman gave birth to a sleeping child, my mother attended the Eating, only to be angered by the single cup of ale offered to her.

"He was never in the world," the child's father had pleaded. "He never knew sin or wrong."

My mother accepted the token payment of a silver coin with icy contempt and left. The following day the man sent a messenger to call us back to his home; his poor wife, unwilling or unable to stay in a world without her child, had died in the night. My mother listened to the message and said her thanks.

Then she went to her room and closed the door.

For two nights and days she stayed in there, ignoring my knocks at the door as I grew ever more anxious. At the last possible minute we left our cottage and travelled to the farmstead.

The feast was much, much larger that time.

Chapter 6

So, yes, I know the lengths to which the queen will go. She, like my mother, plays to win. But time has taught me how to endure them both; it's my speciality. "I understand, Your Majesty," I say. "You're right. I'm grateful for your concern."

"You're my daughter, or as near as, Twylla. How else could it be?"

Her words, too close to my own thoughts, make my skin tighten. "Thank you, Your Majesty."

She nods and stands, having already accepted and disregarded my thanks and I bow deeply to hide the anger on my face, remaining low until the door has closed.

As soon as she's gone I rush to my bed to straighten the counterpane and smooth the dent her finger left. When there's a knock at the door I panic, hastily running my own finger back down it so she can't tell I tried to remove it.

"Enter."

I breathe a sigh of relief when it is only Lief, though again his face is the conduit for my emotions; both fear and worry play across his handsome features. "The queen says Dorin will be away for some time, and that all duty now lies with me."

"Yes."

He looks at me before nodding slowly. His mouth opens and closes as he bites down on whatever he was about to say. Finally, he speaks. "Very good, my lady. Shall I light your candles now? Do I need to fetch your supper from the kitchens?"

"No, one of the maids will bring it to you at the door of the tower. She'll bring both yours and mine – you'll hear her knock. But you may light the candles."

He nods again and bows and I jerk away from him as he walks past me without waiting for me to move.

"My lady?"

"You must. . . You must not walk so close to me."

He smiles. "I'm not so close, my lady."

"You are," I say shakily. "You must always keep an arm's length between us. Always."

When I take another step back he nods.

"Of course, forgive me."

As he turns away I catch his scent, slightly sharp and citrusy; leather, a hint of wood smoke. It's somehow calming and I breathe deeply, taking it into my lungs and holding it there as I watch him move about the room. He takes a taper from above the fireplace and lights it, carrying it carefully around the candles until the room blazes with light, much brighter than I normally keep it. The taper burns quickly and he has to shake his hand to stop the flames from licking his skin. He walks back to the doorway and stands in front of me, taking two steps back and holding an arm between us. When I flinch, he frowns and lowers it.

"I'll bring your supper when they send it then. Will that be all?"

I nod and he smiles at me, that all-tooth smile with his tongue peeping between his teeth, as he bows. As soon as he closes the door I rush to my looking glass and try it myself. I look like a fool.

My supper remains untouched, the grease congealing on the stewed meat doing nothing to tempt me to eat. My old life with my mother loaded certain foods with meaning and though I know the difference between eating and Eating, I cannot help but silently measure the morsels when it's food I remember from an Eating. Most of the food I eat here is castle food – the queen would never eat what the commoners eat – but now and then something comes along that I know of old. A heel of seeded bread is a lie; a wedge of hard cheese is a debt left unpaid. Stewed meat is for obstinacy, and I wonder if the queen had it sent deliberately.

Lief chides me when he comes to take the bowl away. "You've not eaten, my lady."

"No."

"Can I bring you something else?"

"I'm not hungry."

"But . . . it is such a waste."

I look at him in surprise. "They'll give it to the pigs. It won't go to waste."

He stops dead, his eyes stony as he bows stiffly and takes the tray. He says nothing more, sweeping from the room with a disdain that would impress the queen. His foot hooks around the door and pulls it closed, the breeze from the movement blowing out some of the candles. My mouth is open as I stare at the door; I had thought I was immune to disapproval by now.

My skin feels too tight, memories of my mother washing over me. The shadows under her eyes that made her look like one of the corpses she was supposed to atone for. The sound of her voice summoning me into her room, always in darkness. The windows covered in thick woollen blankets so the air was heavy and cloying and full of her reek. She would spend hours washing herself, the cleansing both ritualistic and obsessive, daubing jasmine oil under her armpits and in her groin and along her neck. She kept a fire in her room, burning day and night, no matter the season, and I would sit and swelter on the small stool as she lay back in her bed and instructed me in the words and rites we had to perform. The smell of jasmine would strangle me as she sat sweating in her own private hell and telling me how one day I would do the same. She would look at me down her nose, her eyes cold, as if she knew well in advance what a disappointment I'd be to her.

77

I cross to my window and lean out, taking great gulps of the clean, crisp air, my fingers gripping the cold stone. I am Daunen now. I am Daunen Embodied.

I leave the shutters at the window open all night.

Sleep comes in bursts – light while my body rests and I watch the fireworks behind my eyes – and deeper bouts that leave me gasping for air when I wake from them, tangled in the sheets. Dawn takes a long time to arrive and I am eager to put the night behind me. I wash and dress, waiting for my breakfast. I'm toying with the idea of sending it away immediately, to show him that I won't be bullied by him, when he knocks the door.

But all thoughts of banishing him and the food leave my mind when he enters, the tray balanced carefully on one arm. Instead of porridge, bread and cheese it contains flaky, buttery pastries, their centres bright red with jam, fig marmalade, a small bowl of viscous golden honey, soft, fresh white bread, so different to the seeded loaf I ate at home. All of my favourite foods. He lays the tray unceremoniously on top of Merek's drawings and turns to me, a shy smile on his lips as he pulls a slightly squashed bouquet of flowers from inside his tunic and offers them to me.

"I'm sorry, my lady. I behaved out of turn last night." He bows, brandishing the flowers.

For a moment I can only blink in surprise. Then I remember myself. "So this is an apology?"

He nods and gestures to the tray and I finally notice the

piece of paper resting beside my knife.

"My mother always told me a gentleman commits to an apology in writing," he says. "So the lady knows he doesn't mean to take it back."

I pluck the note from the tray and scan it, ashamed by my inability to read it but determined not to let him know I can't. I pretend to examine the marks, my eyes blurring over the long strokes and round curves, none of it meaning a thing to me. I can only assume from the slightly smug, expectant look on his face that what I'm holding is an eloquent note on the evils of wastefulness disguised as an apology. The kind of apology that admits nothing. When my face begins to heat up, I drop it back onto the tray, not even flinching when it lands in the marmalade.

"Pretty words. I'm sure your mother would be proud." I let my annoyance at myself slip into my voice, directing it at him to try and exorcize it. "But I don't need your apology, guard. You're perfectly entitled to your own thoughts on my wastefulness. However I don't need them detailing to me, not out loud and not on paper. I answer to the Gods, not to you."

He opens his mouth, an argument forming there before something sparks in his eyes. He looks from the note to me, before speaking gently. "Perhaps you would allow me to read it to you? Sometimes it's hard to say what you mean on paper, sometimes the tone of a word is needed . . . my lady," he tacks on.

Again shame flares, I've misjudged what the note contains and he knows I haven't read it; that I can't read it.

When I hesitate he steps forward, his hand extended for the note and I cringe into the wall. He pauses, holding his hands before him. Slowly, slowly he moves towards me and I stay frozen, holding my breath, unable to take my eyes from him. Then he's a foot away, six inches, beside me, reaching past me for the letter and my heart stops, I feel it halt beneath my ribs. The moment stretches out and then it's over, he takes an exaggerated step back and looks at me as he opens it up.

"To the Lady Twylla, I beg your forgiveness. My actions towards you last night were unkind, uncalled for, and undeserved. I know I have no right to question you, and I apologize wholeheartedly for the offence I caused. I know this alone will not atone for my actions, but allow it to be the first of many gestures that will show my loyalty to you. I am nothing but your humble servant, Lief."

He folds the note and places it on the bureau before moving away. He watches me closely, and I have to turn my head to give myself time without his scrutiny, my pulse still thudding in my ears as I recover from his closeness. There was not so much to the letter after all.

"Why?" I ask eventually, conscious he is still watching me, waiting.

"Why what, my lady?"

"Why did it bother you so much, that I didn't want my supper? You're here as my guard, not my guardian. What is it to you if I don't eat?"

Colour rushes to his cheeks. "I. . ."

"Yes?"

"Forgive me again, my lady. It wasn't about your appetite. It was the waste."

That word again. I frown at him, and he continues.

"It made me angry; no, not angry – sad. Sad to see fine food destined for pigswill. I shouldn't have behaved as I did, it was wrong, but my sister. . . We don't have much at home. That's why I'm here to work. So when you said. . ." He trails off, looking miserable and I understand.

I once had a sister who didn't have much at home, and though I know she eats well enough now, because of me, she still spends hours on end at feasts she can't take part in. And yet I didn't think of her at all as I sent the food away, safe in the knowledge there would always be more. I forgot that I don't have to fear hunger any more. I forgot her.

"I'm sorry," I whisper.

He shakes his head, assuming my apology was for him. "No, no. Please. I am sorry. It's not your fault. That's why I needed to apologize, my lady." He extends his arm. "Please, take the flowers."

I hold my hands up to stop him. "You can put them on the bureau."

"Won't you take them from me, my lady?"

"Lief, you know I can't—"

"I won't let you touch me, my lady."

"You don't understand—"

"Hold out your hands and I'll drop them in."

I shake my head. "Please don't do this, Lief. Please put them on the bureau."

He looks so sad, so defeated, and I can't bear it; I want to offer him something in return for his confession.

"I have a sister too," I blurt and he pauses, looking at me. "Maryl. Her name is Maryl."

"How old is she?" he asks after a moment.

"Eleven harvests now," I say. "I haven't seen her since she was seven. Not since I came here."

"Not at all?"

"I can't. It would anger the Gods," I say. "To become Daunen Embodied I had to leave everything else behind."

"But you miss her?" he asks softly and I nod. "I'm sure she misses you too."

"If she remembers me," I speak as quietly as he did. "Seven is very small. And I can't imagine I'm spoken of much, back at my old home. I don't think there would be much to remember."

Lief's eyes rake over me. "People don't forget what it is to be loved," he says finally. "No matter how young or old you are, or for how long you had it, you always remember what it is to feel loved. She'll remember you."

He bows, preparing to leave, and something surges in my chest.

"Wait." I swallow the lump in my throat. I cup my hands beneath his, trying to hold them steady and disguise the trembling in them. He looks into my eyes as he drops the blooms into my hands, sprigs of hollyhocks and anemones and lavender raining gently down, until all he has left is a single lavender blossom on its woody stem. His green eyes flicker to it, then back to mine as he holds it out to me, pinching the very base of the stem in between his thumb and forefinger.

And I take it.

I tip all the other flowers into my left palm and grip it as though it's a lifeline. It's a stupid, dangerous thing to do and my heart is fluttering in my chest like a bird trapped in a fist. But for all I know how wrong it is, it's the right thing to do, I can feel that. He offered atonement for his sin of anger; my confession and taking the flowers from him is atonement for my arrogance and ingratitude. There has to be balance, each sin has to be atoned. Now we are equal.

When he finally lets go, leaving me holding it, I stare at the lavender sprig in wonder as he bows and makes ready to leave me to my breakfast.

"You won't hurt me," he says softly as he opens my door. "I know you won't."

As he closes the door, I think of Tyrek.

Chapter 7

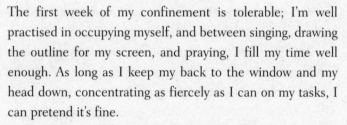

The first week of my confinement is tolerable; I'm well practised in occupying myself, and between singing, drawing the outline for my screen, and praying, I fill my time well enough. As long as I keep my back to the window and my head down, concentrating as fiercely as I can on my tasks, I can pretend it's fine.

But after that first week boredom creeps into my quiet solar and tugs at my skirts and I find it hard to settle my mind to anything other than what's outside my tower. I miss strolling in the gardens. I miss walking the halls. I miss my temple, its peace and simplicity, and, more than anything, the way it felt separate from the castle. I asked for them to bring the totem to me and it's now mounted on the wall opposite my bed. But the light in here doesn't move across it in the same way and the sun is always covering the moon now. I'd like to believe it was a sign, and a good one, but I know it's a trick of the light. I can't pray properly in here, I can't concentrate and I'm scared that despite the queen's words the Gods will be angry that I'm neglecting them.

Lief and I have come to some kind of truce, though truce isn't the right word for it. There's an unspoken something between us since I took the flower from his hand; not friendship exactly, more comradeship, how I imagine brothers-in-arms feel about their fellow soldiers. As if we both know we took a huge risk and survived it, and that brings us together.

Every day I ask him how Dorin is and every day he tells me the same thing, that he is no better and no worse. The healer seems to think the sting knocked his humours completely out of balance. They're saying that's why he remains weak and frail, though the sting site itself is supposedly healing well. I want to go and see him, but obviously that's impossible, so instead I tell Lief to send messages saying I'm praying for his swift recovery. And I do pray for his swift recovery, not least because his return marks the end of my captivity, but then I feel selfish and have to pray again for forgiveness.

I realized it first on the night he told me off for wasting food, but it's now glaringly apparent that Lief has never worked as a royal guard before and has no idea how he's supposed to behave without Dorin here to set an example. He has no sense of protocol; half of the time he forgets to call me "my lady", and he's far too eager to talk to me in a way that Dorin never would, despite knowing me for four harvests.

"How do they make that colour? It's so rich." He hovers in the doorway, pointing to the indigo silks I am unravelling one morning, having decided to abandon sketching a design and instead stitch freehand.

"I don't know, I've never asked," I say, with an edge to my voice, but he seems to miss it, shrugging, watching me separate the strands. I ignore him, but knowing he's watching makes me fumble the needle and tangle the silks and it's only when I tut loudly he remembers himself and leaves me.

When he brings me supper later, he tells me "It's made from sea snails, my lady."

"What?" I drop my spoon into my bowl of broth and he laughs.

"Your purple threads, my lady. The dye is made from the shells of sea snails."

"How do you know that?" I ask, my curiosity piqued.

"I asked," he grins, bowing cockily before sauntering from the room.

And so it continues. The first week becomes the second and he spends more and more time in my doorway, taking my questions about Dorin as his cue to ask his own about the flowers I'm sewing; which ones do I like best, have I seen all of them with my own eyes or only in pictures. He tells me how the dyes for my other silks were made, and ponders aloud what would happen if they became mixed somehow. He tells me about Tregellian flowers and plants in detail and I finally ask him if he'd trained as a herbalist, given his knowledge. But this silences him, a crease forming between his eyebrows, and he makes an excuse to leave the room. I don't make the mistake of asking about his former life again, too unnerved by the ringing silence in my room after he's left it.

"Dorin says I am to send the second swords to the blacksmith for sharpening, my lady," he announces one morning, lingering as is his custom after he's replaced my candle stubs with fresh pillars.

"Very well," I say, my focus half on the gardens below me and half on his words.

"Not very well, my lady. The blacksmith is gone."

That gets my full attention. "Gone?"

"Apparently the queen felt he shod her horse ill."

I offer a silent prayer for the blacksmith.

"Does my talking bother you, my lady?" he asks from the doorway, where he's now cleaning under his fingernails with a small dagger.

"No, not at all."

"You must tell me if it does; I won't be offended."

"You don't bother me, Lief."

He smiles. "I'm glad. So where shall I send the second swords?"

My days fall into a pattern of breakfast, talking – or rather, mostly listening – to Lief, singing, luncheon, praying, supper, and working on my screen until it's a reasonable hour to go to bed. But even having a routine of sorts is not enough. When I send him away in the afternoons so I can pray I find it doesn't fill me with the peace I normally feel. In the evenings I pick up the needle and put it down, glancing at him as he sits in the doorway, reading the same tatty book night after night. After two weeks of this I demand he reads it to me and he does, reciting from what I now know is an outdated almanac, telling me weather forecasts from twenty harvests ago. The worst thing is it's rapidly becoming my favourite part of the day, my needle dangling from my hand as he reads in his sing-song voice.

I wonder if this is how it would have been if Tyrek had become my guard and the thought burns. He reminds me of Tyrek – the way he forgets what I am, or doesn't care. He's as fearless at Tyrek was, and as rash, and I know I shouldn't encourage this, shouldn't have told him about Maryl, shouldn't have taken the flowers from him. I don't want to find myself with my hands on Lief's neck because I have somehow said too much, especially to a Tregellian, whether he is loyal to his country or not.

I tell myself again and again that there can be no harm in what we're doing. As long as we don't discuss the realm or the castle, I can't possibly betray the queen or the country, and that keeps him and me safe, but I'm still not at ease and I can't put my finger on why. There's an itching inside me, an irritant I long to scratch but cannot reach, and it amuses Lief, when he returns, to find me pacing.

"You'll wear a hole in the floor, my lady." He grins his wide-mouthed grin, pretending to examine the cold stone as

I roll my eyes at him. He smiles so easily, as though his face was made to split in two and show all his teeth to the world.

When Lief enters my chambers with my breakfast three weeks after the queen's decree, I am still not up, sitting against the pillows I have piled behind my back. I have been trying to read his note, but the only word I can make out is my own name. Slowly, I have searched through and the letters from it in other words, but I don't know what the letters around them are and it's frustrating. When Lief knocks I stuff the parchment back under my pillow.

"Is it breakfast in bed today, my lady?"

"I must have overslept," I say. "If you'll give me a moment, I will dress."

"Forgive me, my lady, but you might have time to stay in bed and eat if you wanted to. You don't have to be anywhere for a few days."

"The Gods wouldn't thank me for my idleness."

"Even the Gods need to rest, every now and then." He grins.

I realize to my surprise that I'm grinning back at him.

He pauses, tilting his head to the side. "You should smile more my lady. It suits you."

My stomach flip-flops inside me and I look away.

"Forgive me, that was forward. I'll be silent now." He places the tray in front of me, moving slowly, and I stay still as he balances it carefully atop my lap. He looks at me and I nod. I fill a white roll with soft cheese and then, as soon as he leaves, rummage under my pillows for the note, puzzling it through as I eat.

The door opens again – Lief come to collect the tray – and I hide the note away, folding my arms across my chest.

But the face that peers around the curtains of the bed is not Lief's, it's the prince's.

Instantly I lurch out of the bed to bow, upending the tray, and, to compound it all, I get tangled in the covers and land face first on the floor.

Prince Merek stands before me, a smile playing at his lips before he bites them to stop it from spreading.

"Twylla," he says, nodding to me, serious again. "Should I call your guard?"

"No," I say hurriedly, pulling my cloak around my shoulders and standing before him. "Your Highness, forgive me. I was unprepared." My cheeks burn with shame.

The prince looks me up and down, his eyes shining in amusement. "No need to bow quite so low to me, you know. A nod of the head will do. Did you hurt yourself?"

"No, Your Highness," I say firmly, even as my face betrays me. Did he make a jest? "I'm well."

He turns away as his lips contort. "I came to view the progress of your screen. My mother said you had plans to design one. How goes it?"

I wrap the cloak around me tightly, wishing my hair were not falling loose down my back, wishing I had risen, wishing I had not fallen on my face. He peers at the scant embroidery on the screen, before looking back at me, an eyebrow raised.

"I've not had time to work on it of late, Your Highness,"
I offer.

His lips twitch again, another hinted smirk. "I see. That
is a shame. You've had no use for my drawings then?"

"I have. Of course I have, thank you." I hesitate, before
crossing to the bureau and collecting the folder of his
drawings. When I hold them out to him he frowns.

"They were meant for you, Twylla. As a gift."

For a second time my skin crimsons and I duck away,
wishing my body would control itself. "You are too kind, Your
Highness."

"Dine with me later," he says suddenly, speaking so
quickly I'm not sure if I heard him correctly.

"Your Highness?"

"Tonight. Take your supper with me, or rather, I will
come and take my supper with you. I know my mother has
commanded you stay in here until you have your full guard
again."

My jaw gapes, making me look more of a fool than I have
already shown myself to be. I fumble for the words to thank
him and accept but can't find them. Instead my heart beats
too fast and makes my toes and earlobes throb in time with it.

"I'll return at eventide then," he says, as though
I had responded. When he nods and takes a step away I
automatically bow, thankful for the chance to again hide my
confused face. At the door he turns back to me, mischief in
his eyes.

"There is no need to dress for dinner, should you not wish

to," he says, turning away, but not before I see the edge of his mouth curl upwards.

I stare at the door, my jaw slack. Within seconds Lief has entered, a small frown puckering his forehead. He takes one look at me before turning back towards the door.

"Is everything well, my lady?"

"Fine. It's fine."

"You look a little. . ." He trails off, waving his hands.

"I didn't expect him."

"I'm sure he noticed that." He nods at my dishevelment.

"Lief!" I protest, before I realize that he is the second man to see me in a state of undress that morning. "Turn around! No, leave. If you would send for the maids, I need hot water. Lots of it. And can you find out where my red dress is, the heavy brocade one? And my silver combs, they were sent for polishing."

"Are we going somewhere?" Lief asks.

I shake my head. "No, I am dining with the prince tonight. Here."

"You're to be married, Dorin said."

"That's right."

"Does he dine here often then, my lady?"

"No," I say slowly. He knew I'd been confined here and it took him the best part of a moon to decide to approach me. Why come now?

Lief looks at me oddly, his expression asking the same question.

"The prince is busy," I say. Though I've no idea whether

that's true or why I'm defending him.

Lief continues to stare at me, his lips pursed before he nods towards the food-covered bed. "Can I bring you something else? If you didn't like it, you could have said so. You didn't need to throw it about." He smiles at his joke.

I roll my eyes. "I was surprised by the prince," I say. "But, no, thank you, I managed some bread and cheese before he came. You can take the tray and ask the maids to come and change my linens whilst I bathe."

"As you wish."

Though he smiles at me as he takes the tray away it is not mirrored in his eyes and I watch him, puzzled.

The bath gives me the time I need to think, the sweet-scented water soothing my nerves as I sink into it and allow my hair to swirl around my head. We've never dined alone together before; we've never spent any time alone together before. But there's little more than six moons before he turns twenty, so I suppose he must be preparing for our wedding. The thought leaves me feeling hollow, even though I knew it would happen. Our wedding. I will be a wife. I can't imagine being someone's wife. Not only a wife, but queen one day. Merek's queen. Mother of the heirs to the throne. There's an odd swooping in my stomach as I imagine it and I sit up swiftly, sloshing water all over the floor and gripping the sides of the tub, the sanctuary of the bath ruined.

For the remainder of the afternoon I kneel before my totem, staring at it blankly, until the sun goes down and I dress in the red gown and add the combs to my hair. With little else left to do until it is time for the prince to come I return to my sewing, oddly able to focus on it.

When the prince is finally announced, I'm close to calmness.

"Twylla." He greets me and I drop into a bow. "I hope I find you well. I have obtained special permission from the queen to escort you to the portrait gallery while the servants prepare your room. Your guard will remain here to supervise the arrangements."

My mouth falls open and the prince bites his lower lip as it begins to curve upwards. I blink at him, unsure whether I heard him rightly.

"Twylla?" he says when I continue to stare at him in awe. "Are you ready?"

"Yes." I nod shakily, pulling myself together. He doesn't offer me his arm; instead he gestures for me to leave before him. I hesitate, unwilling to present my back to him, but he nods.

"It's fine, Twylla. Please, go on."

Only he could convince the queen to let me leave without a guard.

I feel giddy when I step out before him, knowing he is behind me. Lief's gaze meets mine and for a second I'm sure he has winked at me, before he stares straight ahead, his shoulders held stiffly as Merek follows me out. When I reach the door at the bottom of the tower I realize I'm afraid to step out. I look back and the prince nods at me again.

"Go on, Twylla. The queen has granted permission."

I open the door and step into the west wing of the castle, unescorted save for the prince.

The prince walks at my right, in Dorin's place, and the space at my left leaves me feeling exposed, as though I'm only half dressed. Even when I'm not confined, I rarely go to the heart of the keep and the novelty of the route adds to the surreal sense that what we are doing is not truly happening. My eyes dart around the corridors, seeking signs of anything that has changed during the weeks I've been banished from them. But, no, if I didn't know better I'd swear the vases of white roses that line the halls are the same ones I walked past on the day Dorin was stung. It's as though time has stood still; as though the castle has been in an enchanted sleep. And that makes me think of the Sleeping Prince, and Merek's interest in me after the hunt, and how it waned after he watched me sing for his stepfather. Is that why it's taken him this long to seek me out?

I look at the prince and see his fierce gaze locked on the doors ahead of us, his profile as proud as his mother's. He doesn't speak as we make our way to the portrait gallery and I follow his lead, keeping my eyes on our destination, wondering what prompted his invitation tonight. And whether it's at his own behest or the queen's.

It takes me a while to realize that it's not only me without a retinue. As the sole natural heir to an endangered throne his safety is vital; he, like me, is constantly guarded against threats. Twice I turn, scanning for concealed guards watching from a distance, but see nothing. I ache to ask him where they are, what strings he pulled to have us both seemingly unchaperoned.

We turn into the gallery and at once the two sentries at the end vanish through the doors. I cannot help myself; I turn to look at the prince, my eyebrows raised in question.

"I asked for peace," he says, stepping away and turning to look at the portraits on the wall.

He asked for peace. And it was simply granted. I envy him, until I too look at the walls.

It must be eerie for him to look upon these ancestors who he so resembles. And the women that his sister would surely look like, if she'd lived. I've been here once before, in my early days, when the king himself took me through the room, portrait by portrait, telling me who they all were. I recognize Carac and Cedany, from the song, both of them stern, their proud chins tilted to the sky.

On the far wall the largest painting is of the prince's father, King Rohese. He steps towards it, leaving me behind as I stare up at his family. If there had been any traces of deformity in their features when they lived then the artists wisely ignored them in their work; each one is study in pride and elegance. I join the prince in front of his father's picture.

"Do you remember my father?" he asks.

"I don't, Your Highness. I never had the pleasure of meeting him." I remember spiced ale, and clove-studded oranges, and Guinea peppers and trout. I remember what my mother consumed at his Eating – pride, vanity, anger and jealousy – but I never met the man when he lived. "I was here though. With my mother. For his Eating."

He nods. "I remember. You were singing –" he pauses, turning to look at me "– singing as my father lay dead."

"Your Highness, I'm so sorry," I murmur, mortified.

"You were very small," he continues. "I remember wondering if Alianor had been healthy would she have been as small as you, or tall, like us. Your hair looked like fire. I'd never seen anything like it before. You were the first child I ever saw, save for my sister."

I blink rapidly as I realize what he means, that he followed his stepfather, that he watched me too. I had no idea.

"My mother didn't notice I'd gone. I don't think she heard you. But I had. I heard you. I saw you. You were very different from me," he says before I have time to speak. "You could sing and smile and be free, and I had to mourn and be regal. I was eight years old and I'd already spent almost two moons in mourning for my sister. I wanted to play and run, perhaps even sing, but not grieve again. I barely knew my father; his business with the kingdom kept him well away from our nursery. It's difficult to grieve for an idea."

After four years of silence his desire to confide in me so openly is unnerving and I don't know how to reply, or if I am supposed to at all. I want to tell him I wasn't free, that my disappearance that day had cost me when we were back in our cottage. But he gives me no chance; instead he turns back to the portrait.

"I look like him, do I not? Of course, we all look the same – but then you know why. My sister, Alianor –" he gestures at a soft portrait of a small child, gazing blindly out of the canvas "– would have looked like our mother had she lived."

When he pauses, his eyes moving between the pictures of his father and sister, I finally find my voice. "You must miss her, Your Highness."

"I barely knew her, in truth. She was a sickly child and spent much of her time being kept away from anything that might damage her. I had quite the solitary childhood. How old were you back then, Twylla?"

"Six, Your Highness. It was the year of my sixth harvest."

"And now you have had your seventeenth harvest?"

"Yes, Your Highness."

"Twylla –" he turns to me "– will you do something for me?"

"Of course, Your Highness."

"Stop calling me 'Your Highness' when we are alone. We're betrothed." He half smiles as my heart stutters at his words. "My name is Merek. Sometimes I worry I might forget my own name, I hear it so little. Please call me Merek."

I nod and he raises his eyebrows in prompt. "Merek." I sample his name. It tastes of the peaches I stole as a child, the flavour of cream licked from the bowl when no one was looking. Forbidden.

"Better." He nods before continuing. "Next year marks my twentieth harvest, as you know. Not that the harvest measure means anything in the castle. I didn't help gather the harvest in my eighteenth year. I suppose that means I'm not truly a man yet."

He turns away again, walking back down the gallery and after a moment I turn and follow him. He pauses again in front of a small portrait, the young woman inside it looking eerily like Alianor.

"That's my grandmother, daughter of the famous Carac and Cedany. She was lucky to survive childhood – they never thought she would."

"Did you know her well, Your – Merek?" I test it again.

"Not at all. She died before I was born. Our family tend to have short lives, despite our positions. I can't imagine why." His words are bitter. "She brought the hounds to the court, you know. She heard of them somewhere and demanded to see them in action. She introduced the idea of hunting our enemies. My grandmother. How sweet she was."

I think of how her husband found her finger after she died and wonder if he regretted the dogs then.

Merek frowns, his lips curling, and then he nods. "We should go now. The preparations should be complete and this is not my favourite place to come."

Without another word he sweeps from the gallery, leaving me stumbling again to catch up. Behind me I hear the guards reappear in the room as he crosses the threshold.

He doesn't speak on the return journey. His stride is long and the pace swift, and I have to lift my skirts so I don't fall trying to keep up with him. The corridors are much more crowded now – it seems the rumour has spread that the prince and I are abroad and everyone wants to see us – but he strides through without responding to people's greetings. They greet me too, but they stand back against the walls as they do. I don't pay them much mind though. I'm too busy thinking about why the prince would take me to the portrait gallery when he clearly has no love for it. It seems odd, to request freedom and then go to a place you hate. What would make you choose that?

Chapter 8

Lief stands outside my door, his posture stiff and formal, his face a mask. He opens the door and Merek enters without acknowledging him. This time as I pass he definitely winks, his left eye scrunching deliberately, and I have to press my lips together to stop myself from smiling.

A table has been laid by the window, my bureau moved against the bed. Candles gutter softly in the draft from the door and are reflected in the silver of the plates and cutlery. The light flickers across the totem. There are goblets and tumblers, a vase of tuberose and tansy in the centre. It's sweet and I'm touched at Merek's attempt to create a less formal setting. He crosses the room with confidence, pulling out a chair for me. When he is sat opposite me, he nods at Lief, who pours us both wine as if he had been doing it all of his life. Once the wine is served, he melts away, leaving me alone with Merek.

Merek studies me from across the table, his head tilted. He sips his wine as he does and I try to busy myself examining the flowers.

"If I may be so bold, that colour doesn't do you justice. It looks like something my mother would wear."

"The queen chose it," I admit. "Bright colours, red especially, please her; she says it's the right colour for Daunen. And that it pleases the king."

"My mother doesn't care what pleases the king."

I look away and lift my glass to my lips.

"Do I make you uncomfortable?" he says. "I suppose I must – if anyone else were to say such a thing it would be treason, after all."

"You may speak as you wish."

"'Your Highness.' You might not say it aloud, but I hear it nevertheless." His grin is twisted, hardly a grin at all. "Forgive me, Twylla. I do not have much opportunity to talk freely to people I'd choose to talk to. But then you must understand that; your situation isn't so different from my own. Neither of us has peers, or friends. There is no one like us in the whole of Lormere. It makes one see the world differently, I believe." He takes another sip of wine. "Don't you find it wearying, Twylla? To live so much inside your own head? I know you have your Gods but are they enough? Do they give you the answers you need?"

I don't know if I'm supposed to answer him. He says things I can't possibly agree with, as much as I want to. He speaks as though we're lifelong friends, confidants, and it's too much, too soon. I wish Lief would bring the food, or that the candle would fall and set fire to the tablecloth; anything to stop this.

"I don't enjoy it," he continues. "I can't imagine anyone would. To be so alone, here in a court full of people. I was the only child of rank here until they brought you in. No one else my age, no playmates, no one at all save a never-ending band of tutors and nurses. Surrounded and yet isolated. . . We're alike, you and I."

Still I say nothing, my eyes burning from staring at the table top.

"You will not reply? As you wish. But we are. Even on progress I was kept at arm's length. You would have thought two harvests of travelling together would have brought camaraderie to our party, but sadly not. It's the same for you – people stay away."

"Did you enjoy your progress?" I ask, clinging to the one subject that might tear him away from this dissection of our lives.

He looks at me, his face unreadable. "It was eye-opening," he says.

He raises his hand, clicking his fingers together and Lief materializes in the doorway. "We are ready," Merek tells him before he looks back to me. "And I certainly have a better understanding of how a kingdom works now—" He pauses as Lief brings our food and refills our glasses. Merek ignores him, waiting for him to leave the room and close the door before he speaks again. "It's a simple system: in Lormere the

103

land is governed by the lords who sit on the Privy Council. My mother and stepfather consult with the council, who report on issues in their cantons, potential threats and tenant queries and the like, and then decisions are made about how to manage them. My mother issues a decree, seals it and then the lords see it is done."

"And that is all?"

"In a manner of speaking. A lord governs part of the land – Lortune, Monkham, Chargate, Haga and so on. They appoint the priests, the sheriffs and local peacekeepers, oversee justice and petty courts, hold audiences with their tenants and so on. In return they are paid a tithe in taxes and goods from the communities they govern, and they pay us part of that tithe to assure their continued positions and titles."

I glance at my plate, oysters swimming in butter and chives. Oysters are Eaten for untempered jealousy; all the fruits of the water mean jealousy in some form or other. I decide to ignore the food for now.

"It seems a neat system."

He nods, lifting an oyster to his mouth and pouring it in. "It's neater than Tregellan, certainly."

"In what sense?"

"They have no monarchy – it was never re-established after the war. They are ruled now by a council, one representative from each canton. They vote to pass a decree or law; no one man or woman can make the final decision, so decision-making can go on for days. There have been occasions where the issue hasn't been resolved at all, because a clear winner with a majority vote hasn't been determined. It is inefficient." He smiles wryly and I remember the queen's comment at the hunt when he said the same to her. "However," he continues, "they are years ahead of us in terms of medicine, and they have alchemy, which is one of the reasons I sought to make such good connections there. They won't give up their secrets easily, but if there's one thing I agree with my mother on, it's that we need to harness those things here in Lormere. I'm hoping Tregellan might be a little more inclined to share their knowledge when we rule."

His words make my skin feel prickly. *When we rule*.

"Did you meet any of the alchemists?"

His eyes light up and he leans forward, nearly putting his elbows into his plate. "I did. One man, heavily guarded, but they allowed me to watch some of the process. Nothing of any use to my mother, much to her disappointment, the real work was completed before I was allowed to enter, but I saw the final transmutations. I saw them make gold. Tregellan's treasury will never run dry. I wish that we had that skill here."

He lifts another oyster and tips it down his throat, dropping the shell into a bowl. "We're the only kingdom in the realm that doesn't have the secrets of alchemy. Tregellan thrives because of it. Even Tallith used to employ it and they were richer than we'll ever be without it. In Tallith it was a royal vocation, to be an alchemist. Only those of the blood could practise it."

"Is that what you want?" I ask him. "A rich kingdom?"

"Is that wrong? Wrong to want my people to thrive?

Wrong to want food and medicine for all of my subjects?"

"No, that's good." I hesitate.

"Do you think me greedy?"

"I didn't say—"

"A person can say a lot without speaking," he retorts, drinking deeply from his glass.

"Riches didn't save Tallith from falling," I say softly.

Merek looks distant and takes an oyster, before putting it back on his plate uneaten. "No, I suppose they didn't. I saw it, you know. The old castle. I found the coin I gave to my mother there."

"What was it like?" I ask, desperate to end the tension between us.

He picks up the same oyster and stares at it, before again replacing it. "Desolate. You would never know that five hundred harvests ago it was the centre of the world. The castle is a ruin; only one tower stands and two of the Great Hall walls. Save for the remains of their Hall of Glass, the rest has fallen into the sea, or been overgrown."

"Nothing remains?" For some reason it makes me shiver. How can a whole kingdom die? How could the Gods abandon them like that? Again I think of the hunt and Lord Bennel's question and I hear myself asking, "Was there any trace of the Sleeping Prince?"

Merek narrows his eyes. "Not you too. It's a story, Twylla."

I push my plate away with more force than I mean to, spilling melted butter across the tablecloth. "I didn't mean the fairy-tale version, I meant the history of Tallith. It is real, is it not?" I don't remember much, but I recall the legend sprung up in part from truth; the last heir to the throne sickened and the kingdom eventually fell because of it.

"Forgive me," Merek says immediately, leaning across the table in earnest. "I was rude. You're right, of course, the history of Tallith says the heir did succumb to some kind of sleeping sickness. And obviously without him to rule and refill the treasury, wars and chaos broke out and destroyed the kingdom. So the stories say." He drinks from his glass again. "But it's not a cautionary tale we need to heed," he adds.

"We'll never be like Tallith, Twylla. Especially not in terms of riches, I fear. But we've survived this long without alchemy; I dare say if we carried on without it we'd be no worse off. I do want what's best for Lormere though. I will fight for it." He looks at me searchingly. "Now I have told you of what I have learned, you must tell me what you have done these past two harvests."

I pause before answering. "I sang and fulfilled my duties as Daunen."

"And that was all? Did you learn anything courtly, dancing or to play the harp? Did you learn to read?"

"There was not much time to spare," I say and he frowns.

"No, of course not. I assume dealing with traitors is consuming. Luckily there's no one for you to execute this moon. So far, at least."

His brows is wrinkled, his jaw clenched with anger or disgust and my face burns again.

Then he sighs, pushing his own plate away. "Forgive me

again." He lifts the carafe and refreshes his goblet. "What happened to those two children who laughed at dandelion fuzz?" he says softly. "Are they gone for ever, do you think?"

I can't look at him.

After a moment he clicks his fingers again, summoning Lief, who removes both of our plates. I wonder if Lief will chastise me later for not eating the oysters. He returns within moments with more food: squab, fennel, shallots, parsnips, all in a sauce.

Merek does not speak, or look at me, instead methodically cutting and eating his meal, sipping from his goblet in between bites, and I follow his example, grateful to have something to do. When he puts down his knife I put down my own, though there's still food left on the plate.

"Do you wish for me to go?"

"Your Highness?"

"Merek! I have asked you to call me Merek. If you must ration your speech with me, at least use my name when you deign to talk. You're going to be my wife; call me Merek."

Halfway through his outburst I hear Lief enter the room and then the door close swiftly behind him as he leaves and I glance at it, unsure of how much he heard before he left.

"I'm sorry," I say. "I don't know how—"

"How to what? To talk to me? Just talk. Be at ease, please. We're betrothed, aren't we? We should talk to each other, confide in each other. Gods – we should take comfort in each other! I know how the role of Daunen works, Twylla. I've studied it and I know what it is you do."

I nod, wishing I had told him to go. I don't want to talk about this, not with him and not with anyone.

"You hate it," he says flatly and I look up. "The executions. I don't blame you. My mother told me that you do it, and that you don't like it. She knows."

I'm surprised. Since Tyrek, I've said nothing, given nothing away about it, or so I'd thought.

"I asked her to stop it," he says. I'm stunned by his admission, looking at him with wide eyes. "She won't," he continues. "Not until we're wed. It is one of Daunen's duties but—" He breaks off, his mouth open as he leans forward and I wait. Then he shakes his head, whatever he was about to say gone. Instead he lifts his glass again. "You mustn't feel guilt over it. They are traitors. We will have to pass death sentences when we rule."

"I know," I say finally. "That's not it. Not all of it."

"Then what?"

"Is it a sin?" I ask cautiously. "Isn't it a sin to take a life, no matter the reason?"

"I don't understand."

"When my mother Ate the sins for the old executioner, she had to eat crow. The sin of murder. I don't want my sister to—" I stop myself, pausing and raising my wine glass.

"You don't want your sister Eating crow for you," he says and I nod.

"I don't want her to have to do that." I'm not sure whether I mean the crow or the Eating at all.

It always hurts to talk of Maryl, or to think of her. She

was more mine than she was ever my mother's. Every time a storm raged over our cottage, it would be me she cuddled into, me who held her close as she shook with fear. I tended to the splinters and cuts she suffered. I rubbed her gums with cloves when she was teething. I curled her hair on my fingers so it danced around her face. She was beautiful, my little sister, with white-blonde curls and a sweet smile, a small gap between her two front teeth. She was sunshine and joy and happiness and I cried for her the whole first year I was at the castle. It's only because of her that I can bear doing what the queen asks me to do.

"You miss your sister?" Merek says and I nod. "And your mother?"

I pause as I search for the words I need. "Sin Eating came first, for her. We were mainly left to fend for ourselves. When she wasn't working, she would retire to her room, in repose, contemplating all the sins she carried."

I think of villagers forking their fingers at us to avoid ill luck as we passed their homes. I recall the stares of other children as their parents pulled them away from us. I think of the night my mother gave birth to my sister and how the with-woman wouldn't come to her aid and how I had to help her. I remember blood and the stench of loosened bowels and the way my mother bellowed like a stag at a rut. I see the flesh on her thighs quivering as she squatted and how I held my hands out to catch Maryl as she slipped from my mother's belly. Mine was the first face she saw, I cleaned the mess from her eyes, wiped the caul from her head. And now I can't be sure I'd recognize her in a crowd. Because I left her, and no matter that it means food and money going to the house, it also means she'll be the next Sin Eater. It should have been me, but I left. My mother at least stayed.

"She has a job to do," I add finally. "Her role is her life."

He stares at me, his head nodding slowly. "I said we were alike, did I not?"

"*You* are your mother's life," I say to him. "She adores you, you must know that. She lives for you."

"She certainly tries to live for me," he says, twisting my words.

"I didn't mean—"

"I know what you meant." He lifts his glass again, frowning when he realizes it's empty. "What is your guard's name?"

"Lief."

"Lief," he calls. Lief opens the door, his eyebrows raised in polite enquiry. "We're finished with our food. Clear it. Twylla, do wish for a sweet course?"

I shake my head, embarrassed by the way he spoke to Lief.

"Very well. Remove the plates. Bring more wine."

I can feel Lief bristle even as he does as he is bid, though Merek seems not to notice. When the wine is replenished and the plates gone, he raises his glass again.

"What are your dreams, Twylla?"

"I – I have none. I have all I want."

"I don't believe that. You must have some dreams – everyone does."

"I want . . . I want to be happy," I say, realizing at once that it's a stupid thing to say.

But to my surprise he's nodding, a smile tugging at his lips. "I want to be happy too."

He doesn't stay much longer and we don't speak of death or dreams again. Instead he tells me about his drawings and the lessons he took as a child. I tell him about my worry for Dorin and he promises to look into it, and to make sure he's getting the treatment he needs. It's easier when he talks like this, and if this is how our marriage will be then I'll be able to bear it easily. When he has finished his wine he calls for Lief, asking him to send for his guards and for serving staff to remove the table and chairs from my room.

We stand silently, side by side, watching as the maids scurry in to take the glasses, candlesticks and vase away. Two of Merek's guards remove the table and chairs then return and, with Lief aiding them, replace my bureau by the window. When they are done, they turn to Merek.

"Wait outside for me," he commands and they leave, Lief trailing behind them.

"Have you enjoyed tonight, Twylla?" he asks.

"I have, Merek," I say.

"Liar," he accuses softly. "It will get easier."

He bows to me and then he is gone, the door standing open with me staring through it, hoping he is right.

Lief appears, entering and pulling back the curtains on my bed. He turns down the sheets and lights the candle on my bedside stool, but his movements are brisk and aggressive.

"Thank you," I say softly.

Lief grunts. "My lady."

"Are . . . are you well?" I ask.

"Perfectly, my lady," he says stiffly.

I watch him, shaking the cover of my bed as if it has insulted him mortally before I speak. "I'm sorry," I say. "If he seemed rude to you. He's had servants all his life – they're invisible to him now."

It was the wrong thing to say and he shakes his head angrily. "Invisible? I know he's a prince and I'm a guard but I am a human being, same as him. We're no different, if you take away the title."

I sigh. "Lief, you can't say that."

"It's the least of what I'd like to say," he mutters. "Forgive me, I know he's your betrothed."

"That's not why you mustn't say it, Lief. He's an anointed prince and one day he'll be king. The queen would be angry if she heard you speak like that."

"It's not treason to say someone is an ill-mannered pig," he says and I stare at him.

He's going to get himself killed if he doesn't learn to keep quiet. Whoever Eats his sins will get stomach ache from all the Guinea pepper they'll have to consume for his anger. If he is allowed an Eating at all.

"You need to learn to control your temper, Lief."

"I am controlled."

"No, you're not. You called the prince a pig."

113

"Well, he is," he says.

"Lief, if the queen—"

"Her. . ." he says dismissively and again my mouth falls open.

"Careful, Lief," I say slowly. "Tread carefully. I told you a lord died because he disobeyed her. I didn't tell you how he died. She unleashed the dogs on him. She sent him running into the forest and she sent them after him. For the crime of whispering while I was singing. And they tore him apart as we listened. We could hear every scream, every crack of bones, and every wet sound they made. And do you know what she said? She told me to sing louder. To sing over it."

His mouth opens, and then closes, and I can see the bravado leaking from him as he weighs my words.

"And you know what I am. What I can do. Do you want me to lay my hands on you as you sit tied to a chair? Do you want me to take your life on her orders because you've committed treason? I executed the only true friend I've ever known because he betrayed the throne of Lormere. It could easily be you next if you don't mind yourself. Your recklessness has to stop. I'm one of them, Lief. I'm going to marry the prince."

By the time I'm finished, my breath is coming in pants and my skin is flushed head to foot. Lief looks at me as though I'm a monster, and perhaps I am. If that's what it takes to make him see, then so be it. Without another word he bows and wheels from the room.

Chapter 9

Finally it seems I've got through to Lief and my reward is that he's become the guard he should have always been.

"Have you heard anything from Dorin?" I try to rekindle our almost-friendship with the old opening lines. But Lief keeps his back to me, briskly transferring logs from a basket to the pile beside my small fireplace.

"He remains the same. They're doing what they can, my lady."

"Has he sent any message?"

"No, my lady."

"Tell the maids to pass on my best wishes. Tell them to tell him I ask after him."

"Yes, my lady. Will that be all?" He turns and looks at me blankly and I nod, flinching when he closes the door behind him.

It hurts. What's worse is that I feel like a hypocrite for telling him to control his anger. I'm angry at my mother, and at the queen, and at Dorin, and at Tyrek. I'm angry at myself. And sometimes I'm even angry at the Gods, because I can't feel them trapped inside this room and I need them. What do they want from me? What am I supposed to learn from this?

"Ours is not to question," my mother had said once. "Dæg gives life where he deems it best, and Næht, in her infinite jealousy, takes it away when she deems fit. They alone know the secrets of the balance we live in. It is a perfect circle. It's not for us to understand their decisions, only to accept that it's the Gods' will."

I've asked their forgiveness time and again for my anger, but I suspect Lief won't be the only one who will have Guinea pepper Eaten when he passes. And though it pains me, he needed to understand how the court works. I won't kill another friend. I wouldn't survive it.

I am standing in my room singing "The Ballad of Lormere" to myself as I dress. My voice sounds strained and it's not helped by the black smoke that curls in through my window; another funeral pyre. I don't know who it's for, nor why they died, but I pray they have more peace than I've known lately. When there is a knock at my door I expect it to be Lief but it's not. A strange guard stands there, white-faced, the corners of his mouth turned down with disgust as he informs me that the queen has ordered him to come and escort me to her. Hope rises inside me that she's assigned this new guard to me and that I'm about to win my freedom back, but the look on his face tells me I couldn't be more wrong; it seems the queen wasn't lying when she said there was no one else willing to act as my guard. I wonder what this one did, or what he was threatened with, to draw the short straw of guarding me today. Then I realize he is alone and panic grips me, this is why I've been summoned to her; Lief has resigned too. He's left me here; I pushed him too far; I've lost him.

"Where's my other guard?" I ask shakily.

"Here," he calls, jogging up the last few steps. "Forgive me, I was sharpening my sword."

My relief at seeing him there takes me by surprise.

We walk through the halls, silent but not peaceful. The corridors reek of charred flesh from the pyre, the odour horrifyingly similar to the smell of a pig on a spit. There is something in the air, something sharp that cuts through the stench of cremation, making a scent all of its own. The sun is shining, lighting the dust that my dress disturbs on the carpets, and the sky is clear, but it feels as though the castle is holding its breath.

I turn automatically towards the long gallery but the queen's guard does not do the same. It happens so quickly that I don't have time to stop. But Lief is fast, faster than either of us, and he shoves the guard aside with only a fingernail's grace saving him from contact with me. I slam myself against the wall in shock, knocking the air from my lungs, but the guard draws his sword, pointing it angrily at Lief, whose own face is lit with rage.

"You dare—" is as far as he gets before Lief rounds on him.

"You fool," Lief hisses. "Do you want to die?"

With a look of terror the guard sheathes his sword, but Lief has not finished his tirade yet, his fists bunched, his arms shaking with the effort of not lashing out.

"What kind of idiot does not know how to escort a lady, particularly this lady? To get to the south tower where the royal solar is we turn south. Your mistake would have cost you your life had I not saved you. You'd be on the floor, shaking and bleeding through your nose, dying like a poisoned rat."

The guard looks back and forth between Lief and me. My hands are clenched by sides, my body flooded with horror, and I cannot catch my breath. It was so fast, I didn't see it coming.

"Forgive me," the guard's voice wavers.

"Why did you not turn?" Lief demands.

Again the guard shakes his head. "I – we do not go to the royal solar today. We go to the Great Hall."

"Why?" I find my voice, though my throat is taut. "I thought you said the queen wished to see me."

"She does my lady. In the Great Hall. All of the court is there."

"Why?" Lief asks. "And why did you not say before?"

"I thought you knew," says the guard, glancing at Lief, who shakes his head with puzzlement. "There is a trial. One of the ladies is charged with treason."

My stomach drops as I look at Lief. He stares back at me, all formality faded from his gaze. For too long we stare at each other, both confused, both afraid. Then he nods, taking control and returning to my left.

"We'd better go then," he says grimly, waiting for the other guard to stand at my right, though now he keeps an embarrassingly large distance between us, especially in contrast to how close Lief stands to me. It strikes me that though Merek can touch me and not be hurt, he takes such pains to never come too near, to never risk contact. Whereas Lief comes dangerously close, sometimes leaving only an inch or two between us.

It's with further shock I realize I like it.

In the Great Hall the long tables have been pushed back and there is no fire burning in the fireplace. The court sits on benches, row after row of pale, waxen faces, all facing the dais where the king, queen and prince sit on intricately carved chairs. They're talking amongst themselves, and I watch them as I search for somewhere to sit. The king looks angry; he's speaking to the queen, who keeps shaking her head. Finally, the king turns away from her sharply and she stares at him, before turning to look at Merek, who also looks away.

Lief and the other guard move to stand at the rear of the room. On the right the wall is lined with chambermaids, pages, spit-turners and kitchen servants. I see Rulf, and my skin tingles with guilt. The entire castle is here to bear witness.

Merek looks at me as I walk to my seat and frowns. He

leans over to the queen and says something and she shakes her head. On her left, the king leans across again, also talking urgently. But again the queen shakes her head, and both men sit back in their seats, the king chewing his lip and looking angrier than ever. Merek looks back at me and subtly raises his shoulders and then drops them, before he turns his gaze away. Then it is the queen's turn to seek me out and I hurriedly sit down, towards the back, on the bench next to Lady Shasta.

She blanches when she sees me and slides across the bench, though I could have fitted six of myself into the gap between us. I close my eyes when she clutches her husband's elbow and he slides a protective arm around her waist. Whoever is being tried is on trial for treason. And for treason I am the executioner. After the next Telling in a week's time, I'll be killing one of our own.

When I open my eyes the queen is standing, staring down at us all, and I know I am not the only one whose shoulders hunch and whose eyes lower. When she has completed her survey of the room she turns to the side and nods. The door is thrown wide and a woman, shaking, sobbing quietly, is dragged in. At her sides two guards are struggling to control dogs leashed on thick chains.

As one we all shudder. Lady Shasta gasps and I see her husband's knuckles whiten as he holds her tighter. It is Lady Lorelle.

Poor Lorelle's eyes are black holes in her face; her hands are clasped before her as though to beseech the queen. She is not bound; there's no need with the dogs there. I search the crowd for her husband, Lord Lammos, but cannot see him. He must be here somewhere – the whole court is – but not even love will be enough to make him risk the queen's wrath.

The accused is brought to stand before the queen, who gazes down at her with no pity, no recognition of her so-called friend, and we hold our breath as one, waiting for the charges.

Then the queen speaks. "You are brought before me on the charge of treason against the crown of Lormere. If you are found guilty you will be sentenced to death and there will be no Eating for your soul."

Lorelle lets out a terrible wail and one of the dogs growls, a guttural, chilling sound. I look at Merek, but he looks down at the table, as does the king.

"I find you guilty," the queen says, as softly as a girl confiding secrets to her best friend.

A shiver moves through the crowd like a disease, passing along the benches from the front to where I sit, and I feel my stomach lurch. A noise behind me makes me glance to the side and there is Lief, standing at my back, one hand on the hilt of his sword, his fingers flexing.

As the queen speaks again, I turn back to the front, frightened Lief's movements will draw her attention to me and remind her that her executioner is sitting in the room. But she has eyes for no one save her former friend quivering before her on charges too heinous to be named.

"As you have been found guilty of treason, I sentence you to a traitor's death. Come the—"

"Helewys, please!" Lady Lorelle cries. "We were children together. I have done no wrong. . . I thought I was too old. . . I didn't know—"

"Come the next Telling," the queen continues, her voice raised to drown out the other woman's appeal, "you will be taken to the Morning Room and there your life will be forfeit for your crimes against the throne of Lormere. May the Gods have mercy on you."

"No," a voice says firmly.

We all look around to see who spoke and then with a slap of shock I realize it was the king.

"No, Helewys," he says again, standing, and every pair of eyes in the room turns to him. Merek stares at his stepfather, his face unreadable, as the queen turns to her husband.

"You dare?" she whispers, but the stone walls carry it and we all hear it. "You dare contradict me?"

"It's not treason, Helewys," the king says. "It's a gift from the Gods."

The queen and the king lock eyes and then I know what Lorelle's supposed crime is. She's with child. She and Lord Lammos are going to have a baby. Alianor was the last child born to this court; since her death no one has dared to conceive. Not when the queen has not. It's been an unspoken pact between the ladies of the court that if the queen cannot get with child then they cannot either.

And she would have me take both Lady Lorelle's life and the child's because of it. I could never . . . not that. I couldn't take the life of an unborn child.

"I say it's treason and I sentence her to death," the queen says.

"Then I pardon her. Lady Lorelle, you have my pardon," the king says firmly and I cannot tear my eyes from them. The queen has turned bright red and the king's shoulders are rising and falling rapidly, as though he's been running. I would never, ever have made a wager on this happening and from the look on the open-mouthed faces around the hall, no one else would have either.

"You cannot. . ." the queen says.

"I am the king. I can," he replies. And then he kneels before the queen.

Shock causes me gasp loudly, and I see everyone else in the room reel too. It is an old custom – though never, to my knowledge, used – that the queen can intercede with the king to plead for clemency for the condemned. But a king has never, ever knelt before a queen. This is history, being made as I watch. A king begging a queen.

He looks up at his wife and holds his arms out to either side. "Please, Helewys, I beseech you to spare her life."

"You would work against me?" she asks and there is real curiosity in her voice.

"In this, yes." He bows his head. "I will not sanction the death of a woman for the crime of getting with child."

The queen glares at him and, with utter disgust warping her face, she stalks out through the royal doors, taking the passageway to the royal solar. The king stands slowly and looks about the room.

"Take the dogs away," he orders the Master of the Hounds, who hesitates, looking towards the door the queen left through before he obeys. Then the king looks at the weeping Lady Lorelle, finally in her husband's arms. "Lord Lammos, please take Lady Lorelle from the castle. Tonight. Horses will be made available to you and you may return to your hall in Haga."

Lord Lammos stammers his thanks and Lorelle sobs, her hands shaking as she clutches her husband. The two leave the room, their arms entwined.

The king ignores the astonished court and follows the queen out of the Great Hall, his shoulders slumped wearily, though he pauses to clasp Merek's arm as he passes. Merek's eyes meet mine as he stands, and he raises his eyebrows once, before he follows his mother and stepfather from the hall.

The moment the door is closed behind them the murmuring starts.

Lief crouches down behind me, whispering urgently. "My lady, I would be so bold as to say we should go now."

I nod, utterly stunned, rising to follow my guard. The king stood up to her. And he won. I look at Lief to see what he thinks and his eyes are bright and manic as we walk, his pace swift as I struggle to match his stride.

"The other guard," I begin but he talks across me.

"Forget him. He doesn't matter now. Turn left."

I stop. "Where are we going?"

"To see Dorin. While we have chance."

124

"We can't—"

"The other guard isn't likely to tell the queen he lost you, is he? This is your best chance if you want to see him."

I gaze at him, weighing up his offer, before nodding. "We must hurry."

When we reach the bowels of the castle, he pauses, closing the door to the stairwell behind us. "Wait. I owe you an apology. Another one. I haven't written it down so you'll have to take me at my word."

"Not now, Lief—"

"Please. I'm not – I want you to understand why I am the way I am. I'm not used to being a servant; I'm used to being my own master," he shrugs, glancing up at the ceiling before meeting my eyes again. "I come from a farm and I was to inherit it eventually. But my father died unexpectedly. With a mother and younger sister to provide for, it fell to me to make ends meet. So I came here. As fate would have it you needed a new guard and I arrived on the day of the trials. I am making mistakes, I know, but I am trying, my lady. I am trying."

I look at him, fear and pity warring inside me. "Why are you telling me now?"

He chews his lip before he answers. "Because you deserve an explanation – the way you put up with me." He smiles sheepishly. "And if the king can be brave then I can too."

"What do you mean?"

"She would have killed that woman if he hadn't stopped it. She would have made you do it. And for what? Because she is with child. That was her crime against the throne of Lormere. She did what the queen can't."

I clap my hands to my mouth as though I were the one who'd said it. "Lief, you cannot—"

"I know I cannot! You keep telling me I cannot. And I know you're right. I don't know how you stand it."

"What makes you think I do?" I stare at him. "What makes you so sure that I do stand it?"

"You never speak of it."

"That doesn't mean I don't think of it. I spend hours in prayer, asking the Gods to help me understand it all."

"Have you tried asking them to do anything about it?" he says and I don't know if he's mocking me.

"What could they do?"

"I don't know. Maybe they want you to do something about it. If all of you stood together then—"

"Like in Tregellan," I say and he turns pale. "Do you think we should we start a war we cannot win? Should we stage a coup, gather what's left of our meagre forces and rise up and kill her, and the king and the prince? Are you suggesting treason as an answer?"

"No," he says quickly. "I didn't mean that. Petition her, present it to her reasonably?"

"Do you honestly think people haven't thought of it? When I was in my fourteenth harvest, Lord Grevlas planned to plead for the dogs to be banished. From all accounts he had a lot of support. Until he tried to enlist the wrong supporter. Whoever it was went straight to the queen, and the rest of his supporters did the same. Had it been a year later I would have been the one to execute him."

Lief looks away from me, his hands clenched tightly, before he exhales, a long, drawn-out breath as his fingers uncurl and his eyes meet mine once more.

"You're not like them," he says slowly.

"I am their executioner, Lief."

"Because they make you."

"It doesn't matter—"

"It does to me," he says softly. "More than I can say."

Then I look away, the intensity of his gaze reminding me of Merek, making my stomach twist.

"Nothing can be done to make things right," he says after a moment, so quietly I wonder if he meant to speak aloud.

"Nothing," I agree and he closes his eyes briefly. "All we can do is stay quiet and do our best. We must be ghosts. That's how you stay alive in this castle. You become a ghost. You keep your head down and you stay out of her way as much as you can."

"You should leave."

"I can't. You know what I am. I have poison in my veins, Lief. It's only the God's will that stops it killing me. If I defied them, if I turned away from them, I'd be dead before I got out of the castle. They'll forgive my doubts because I'm mortal and I must be tested, but they'd never forgive my walking away. And even if they didn't strike me down straight away, the queen certainly would – you know that, you saw her now. She'd do whatever it took to revenge herself on me for it. Hurting my sister. Hurting you. You'd be killed, for not keeping me here. Chances are they'd have me kill you before they took my life. Perhaps rightly so, because this is definitely treason, Lief."

"I didn't hear you say a word," he says softly. "I heard nothing."

I nod and he looks at me, his eyebrows raised and his mouth pinched. "Go on," he says finally. "I'll wait here. He's in the room at the end. Go and see Dorin."

I can't look at the door of the Telling Room as I pass it.

The room is dim, scantly lit by the candles guttering beneath a copper pot that simmers and fills the chamber with the woody, spicy scent of cypress. There's something else, some odour under it that makes my skin crawl. Dorin lies in a corner on a raised pallet and it's clear from his face that he is deeply ill, his features taut under skin that looks like tallow. At first he looks asleep and I am about to turn and leave him to rest.

"My lady," he says thickly. "What are you doing here?"

"Hello, Dorin," I say. "I came to see how my most trusted guard fares."

"My lady, it is good of you to come. I apologize for the inconvenience of it. I know I've let you down."

"You've never let me down. How do you feel?"

"I go from strength to strength each day. I'll be back within a day or two, I assure you. I can only beg your forgiveness that I am here at all."

He doesn't look as if he goes from strength to strength. He looks like a corpse, gaunt and wasted. I'd never have known it was him if he were not the only man in the room. What kind of illness can shrink a man to this in three weeks?

I smile at him. "I don't doubt it," I lie. "Though Lief is doing well. I'm in good hands; you need not fear. I've been praying for you."

He nods, his eyelids fluttering, and I realize he is losing consciousness.

"Stuan, no more ale tonight," he slurs.

"What?" I stare at him, wondering why the name is so familiar. Then I remember. Stuan was the guard who left after I killed Tyrek. He hasn't worked here for more than two harvests. And that's when I realize what the creeping scent is under the cypress. It's poppy tears. They're giving Dorin poppy tears.

I'm in my ninth harvest and we've been called to the town hall in Monkham. The mayor's mother has died, which was expected as she was in her eightieth harvest year and had been ill for some time. I was excited to go to the town hall and see it, craving some of the luxury I'd seen in the castle, but it was starkly different. It was dim and dark and the room for the Eating smelt sickly sweet like rot. The coffin was in the centre of the room and the mayor had only supplied a stool for my mother, so I stood at her side as she performed the Eating. It wasn't a large spread, but right in the centre of the coffin was a dish of cream with a sprig of rosemary on top.

I watched as my mother ate around the cream, never dipping into it, never taking a spoonful. She left it right until the end, avoiding it until she'd cleared the coffin of everything else. Then, to my surprise, she spoke to me.

"Do you know what it is?" she asked.

I nodded, too scared to reply. She'd never, ever spoken during an Eating, ever. Before now she'd only explained her actions once we were back in her room, with me breathing through my mouth to lessen the reek of the jasmine. Never while we were still at an Eating.

"It's not fresh cream, Twylla," she'd said. "It's soured cream."

I frowned. "Why did they offer soured cream?"

"It means the woman lost a child," she'd replied.

I'd shaken my head, not understanding. Losing a child wasn't a sin; everyone knew the Gods could take away as they saw fit and sometimes they called an unborn back to the Eternal Kingdom. Sin Eaters are privy to all the secrets of the dead; we know every sin a person ever committed from the feast, and from that you can piece together their life and the kind of person they were. I'd watched my mother Eat coddled eggs for thieves and boiled horse liver for scolds and nags. But I had never seen soured cream on a coffin before.

"It isn't a sin to lose a child," I'd said.

"It's a sin to take the herbs that would make you lose a child," my mother said, her voice tight. "Pennyroyal, yarrow, blue cohosh . . . rosemary. That is what soured cream is for. The milk of life gone bad. Only Næht may decide when it is

130

time; no man nor woman should."

I'd stared at the coffin, still a little too young to understand, as my mother rose and left the bowl atop the coffin without saying the words that completed the Eating. I had been about to follow her when a hand gripped my wrist.

Looming out of the dark corner was a cadaverous, leathery face, its mouth and nose covered in lesions. Its eyes were black, I could see no iris in them; I could see no reason in them. The man held my wrist in surprisingly strong fingers, bone covered in thin skin. And he stank of something heavy and sweet.

"She's not in there," he'd said, saliva pooling in the corners of his mouth, his words slurring. "She's a witch. They have to burn her or she'll come back. She killed a baby. She said no, no, no, but I put a baby in her anyway and then she magicked it away."

I'd screamed and the mayor flew into the room, my mother after him.

"Let her go, Papa," he'd said to the old man but he wouldn't and gripped me tighter.

"She's a witch!" he'd roared and then my wrist was free. The man slumped to the floor and the mayor herded me from the room.

"He has growths," he said to my mother, wringing his hands in apology. "We give him poppy tears for the pain. He doesn't know what he's saying. He wanted to be there, to say goodbye. I thought he'd be quiet. Forgive me, Madame Eater."

My mother had looked at me. "What did he say?"

"That – that she said no but he put a baby in her. And that she's a witch," I added, my voice shaking.

My mother looked the mayor up and down, as if she was reading him the way she read the food at the Eating. Then she marched past him into the Eating room. When she returned she had the bowl of soured cream in her hands and as we watched she tipped it down her throat, dropping the bowl to the ground where it smashed.

"I give easement and rest now to thee, dear lady. Come not down the lanes or in our meadows. And for thy peace I pawn my own soul." She spat the words, keeping her eyes on the mayor the whole time. "I'll expect to see bull's eyes at your father's Eating," she said and the mayor had gasped. "But I won't Eat them. I will not take that sin."

He held out the silver coin to her but my mother didn't take it. It was the only time she didn't.

"My lady, we must go," Lief says, pulling me back into the present, though I can still feel the old man's hand on my arm.

"My lady?" He peers around the door. One look at my face and he's half drawn his sword.

"I'm fine, Lief," I say shakily. "I just. . ."

Lief looks at Dorin, slack-jawed and wan against the pallet. "Wait outside, my lady. I'll try to make him more comfortable."

I nod, grateful to leave, taking great gulps of clean air and leaning against the damp stone walls. Poppy tears. Lost children and monsters in the dark. The sin my mother would not take. I shudder, trying to shake it off.

When I look back into the room I see Lief moving Dorin's head with a practised hand, his actions deft and tender, and I wonder how his father died.

Chapter 10

"What shall we do today, my lady?"

I am staring out of the window, my thoughts flitting between Dorin, the king and queen, and Lief himself, and his question flusters me. "We?" I ask.

"I don't mean to presume. But I thought . . . we're both here, and it seems foolish for us to not use each other's company. Not that it's my place to use your company. But . . . if you wanted company, I am here."

"Well –" I smile sweetly "– I'd planned to pray."

"Ah." His face falls. "I might leave you to it then. No need to gild the lily with too many prayers."

"You don't believe in the Gods, do you, Lief?" I voice a suspicion I've held for a while now.

He looks at me before shaking his head. "Not really, my lady."

"Do many Tregellians not believe in them?"

He shrugs. "It's not like here, if that's what you mean. But then Tregellan is governed by a council, not a monarchy. We place a lot of value on science and medicine. There's not a lot of room for Gods in that."

"Is there not? Can you not see the life that Dæg brings in your sciences and medicines?"

"I see the work of men in our sciences, my lady. And the Gods have never answered a single prayer of mine," he adds bitterly, before he shakes his head. "Forgive me, my lady. I speak out of turn."

"No," I say before I can stop myself. Lief looks at me, his eyes wide. "You may have your opinion. Just be careful where and with whom you speak it."

"In here, it is safe?" Lief asks.

I nod.

"With you, it is safe?"

I nod again.

"Even though you're the incarnation of a Goddess?"

"Daunen isn't a Goddess," I say. "She's the daughter of the Gods, but not a Goddess herself."

He shrugs lightly and smiles. "Maybe that's why I like her best."

When I lived with my mother, my sister and I built a den of sorts in the garden, hollowing the innards of a bush, painstakingly snapping branches back to carve a space inside. When our brothers went to market and our mother rested we would crawl inside our den and sit, hiding our treasures amongst the leaves and telling stories. No one else knew it was there and it was our place. It was a safe space.

Now my room is the same, a den for Lief and me to hide in and tell our stories. We chat about our childhoods, exchanging tales of misdeeds and tumbles and the folk from our villages. When he asks, I tell him how I came to be at the castle and he is suitably awed.

"Perhaps I should look into becoming dedicated to a God."

"You'd have to believe in them first." I smile.

"I could learn to." He smiles back.

"Can you sing?"

He draws himself up to his full height and rests a hand over his heart.

In mountain's shadow, Lormere stands,
Most blessed of the western lands,
Through snow and ice it doth endure,
A land of might for ever more."

A smile creeps across my face at how badly he does it.

"What do you think?" he asks once the song is over.

"You make an excellent guard, Lief."

"You wound me, my lady," he sniffs, pouting at me before grinning. "Though I confess I wouldn't be keen on being poisoned once a moon."

I answer him softly. "Daunen is the daughter of two Gods. One giver and one taker. It's because of Næht that I have to take life, as she did when she took the skies from Dæg."

He nods, looking thoughtful before he speaks. "What would you do if you weren't Daunen Embodied and betrothed to the prince?"

"I'd be the next Sin Eater."

"No, my lady," he sighs. "I mean what would you do if you didn't have a destiny? What do you wish for?"

I close my eyes, replaying my life in my mind. I've never thought of not having a destiny. I've always had one. Last time I wished for something I believed I'd never have, it brought me here. I tell him I don't know what people do when they're free.

"What do you mean by free?" he asks.

"Like you. You can go where you please and do as you wish. I don't know what that's like."

"I'm not free, my lady," he says slowly. "I can no more wander off and do as I will than you can. You think of having choices like people think of flying. They see a hawk soaring and hovering and they tell themselves how nice it would be to fly. But pigeons can fly, and sparrows too. No one imagines being a sparrow though. No one wants that."

Lief looks at me with such sadness in his eyes that my breath becomes caught inside me. I want to reach out and wipe the expression from his face.

He rises to his feet and turns away. "I'll go and see if our supper has been brought."

With sudden, horrible clarity I realize that one day Lief will leave; whatever his thoughts on freedom are he's at liberty to leave if he chooses. But I'm not; I'll stay here in the castle for ever. My entire life has been mapped out before me. I won't even have sparrow-like freedom.

I didn't realize tears had fallen until Lief returns. His gasp is enough to check me, and I turn away, wiping my cheeks as he clatters the tray down and sinks at my feet.

"My lady?"

"I'm fine, Lief."

"Was it me? What I said? Can I fetch you anything? Send for anything?"

"No. Wait, yes. Could you bring me some wine?" I say, ignoring the quirk of his eyebrow. "Honey wine, please. Only a little."

"At once." He nods and speeds from the room. A short while later he's back, a small bottle and glass on a silver tray in his hands. He pours my glass and places it on the bureau before me. I don't want the wine, not truly, but I can think of nothing else that will take the edge off my melancholy. The wine is sweet and warm and doesn't help at all. I don't know what's wrong with me.

He sits on the floor in front of me, gazing at me with an unusually grave expression.

"I don't want to upset you further, but the maid who fetched the wine also had news about Dorin. It's not good," he says hurriedly before I can interrupt. "He's fallen into a sleep. He won't wake up. The healers don't believe there is anything that can be done, but the prince says they're wrong. He's insisting they send for a physician. A Tregellian one."

"A Tregellian physician? Here?" Relief and fear war

inside me. Would Merek really do that for a mere guard? A cruel voice in my mind whispers that this provides Merek with the perfect opportunity to bring his much-wanted Tregellian medicine into Lormere and I push it aside, trying to concentrate on what Lief is saying.

"The prince has apparently told the healers they are to send for one. They're in an uproar about it. I'm not sure what bothers them more, that a physician may come or that it will be a Tregellian." His face darkens and then it clears. "Forgive me, I'm being stupid. Now isn't the time."

"Will a physician be able to heal him?"

"It might be his only hope. I saw inside that sick room. Waving a censer over him isn't going to heal anything. He needs a proper diagnosis, not all of this talk of imbalanced humours. If they can find what's wrong with him he might at least stand a chance of getting the right treatment and recovering."

Again he speaks as though he knows about healing and I remember his hands on Dorin, firm and practised. He said he was going to be a farmer but surely no farmer knows so much about plants and their properties? For now I swallow my questions, looking down at my hands as my mind turns towards another problem. "I hope my mother doesn't find out they're sending for a physician," I say quietly.

"What does your mother have to do with it?"

I keep my eyes on my hands as I try to find the words to explain it, knowing he'll want all of it and not sure if I can tell it all, even now. "She doesn't hold with it. She believes that if

Næht has marked a man for her own, it's wrong to intervene."

"Intervene? As in to heal him?"

"To undo the will of the Gods. Some healing is permitted, certain herbs and prayers, but if it goes too far . . . she thinks it's wrong to take from the hands of the Gods. And that's what physicians do. They use unnatural ways. At the least she'll want it balancing or she won't do the Eating if he does die."

"Balancing?"

I sigh. "When someone is gravely ill, another death can be offered to Næht to try to appease her so she doesn't take the life of the dying person. A sacrifice can be made, usually a sheep or a pig." *Or a goat*, I say to myself. "If Næht is satisfied then she'll spare the life of the person who ails and my mother will accept Næht's will and not hold it against the soul of the survivor."

"I don't understand what that has to do with healing."

"Physicians tether the soul with their cures and keep it here when it should have gone to Næht."

"But who's to say that it's not Næht's will that they're healed?" Lief says.

"You don't understand," I say, turning from him, a headache starting behind my eyes.

"Forgive me, my lady. I was being churlish. So when this healer comes, we'll kill a sheep and if your Goddess accepts, then Dorin will get better? Is that how it works?"

I nod, unwilling to think about it, to remember.

"Well, then, we'll do that. Will that please your mother?"

I shrug. "It has done, in the past. As long as a cut of the

meat is sent to her as a tribute when the animal is killed."

"Does it happen often?"

"No, not often. There aren't many families who can afford to lose an animal, even at the cost of a loved one."

"When was the last time?"

I look away from him. The last time that I knew of was for my sister and it did not happen in the way I had described to Lief. Maryl had been feverish for days, and no amount of cold compresses would bring down her temperature. We could get no fluid into her; her bones were small under my hands and she was fading from us. My mother, ever the dutiful servant of Næht, shrugged when I cried.

"If Næht wants her, she shall have her."

"Can we do nothing?"

"We must do nothing. It's Næht's will."

Then she was gone, away to an Eating, leaving me behind to be with Maryl as she died. I had screwed up my courage and gone to the with-woman in Monkham, begged some feverfew and willow bark from her. I ground it and boiled it and fed it to my baby sister, drop by drop, until she was cool and lucid again. When my mother returned I told her it was a miracle.

"Næht didn't want her after all," I said, unable to meet my mother's eyes.

We dined on roast goat that evening, a rare treat cooked by my mother herself – a celebration, I had thought – and I swallowed it all down. An hour later, I brought it all back up in the goat house beside our home. Penny had been my favourite, my darling. She had chewed delicately on my skirts and snuffled her hairy nose into my pockets. She came when I called her.

But I kept my sister and Næht had her sacrifice. I push away the thought that the sacrifice is only ever meant to appease her for a little while, and that I don't know how much time was bought for my sister.

"The last time was a long time ago," I tell him. "As I said, it's not often practised – there aren't many who could afford to lose a moon's mutton or lamb."

He shakes his head and sighs. "It's not a sin to heal people, or to help them. It's not defying the Gods. How can it be, when the plants physicians use grow in the earth and the knowledge comes from the people the Gods supposedly created? I was saying all of this to Dimia yesterday."

"Who's Dimia?"

"She's the maid who brings our food. She brought your wine to me. She's been finding out how Dorin fares for you. She—"

"That's kind of her." I speak over him.

Lief looks at me curiously, before continuing. "She has been checking on him and reporting back to me. And I promise you that Tregellian physicians are the best. If anyone can do something for him, they will . . . and then we'll sacrifice a sheep to your Næht to balance it if we have to. My lady, is it not worth it for Dorin?"

I stare at him. "He's going to die, isn't he? Without this physician?"

Lief nods. "He can't be helped if they don't know what's wrong with him."

I recall his thin skin, the smell of cypress, his delirium. He looked barely alive. "But I've been praying so hard to the Gods. I'm dedicated to their daughter, anointed in her name."

Lief notes the panic in my voice and rises to his knees, leaning past me to top up my glass. As he moves back he pauses, his face close to mine, and my stomach aches strangely. "It's not over yet," he says. "It's all down to the physician."

I turn away to lift my glass and when I look back he is at my feet, a safe distance away again.

"Either way, it marks the end for us," he says softly.

"What do you mean? Are you leaving?" The panic returns, my voice becoming shrill.

"No. No," he says hurriedly. "I'm staying with you. But this . . . time that we spend together will have to come to an end. Whether Dorin returns or someone else is sent to guard you. I'm not completely stupid, I know it shouldn't happen. I know it can't continue."

His brow furrows and I drink some more of the wine, understanding why Merek is so fond of it and the numbness it offers.

"I can't think about this now, Lief. I need to think about Dorin. If I pray harder, if I could go to my temple. I can't pray here, it's not right," I babble, but already I'm imagining losing Lief, returning to my old ways, with him outside my door and never in here with me. No more talks, no more

143

jokes. No more questions. Just my guard. "What can we do?" I moan.

"The only thing I can think of is ask the queen to permit me to be your sole guard. That way you can go to your temple, and see Dorin."

"And if he returns?" There is a brief, delirious moment when I imagine all three of us laughing together in my room.

"We'll deal with that if it happens," Lief says. And I know from his tone that he doesn't think it will.

"She'll never allow it," I tell him, pushing my confusion aside. "You know what she said. She wouldn't trust one guard to keep me safe."

"Then let's not ask her. Let's ask the prince."

"Merek? Why would he help?"

"Because he's your betrothed. Because he has a vested interest in your well-being and you being cooped up in here is not good for you. He knows how much you value your temple and being there. And he knows what it's like to be shut away."

"You were listening when we had supper!" I accuse him.

"I couldn't help it, my lady. I had to stay within earshot so I could hear him summoning me," he says. "I might be invisible, but I have ears."

I shake my head at him. "The queen will hate it if I go over her head."

"But will she deny Merek if he asks her for it? She allowed you out with him, without a guard, after all. She's allowing him to bring in a Tregellian physician for your guard. If he says it's what he wants, is she likely to deny it to him?"

"Are all Tregellians as cunning as you?"

"I am not cunning, my lady. I promise you that. I'm good at seeing around obstacles, is all." His eyes are larger than usual as he looks up at me and my heart races in my chest. It would solve all of my current problems. I would be able to leave these rooms, but keep my time with Lief. I can deal with Dorin if – when – he returns. It wouldn't be hurting anyone.

"Would you send word to the prince?" I say slowly. "Tell him I'm thinking of him, and that I'm grateful for his trying to help Dorin. Ask him to send someone to my temple to pray on my behalf, seeing as I am isolated in my room." I think back to what he said during our supper. "Tell him I fear I'm spending too much time in my head. Say that I'll be sad to miss the dandelion seeds this year, but that I hope he enjoys them."

He grins at me and I'm sure now that he heard much of the conversation during the supper. "Are all daughters of Gods as cunning as you, my lady?" he asks.

I smile grimly. "Perhaps I'm good at seeing around obstacles too."

He grins again and sets to work and I watch his long, slim fingers curl around the quill, gripping it tightly as he writes. His knuckles, too large for his hands, whiten as he grips the pen, guiding it across the sheet. I am transfixed by the movement and I don't hear him when he speaks.

"Shall I send it?"

"Yes . . . before I lose my courage."

His smile is wide as he leaps to his feet. He departs with haste and returns as quickly.

"Dimia's taking it to her brother now. He's one of the queen's men and he'll be able to get it to the prince."

I feel a sharp pang in my chest when he says Dimia's name. "How long do you think it will take for a reply?"

"I wouldn't know. Shall I wait downstairs?"

"No," I say swiftly. "We'll wait here. It might be a while yet."

"As you wish." His voice is low.

But we don't have to wait for long. Less than an hour has passed before there is a timid knock at the door. Lief and I look at each other and he draws his sword, motioning for me to stand behind him.

When he throws open the door a small, curvy, dark-haired girl stands there, gazing up at him.

"I waited downstairs," she addresses him quietly, "but you did not come, so I thought. . ."

"Dimia, you must never come here," he chides, though his voice is soft.

"Forgive me," she says as she looks at me. "My lady, my brother was asked to deliver a reply immediately."

She's very pretty. I don't like her. "Thank you, Dimia. You may go."

She dips her head before looking at Lief and smiling shyly. He returns her smile, gifting me with another sharp jab beneath my ribs before he closes the door.

He brings the note to me, waiting for my eager nod before

he opens it, frowning before his face splits into his familiar wide grin.

"Lief! What does it say?"

"The prince has challenged me to a duel. Tonight. For your freedom."

Chapter 11

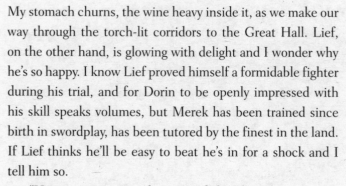

My stomach churns, the wine heavy inside it, as we make our way through the torch-lit corridors to the Great Hall. Lief, on the other hand, is glowing with delight and I wonder why he's so happy. I know Lief proved himself a formidable fighter during his trial, and for Dorin to be openly impressed with his skill speaks volumes, but Merek has been trained since birth in swordplay, has been tutored by the finest in the land. If Lief thinks he'll be easy to beat he's in for a shock and I tell him so.

"Have you ever seen the prince fight?" he asks.

"No, but I expect he's good."

"You've never seen me fight either."

"Lief, he's been taught by the best the kingdom has to offer."

"But he's never fought for his life, my lady. His tutors

won't have been as hard on him, because he's the prince. I doubt he's ever been bloodied at all."

"And you have?"

"I have." He grins. "The Lormerian guards did not go easy on me at my trial. They aimed to disarm me, even wound me. And I beat every single one of them."

"Just . . . don't be too sure," I say. "He's not a novice. He wouldn't challenge you if he didn't think he could win."

"Why challenge me at all?" Lief says. "Why not simply tell the queen he thinks you should be allowed out with one guard?"

"No one 'simply tells' the queen anything, Lief. Not even the prince."

"I think it's for your benefit," he says slyly. "I think he wants an opportunity to show you what a fine husband he'll make, beating your loyal guard in combat as you watch."

"Being the best at duelling isn't all that high on my list of qualities a husband should have," I say tartly.

"Then you're in luck, as he's going to lose." Lief smiles and in the torchlight it's sinister, distorted by the play of light and shadow on his face.

"Don't hurt him," I say and Lief pauses.

"I wouldn't," he says slowly. "I wouldn't do that to you."

I flush and nod. "Come, we'd better not keep him waiting."

Merek is waiting in the Great Hall when we arrive, the sleeves of his tunic rolled up and a sword slung from his belt.

He bows as we enter and I pause and bow back, Lief doing the same at my side.

"How are you, Twylla?" Merek says as he approaches.

"I'm well, Your Highness. May I ask how you are?"

"I'm well, though it's been a strange day." His eyes glitter as he speaks. "We can talk more of it another time. Thank you for your note. I thought you said you had not learned to write."

"Lief wrote the note. I dictated it," I say.

He nods and turns to Lief. "You are charged with protecting the lady, a role which you currently undertake alone?"

Lief bows again. "Yes, Your Highness."

"You are Tregellian, are you not? Where did you train in combat?"

"I'm not formally trained, Your Highness."

"Then who taught you to fight?"

"My father, Your Highness," he says stiffly.

"And who trained your father?"

"His father."

"Were any of your family formally trained?" Merek asks, incredulous.

I will Lief to keep his temper. "No. My father was a farmer. As was his father," he says, his fingers on the hilt of his sword.

Merek looks him up and down. "I hear you bested everyone at your trial?"

"I did, Your Highness."

Merek nods. "The rules are simple. If you best me, then I'll grant Lady Twylla permission to leave her quarters with you as her sole guard until the other one is able to return to his duties or other circumstances intervene. I must be able to assure my mother that you're able to protect her." He turns to me and I dip my head.

"Forgive me, Your Highness, but who will judge if I've bested you?"

Merek raises an eyebrow. "We fight for first blood."

My eyes widen in surprise and even Lief looks astounded. "I can't accept the terms, Your Highness," he says slowly. "It's treason to wound an anointed member of the royal family. I can't win either way."

"I give you my word no harm will come to you should you beat me," Merek says solemnly. "These are my terms and my guards will be my witnesses." From the shadows two men step forward and bow. I hadn't known they were there. "But you have to beat me first."

I can see Lief puffing up at the slight. "And if I lose, Your Highness?"

"Then the lady will remain confined to her quarters until the other guard returns to his post or another one can be found for her. I have to be confident that you are able to take sole charge of my future bride's safety. And I can only be confident in that if I see for myself that you are as good as I'm told. Or not, as it may be."

Lief's face hardens and his fingers curl into his palms. He looks at Merek for a long moment, then finally he nods once and jerks his head in the smallest of bows. "I accept the terms."

Merek turns to me. "If I could ask you to clear the floor, Twylla?" he says and I curtsy, making my way to the dais and taking a seat before it.

Lief and Merek take their places in the centre of the room, bowing, Lief deeply and Merek with a nod of his head. Merek draws his sword and Lief does the same, both keeping them pointed towards the floor. Then, without saying a word, they raise their swords at the exact same moment and begin to circle, their footsteps crossing over as they take the measure of each other, stalk each other like prey, their eyes only for their opponent.

Then Merek breaks the circle and attacks, Lief swings his arm to block the strike and the fight is on.

Merek feints at Lief, who darts away, whirling around and thrusting his sword towards Merek's left arm. Merek manages to parry the attack, making a jab of his own that forces Lief back. To my eyes it seems they're equal in skill; neither one has more than a split-second advantage on the other before an attack is thwarted and they have to retreat before pushing forward again.

The room rings with the sound of steel against steel, swords swinging high, then low, then high again. Merek makes a sudden stab at Lief and again Lief whirls away, but not before Merek's sword has caught his tunic in the shoulder and made a small tear.

"Almost, Your Highness," Lief calls cheerfully, twisting around to see his shoulder and Merek snorts.

Merek moves again, swinging his sword across his body at Lief's middle, and my heart is in my mouth, but Lief swings his own sword and smashes it against the flat of Merek's and I see Merek move back and grip his forearm with his other hand.

That is when I see how good a warrior Lief is.

They're not equal in skill, not by a long shot. Lief was toying with him, taunting him as a cat does a mouse, allowing him to make jabs and attempts, making Merek believe he had a chance. But now he's fighting back. Lief's attack is relentless. Merek has no time to try to counter as Lief gives him no choice but to defend himself. Lief's sword rains down blow after blow on Merek's and I can see Merek tiring as Lief backs him across the hall. At my sides the guards stand, their own swords drawn, and I don't blame them; Lief's attack is terrible.

Then Merek drops his sword to the floor and holds up his hands.

"I yield," he calls through pants. "I yield."

At once Lief lowers his sword and bows and after a moment Merek makes a slight incline of his head. Both men stand, breathing heavily. Lief sheathes his sword and Merek lifts his from the floor and does the same.

I stand and approach. "Are you well, Your Highness?" I ask.

"I'm fine. Unbloodied, but given your guard's skill I decided I'd prefer to stay that way." He nods sulkily at Lief, who bows. "As per my terms you may leave your tower with him as your sole guard. I have no fears for your safety with him."

"Thank you, Your Highness. Will I have Lief write to the queen to thank her?"

Merek looks embarrassed. "It might be best if I talk to her."

"Merek –" I forget we're not alone "– you said you had to be able to assure her I'd be safe. Assure her, not tell her. Does she know about this?"

He shakes his head. "She's rather busy with my stepfather. So I took the bull by the horns, as it were." The corner of his mouth twitches. "I'll try to talk to her tonight, but in case I have no opportunity, you'll need to be discreet in your travels. I won't ask you to stay in your room any longer."

"Thank you," I say softly.

He bows to me, his eyes lingering on mine before he turns to Lief.

"I enjoyed that. I confess I spent some of my time in Tregellan sparring with their soldiers. Your people fight well. Perhaps we could fight again sometime?"

"Your Highness." Lief bows.

"I'll see you soon, Twylla." Merek dips his head and then sweeps from the room, his guards marching after him.

Lief and I walk back through the corridors, my heart still hammering in my chest, and it's not until we're well clear of the Great Hall that I realize I've been holding my breath.

"I thought you were going to be a farmer?" I say as we approach my tower.

"It doesn't hurt for a Tregellian to be battle-ready. Since

the war, every father has trained his son to fight with sword and knife and bow, whether they're in the army or not."

I nod as he opens the door of the tower for me. "You're good," I say as we climb the stairs to my room.

"He was too. It surprised me."

"But not as good as you." I lift the latch on my door and cross to the bureau, pouring myself another glass of wine, determined to calm myself.

"My lady, would you agree I have earned a glass of your honey wine?"

"You've earned the carafe," I say, pushing it towards him. "And you've earned me my freedom."

"All in a day's work." He winces as he lifts the carafe to his lips, drinking deeply.

"Are you well?"

He smiles strangely. "I believe I may have been cut."

"What? When?" I take a large gulp of wine, horrified.

"When he caught my tunic he may have nicked my skin. I can't be sure until I look."

"That would mean you lost. Lief, you have to tell him, it's dishonourable. . ."

He looks at me with a closed expression. "If I tell him, you'll be confined here again."

I open my mouth to speak but no words form on my tongue. I don't want to be confined.

"It might not be cut," Lief says, trying to peer over his shoulder. "I need to go to my room."

"Why? What is it?"

"I can't see properly because of my tunic, my lady," he says. "I need to look at the wound."

"I want to see it too. I – oh." I redden when I realize what he means. "Well – but I mean – I don't – yes, I see. Of course."

"I'm happy to do it here, my lady, if you wish to bear witness."

I can only nod, my cheeks blazing.

"Very well," he says. He turns away from me and pulls off his sword belt, dropping it to the floor. In one swift motion, accompanied by a grunt, he pulls his tunic over his head.

"Well?" he says. "Do I bleed?"

But I can't answer because I'm not looking at his shoulder.

I can't stop staring at the shape of his back, the line of his spine. He's much broader than I am. How can he look so different without a tunic on? How can that one simple piece of fabric alter him so much?

"My lady?" he says, twisting to look at me, and my whole body burns as I notice the way his muscles move under his skin.

"Sorry," I mutter, too embarrassed to meet his eye. "Turn around."

I have to stand on tiptoe to look and when I do the relief at what I see is overwhelming. Though there will be a bruise, and the skin has been scraped, there is no blood. He didn't cheat.

"No blood," I say huskily, hurriedly clearing my throat.

"It's grazed, but it didn't bleed – though you'll have quite a bruise by morning."

He turns to the looking glass, peering at the wound, and I blush again as my eyes fall on his collarbones. I cross the room, keeping my back to him as I drain my glass and then refill it. The room feels too hot and I push the window open, breathing in the cool night air.

"I'm sorry," I say again, unsure what I'm apologizing for.

I can't look back at him until I hear the rustling as he replaces his tunic.

"No harm done. It means I didn't lie, or cheat. That's good. You won't have to report me."

"I wouldn't have," I admit.

Lief's face is surprised when it emerges from his tunic. "But it would have been a lie, a sin."

"A small one," I say, my heart thrumming, and when I raise the glass to my lips and drain it for a second time my fingers shake.

"Thank you, my lady."

"Twylla," I say quickly. "When we're alone you may call me Twylla. You've earned that too."

"Twylla," he says softly and it makes me shiver to hear my name on his tongue. "You should rest, Twylla. We have a busy day tomorrow. After all, it's your first day of freedom."

I look at him. When he pulled the tunic over his head he loosened the ribbon that holds his hair back and I wonder how it would feel to touch the freed strands, to wind them around my fingers. Like a sleepwalker I walk towards him,

157

my hand rises and hovers near his chest. We both look down at it, and then it is he who takes a step back as my fingers curl like claws, as though they don't belong to me.

"Goodnight, Twylla," he murmurs. "Dream of good things." He dips his head and turns, closing my door gently behind him.

I look down at my treacherous, trembling hand.

It is a restless, wretched night. All I can think of, dreaming or waking, is his hair and how much I wanted to touch it, his shoulders and his back and how smooth the skin was. I wanted to touch him and if I had he would be dead now. I can't find a comfortable way to lie, but whenever I move the room lurches and I have to sit back up, staring into the darkness. It must be the wine. I drank three glasses on an empty stomach and after the worry of Dorin and the duel, no wonder I forgot myself. But I know it's a lie, another lie. It's not the wine or the shock, that made me want to touch him. When I peered into the looking glass after he'd left, I saw the look in my eye. It was the look of wanting: lust, bright strawberry-flavoured lust. And I can't allow myself to want, because I am betrothed to the prince and if I touch anyone else I will kill them.

Chapter 12

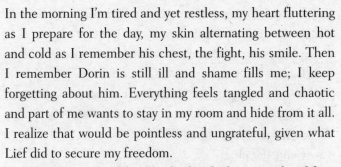

In the morning I'm tired and yet restless, my heart fluttering as I prepare for the day, my skin alternating between hot and cold as I remember his chest, the fight, his smile. Then I remember Dorin is still ill and shame fills me; I keep forgetting about him. Everything feels tangled and chaotic and part of me wants to stay in my room and hide from it all. I realize that would be pointless and ungrateful, given what Lief did to secure my freedom.

"How's your shoulder?" I ask when he brings my breakfast.

"Bruised." He smiles. "As you predicted. And a little stiff. Though not stiff enough to stop me going another round if need be."

I smile weakly as my head fills with the image of his bare shoulders.

"Now," he continues, "if you are ready, the weather is

pleasant, though there is a chill in the air. You should take your cloak." He doesn't wait for my agreement, crossing instead to my wardrobe and removing the crimson cloak. He holds it out as if he plans to put it on me.

"What are you doing?"

"I'm holding your cloak." His eyes glint wickedly.

"Lief, don't be foolish. Please give it to me."

"Don't you trust me?" he says.

I hear an edge in his voice. "Lief, you can't touch me."

"I won't. Do you trust me?" he repeats, watching me closely.

I turn away from him, holding myself stiffly, painfully, achingly aware of him behind me, his breath on my hair. The weight of the fabric falls on my shoulders, covering me. He moves to stand in front of me. "I would not risk you. I thought I made that clear last night."

I pull at the toggle and slip it through the loop, unable to look at him.

"So where do we go, my lady? The castle is yours." I note the return to my title and again my feelings war against themselves, ease and disappointment.

"To my temple."

"Very good." He strides to the door and throws it open, sweeping into a low bow, and I can't help but smile. He returns my smile, his tongue peeping from between his teeth, and my stomach tightens.

Despite my confusion, my freedom bubbles inside me and I can feel a un-Daunen-like smile on my face as we leave the tower and walk down the corridor. Though I doubt any child has ever skipped or run through these halls, in this moment I want to. "Goats skip, little girls walk," my mother once said to me in a rare moment of parenting. Nevertheless, if I thought I could skip, I would.

I can feel Lief at my left, as if there are threads between us, connecting our hips and knees and elbows, our necks and ankles. When his hand moves to adjust his belt I feel the motion, passed to me on the air that separates us, as aware of him as I am of myself.

"Might I suggest a detour, my lady?" Lief says when we reach the gardens.

"To where?"

"I'd like to show you something, if I may."

"Show me what?"

"It's a surprise," he says, smiling at me. "You'll be safe."

I saw him fight Merek; I'm not worried for my safety. "I don't want to push my luck, Lief. The prince said to be discreet."

"It is discreet, my lady. I can promise you that no one will know you're there, or that you've been."

"I can't, Lief."

"I understand, my lady. Forgive me. It was nothing important, just something Dimia showed me."

Dimia again. "If we're swift," I say quickly. "For a few moments."

I can hear him smiling.

He leads us past the walled garden and through the

stables. I stop to give my horse a pat on the nose and then we continue, through the kitchen gardens where the offending dandelions once grew, and beyond. This part of the castle is new to me. Dorin would never have brought me here. I feel another pang as I think of him.

"There."

Then I forget Dorin, Merek, even Lief. Every thought that has worried and plagued me falls away, and all I can do is gape at the garden before me. All of the wildflowers I thought had been banished from the castle are growing before me; poppies and coltsfoot, hellebore and flax, tuberose and tansy. All there.

"This is where you got my flowers that morning," I breathe.

"It is. It's the castle apothecary garden."

"Does the queen know?"

"Yes. It's where all the plants for the healers are grown. She might not like their look but even she can't deny their usefulness. Come –" he holds his arm out to guide me "– follow the path to the centre. Be careful, hemlock and nightshade grow at the far end. Though I don't think they grow your Morningsbane here."

I walk through the plants, some as tall as my knees, trailing my fingers through their leaves, a smile on my face. If I'd known this was here I could have drawn flowers for my screen myself. I'd wager Merek doesn't know of it; none of his drawings of cultivated blooms match the plants that grow before me.

When we reach the centre I sit on a small stone bench,

my gaze travelling around all of the plants as they sway in the light breeze. The garden is a riot of colour – red, purples, yellows, oranges and greens – and I love it. Nothing grows in a row; though I can see that there ought to be beds, there seems to have been little effort made to keep the plants within them. Poppies bloom everywhere and I cannot help but grin when I see a clump of dandelions.

"May I have your cloak, my lady?" Lief asks and I frown at him.

"Why?"

"Trust me. You'll be warm enough. I lied about the chill."

Puzzled, I unhook the clasp and pull it from my shoulders, holding it out to him. To my surprise he shakes it until it billows and then lays it on the floor.

"Lie down."

"I can't!" I say.

"Why not?"

"Because I'm Daunen Embodied."

"No one will know, save you and I."

"What if someone comes?"

"They won't. The servants are working indoors and they only ever gather the plants at dusk and dawn. An apothecary never gathers under the midday sun. You'll be safe."

"Lief, I can't."

"Ouch," he says, raising a hand and rubbing his shoulder. "If I hadn't such a bruised shoulder, you know, the one I bruised fighting for your freedom, I certainly would."

"That's not fair," I protest.

"I know." He smiles. "I'll keep watch, I promise."

I look at him, his play on my feelings working more than I'm willing to let on. "All right," I say. "But you must never tell anyone."

"Cross my heart," he says with a grin.

I sink to my knees, before I sit down daintily on the cloak.

"You need to lie down."

"I can't."

"Just for a moment."

I roll my eyes and sigh, leaning back and folding my hands primly on my stomach. And then I gasp.

The sky stretches above me, blue and clear and endless. If I turn slightly to the left or the right I can see the stalks and undersides of the flowers around me. But what I cannot see is the castle; the perspective down here hides it and it thrills me.

"I could be anywhere," I murmur.

"Anywhere at all," he says, sitting on the stone bench above me. "Do you see now why I wanted you to see it?"

"Yes," I breathe. Everything is perfect and I close my eyes. The sun beats down on my face and I pretend I am alone, not because of him, but because he is my guard. I am just a girl lying amongst the flowers on one of the last days of summer.

There is movement beside me and my eyes fly open as I sit up. Lief has moved to sit beside me and I have to blink, the world turned blue from the bright sunlight.

"What are you doing? You must keep watch."

"I have big ears, my lady. If anyone makes so much as a

move towards the garden I'll hear them and be on my feet before they notice us."

I look at him with unease. "We should go. . ."

"Stay a little longer. I want to see what you see."

I give him a long look before I lie back down, my heart pounding so loudly I can hear it in my ears. After a moment he lies beside me, keeping space between us but close enough that I can hear him breathing.

"Is this all right?" he asks.

"Yes."

"I used to do this with my sister, you know, on the farm."

I hold my breath. He rarely offers information, real information, about his past and I don't want to startle him. But his words feel like an opening and I reply quietly, so he can ignore it if he wants to. "Did you? What's her name?"

"Errin. She's a year younger than me, the same as you. In the evening, after supper, we used to go and lie in the garden and watch the sun go down and the stars come out. Sometimes our parents would join us, mother would bring blankets and mugs of cocoa and father would play his mouth organ. It was good."

His words bring a lump to my throat. How can he bear it? "You must miss them."

"All the time. It's hard being this far away, not knowing exactly how they are. My mother took my father's death badly. He was the love of her life; she'll find it hard to be without him. And poor Errin was almost finished with her training. She was apprenticing as an apothecary."

165

My eyes widen as the information slots into place. So that's how he knows so much about plants.

"She's had to stop, for now," he continues. "Our mother needs her. But one day I'll have enough money and she can carry on. As I said, I can do more for them here. Like you for yours," he sighs. "We both have to do whatever it takes to take care of our own."

"Lief," I say softly, rolling on to my side to face him and smoothing my skirts down. "How did you lose your father?

He sighs, wrinkling his nose and I think he won't answer, that I've exhausted his desire to confide in me.

"There was an accident on the farm," he begins. "He was trying to move our bull; it was a grumpy old thing that hated the lot of us. My father was trying to tempt him into stirring himself and the bull charged him. He escaped the bull but landed badly on a rusted pitchfork we hadn't put away. My sister cleaned the wound and dressed it – she's good at that kind of thing – but by the time the physician came my father had the lockjaw. It can't be cured, not even by our physicians." He smiles sadly. "He knew he would not survive."

"I hope it was swift," I say.

"It could have been swifter," he says softly. "But he wasn't in so much pain, thanks to the poppy tears. I stayed with him most of the time; my mother and sister couldn't bear it."

"I'm sorry, Lief."

"Thank you, Twylla."

We look at each other and I notice he has freckles on the bridge of his nose, a few faint marks, but I'm charmed by them. I have freckles too, on my face and shoulders, chest and back, and then the image of his naked shoulders fills my mind, the smooth, unblemished skin there, and then I feel too hot, my skin on too tight. When I look back into his eyes the world stops, and I have never been so aware of the blood in my veins pulsing through me.

"Can I ask you something secret, Twylla?" he speaks softly.

I nod slowly.

"Do you love the prince?"

I did not expect that. "Why would you ask that?"

"Something Dorin said when I first came."

I sit up hurriedly. "What did Dorin say?"

Lief sits up too and raises his hands to placate me. "Nothing bad, I promise you. He was telling me the history of the castle, and he mentioned your betrothal and said. . ."

"Said what?"

"He said that your role weighed heavily on you, and it was his job, and mine, to ease it where we could. He said you used to be less serious, but then there was an incident with a boy, and that it changed you. And so we had to do what we could to make your life pleasant."

I turn away from him.

Lief nods. "It's not your fault – what happened with that boy – you know?"

I laugh harshly, my stomach aching. "Isn't it? Because they were my hands on his skin."

"No," he says firmly. "You were doing what you were

ordered to." He pauses. "So do you?"

"Do I what?"

"Do you love him?"

I look at Lief before I lie back down and close my eyes. I don't know, in truth, what I feel. I've never thought about it in terms of love. We are betrothed; we have been since I came here. I always knew we would be married one day. It's like knowing the sun will rise, or the sky is blue. It simply is. "I don't know," I say finally. "It's not . . . it doesn't matter anyway."

"That's a 'no' then," he says, lying next to me again.

"Why?" I open my eyes and turn my head.

"Because when you're in love, it does matter. Very much."

"How do you know?"

He looks me straight in the eye. "You just do."

His expression is terrifying and I think of last night. How I wanted to touch him; how my eyes were dark and round in my face when I peered into the looking glass after he'd left. "Have you ever been in love?"

"Twylla. . ."

The sound of a horrified gasp sends us both scrambling to our feet, Lief with his sword half drawn.

Dimia stands there, white as old milk, her huge eyes accusing as she looks back and forth between us.

Chapter 13

Her hand rises to her chest as she stares at us, clutching at the neck of her smock.

"Get out of here," Lief says roughly, sheathing his sword. "You ought not to be here."

"Forgive me, I. . ." She turns but Lief catches her arm.

"No, Dimia. Please. Forgive me," he says emphatically. "You startled me. I did not mean to be so abrupt."

She nods, though her eyes narrow as her gaze moves between him and me. I bend to pick up my cloak, throwing it around my shoulders as if it were a shield.

"Why are you here?" I ask her.

Immediately she drops her gaze. "Forgive me, my lady. The prince sent me to find you. I have searched everywhere for you."

My stomach lurches with the terror of what this could

have meant. What if Merek had come to these gardens himself, what if he had overheard Lief and me talking? We were fools. . . "The prince?" I say as calmly as I'm able.

"Yes, my lady," she says quietly. "He came to your tower as I cleaned and told me to find you at once."

"No one must know the lady was here, Dimia," Lief says firmly.

"But the prince. . ."

"Dimia—" Lief begins but I cut him off.

"You will say nothing," I say coldly, stepping towards her, my skin already crawling with what I'm about to do. "You will forget you saw us here and you will lie if anyone asks you about it. You will forget anything you heard. Because if you don't, I might find myself accidentally bumping into you. Or your brother." To emphasize my point I hold my hands up.

If possible Dimia pales even further and Lief turns to gape at me. I ignore him, focusing on her. "So if I were you, I'd learn to be silent. Do you understand me?"

She nods mutely.

"Go," I say. "You haven't seen us."

She nods again and scurries off, leaving Lief staring at me. I turn away from him.

"That was unkind," he says quietly.

"I had no choice," I reply, though I've sickened myself doing it.

"Yes, you did. She was terrified. Couldn't you see that? She wouldn't have said anything."

"You don't know that. I couldn't take the risk, Lief."

When I force myself to look at him, the reproach in his eyes makes my face feel as though slapped. "So you threatened to execute her? And her brother?"

"I would never actually do it. Never," I say. "I know better than anyone what it means and I would never, ever touch them. But it's the only power I have in the world, Lief. All I have is fear. And if I have to say such things to protect you then—"

To my surprise he cuts me short with a bark of laughter. "Protect me? Why would you want to protect me?"

"Because – because I do."

He looks at me, his brow furrowed before he nods. "Come, we'd better get you back."

"Don't be angry with me."

"I'm not."

"I was trying to protect you," I say softly.

"It's *my* job to protect *you*. It's also my job to protect them from you."

His words feel like a slap to my face. I had never thought of it in that way.

"Will you apologize later, to Dimia?" I say in a quiet voice. "Tell her I'm sorry and that I didn't mean it and that I never would."

"No," he says simply. "You should apologize."

"I can't."

"Can't? Or won't?"

He walks ahead of me and I feel sick inside, the feeling only growing when I see Merek standing in the threshold of

171

my tower with a grim expression. I bow to him hurriedly.

"I've been looking for you," he says, and though his voice is hard his expression is soft and I pull my cloak tighter around me.

"Forgive me, Your Highness," I say. "I was walking the grounds."

"I thought I told you to be discreet," he says.

"I was, Your Highness," I say. "I wanted a little sun on my way back from the temple."

"It doesn't matter now," he says curtly. "That's not why I'm here."

My heart sinks as I look at him.

"We'll go to your quarters." He gestures for me to pass him but stops Lief as he tries to follow. "Bring wine," he orders, before herding me up the stairs.

My legs are heavy as I climb. I feel as though I've aged a thousand years since we saw Dimia. When I open the door, I catch the sunlight being extinguished by a cloud through the window and I turn to him.

"What's happened?" I have to choke the words from my suddenly dry mouth.

"I wanted to tell you myself. . . Dorin is dead. I'm so very sorry."

I blink at him, the walls of the room closing in and pressing against me, squeezing the life from me.

"Twylla?" I hear him say and then I'm flat on my back, staring at both my guard and the prince, confused that there is a roof above my head when all I should be able to see

172

is flowers and sky. It takes me a moment to realize I must have fainted and that I'm back in my room. I've never fainted before.

"What do we do?" Lief asks. "I can't touch her."

"I can—"

"No," I hear myself say, my voice coming from far away as I struggle to sit up.

The relief in both of their eyes is naked and Lief rushes to fetch a glass of water. Merek kneels beside me and holds his hand out for the cup. Lief briefly hesitates before he shoves it, somewhat roughly, into Merek's hand, glowering down at him, but Merek doesn't notice, instead holding the cup to my lips.

"Drink," Merek says and I do.

"When?" I ask, once he's taken the cup away and placed it beside us.

"A short while ago. I came to tell you the end was near but could not find you. By the time you returned here I'd received word he'd passed."

I finish the water and think of poppy tears. If I hadn't gone to the gardens with Lief, Merek would have found me. . . I could have at least been there with him, got there in time to say goodbye.

"Was he alone?"

"The healer was with him. I don't believe he suffered in the end."

"May I see him?"

Merek looks pained. "I don't believe he'd want that,

173

Twylla. A man like Dorin would rather you remembered him as he was."

I nod, a lump back in my throat and this time I cannot swallow it down.

"Thank you," I say. "Again."

"You owe me nothing, least of all your thanks," he says softly and Lief shifts his weight from one foot to the other behind him. It reminds Merek he's there, acting as the reluctant chaperone, and he stands.

"I'll leave you to rest," he says. "I'll call on you soon."

He nods to me and Lief bows as he leaves.

"I'll stay with you," he says softly when Merek is gone. "You shouldn't be alone now."

I wonder why it is I can only have one friend at a time. I had Tyrek, and then he was gone. Now Dorin is gone and all I have is Lief. Who will take Lief from me?

I cannot sleep, cannot even pretend to, and instead I pass the night staring out of the window. When the sky is at its darkest I spot three comets blazing across the sky like birds fleeing winter. It comforts me somewhat, as if it were a sign from Dorin that he is at peace, or from the Gods to tell me they love me still. I watch them until the sun starts to rise, the light hiding them from me, and again I feel comforted, to know they're still there, though I can't see them. Lief stays with me, sitting silently on the chair in the corner. Occasionally I turn to him but he doesn't sleep, sitting with his sword across his knee, watching me, nodding gravely when my eyes meet his.

While he fetches my breakfast and I wash and change my gown, the motions are more habit than deliberate. I don't understand how a man as strong as Dorin could fall to a bee sting. It seems so stupid.

"Will we stay here today?" I realize Lief is standing in the doorway, holding a tray.

"No. I'm sick to death of these walls."

Lief nods. "I'm so sorry, Twylla."

"As am I," I say. I'm sorry I forgot about my most trusted ally and left him to die alone in the bowels of this castle. The Gods did not save him for me.

Music plays softly somewhere outside of the castle as we leave the tower and it soothes me, spreading a balm over the raw edges of my grief and smoothing it into something less jagged. As I turn towards the long gallery, hoping to catch a glimpse of the player through the windows, I see another girl, small, dark-haired, has already had the same thought.

"Dimia," I say and she turns, the glazed look in her eyes clearing as she realizes who talks to her. She cowers against the wall and in that moment she reminds me of myself, the way I draw myself in when I am around the queen. I feel sick again.

"I'm sorry," I say firmly before she, or Lief, has time to speak. "I was wrong to threaten you. I would never touch you. Ever. I'm sorry for saying what I did."

She looks from me to Lief, before she nods.

"I won't say anything, my lady. I wouldn't have done. You

didn't give me time to finish." She pauses before she looks me in the eye. "I had two brothers in the queen's service once. The queen took against one of them, Asher, because she said he smiled too much."

My mouth falls open and we're both silent. The flautist in the gardens plays a trilling melody, the sound both sweet and melancholy, and I want to go to them, to lay my head in their lap and let them play my worries away.

"So you see," Dimia says quietly after a moment, her voice laced with longing. "I know."

"I'm sorry," I say softly. "Could you pass on my thanks to your other brother, when you see him? For taking my message to the prince."

Dimia smiles sadly. "I will, my lady. I'm on my way to see him now, as it happens. He has the afternoon free while the king and prince hunt and the queen is away. He likes the prince, my lady."

I am nodding again, when I realize what she's said.

"The queen is away?"

"Yes, my lady. She's gone to the mere. The king and the prince are hunting, but they let Taul stay behind. There's hardly anyone in the castle. I expect that's why someone is brave enough to play their flute in the grounds." She turns again towards the window. "It's beautiful, isn't it?"

I nod and try to keep my expression calm, both the music and hope filling me with warmth. We can move as we like; there is no one here to stop us. "It is. Well, I hope you and your brother make the most of your freedom today." I smile.

176

"Yes, my lady." She dips into a curtsy before turning back to the window. "I will."

As I continue down the long gallery my smile widens, and Lief glances at me curiously. When we have rounded the corner he speaks.

"What has pleased you so?"

"We have the castle to ourselves."

Lief smiles at me. "What shall we do? Would you like to go back to the apothecary gardens?"

I think of Dorin and shake my head. "Not today. I want to go to my temple, but we may as well take advantage of being able to roam the grounds. Have you seen the walled garden?"

He shakes his head. "I have not."

"It's not much, flower beds and spiralling walkways. We could sit there and listen to the music for a while."

Lief looks confused. "What music? I can't hear anything. I wondered what Dimia meant. I thought maybe her fear of you was making her hear things."

"What do you mean you cannot hear it?" I step to the window and tilt my head to the side. "Oh. It's gone. But it was there, a flute, or pipes of some kind. It was lovely. I would have liked to learn the tune, made a song for it."

"I'll take your word for it, my lady." Lief smirks and for a second I want to shove him. But I don't, too mindful of the consequences. I flush though and he looks at me. "Are you well?"

"A little warm," I say. "The fresh air will do me good."

"Perhaps you should have gone to the mere with the

queen. Mountain air is cool, so I'm told."

"I wasn't invited. I never am."

"How rude. But don't you normally sing for the king while she is away?"

"Usually, yes. But today isn't her usual day to go; she must have some other reason for wanting to go to the mere. And I can hardly sing for the king if he's on a hunt."

"I'd rather hear you sing than hunt," Lief says. "If I were him, I would have summoned you to sing for me instead of chasing deer."

"The king enjoys hunting," I begin, flustered by his compliment. "Besides, I'll sing for him in two days when the queen goes to the mere and—" I stop dead. Why does she go to the mere today? Her visits there are connected to her own moon cycle, today is still the waning moon. She would never go to the mere during the waning moon; it's the death moon; it's my moon. So where is she? And though the king loves hunting I don't believe I flatter myself by thinking he'd rather have had me sing for him if he could. Why has everyone suddenly vacated the castle?

Three beats of my heart and then it's as if the hounds from the hunt are with us. All of the calm from the flautist's melody is gone. Instead there is dread, the hot breath of a pursuer on the back of my neck, the snapping of jaws at my ankles. I freeze in the corridor, fear holding me captive.

"My lady?" Lief says. "What is it? Are you well?"

"I need air," I say, my legs shaking as I move with speed through the castle, Lief keeping pace with me. I stumble down the stairs of the keep, but right myself and continue, not stopping until I'm in the walled garden. I sink to my knees and bury my face in the fragrant lavender.

Something isn't right here. Every bone in my body is telling me something is terribly wrong. Merek would have said last night if a hunt were planned. He may even have invited me, had he known. Hunts happen rarely; this is twice now within a moon. And the queen shouldn't be going on her pilgrimage today. It's always the day after the Telling, always. Death on one day, life on the following. Why has the castle been emptied? Why has the order been changed? Why have I been left behind? Then it hits me. I have always had two guards, and now I have one. I was confined to my room and now I am allowed out. Who would aid me if I were attacked? I have no one save a guard whom I have encouraged to be more friend than protector. A guard who fought the prince a few nights ago to win me my freedom. Freedom won against the queen's command and behind her back. She must know what Merek did.

It's a trap. This is a trap. But for whom? Me? Lief? Does she know Lief and I have become friends; that we've spoken of things that are treasonous?

Then I realize. Merek went behind her back to grant me my freedom. Merek, Prince of Lormere, who yielded to a Tregellian farmer's son. And now we will pay for it. The waning moon. Somehow today we will pay for it and I will lose another friend, a friend I shouldn't have. I will have killed my only friend again.

I look at Lief, standing over me, his face lined with concern.

"Twylla?" he says cautiously.

"No," I say. "You must address me as 'my lady'."

He jerks as though I've slapped him, blanching before my eyes. "Have I done something to offend you?"

I ignore the note of panic in his voice. "You're too familiar," I say, my voice shaking. "It can't be – I can't be your friend."

"Twy— My lady? Are you quite well?"

"No," I say. I push my hands into the earth beneath the lavender and grip it in my fists to disguise the trembling. "This is a mistake. Anyone could be here and you are too busy chattering at me to notice. You must stay alert. You cannot be my friend." I tear my hands from the soil and stand.

I can feel his stare on me, the weight of it pushing at me, and I focus on breathing steadily, in and out, counting my breaths until my heart is steady. I look at him, the pain on his face giving me pause.

"What's wrong? Twylla, talk to me." He is plaintive, childlike in his bewilderment.

"Stop it, Lief. We can't do this. We cannot." I turn on my heel and walk away, trying to think.

Surely the queen would want to be here to witness this? She does love a spectacle. I scan the garden left to right, looking for movement, a sign that we are about to be overcome. How many men would she send against him? Ten? Fifteen? More? I pace the garden with my fingers clenched.

I can feel Lief behind me, can taste his confusion as he

breathes it into the air around me. The weight of his tread is heavy; he is angry too and is making no attempt to hide how he feels.

To the temple or to my room? My room, I decide. The temple still leaves us vulnerable. We'd have to leave it at some point. "We're going back," I say sharply. "Hurry."

As I climb the steps I hear him behind me, his boots thudding against the wood, and again my heart quickens with the feeling we're being chased, hunted. I move faster and he does the same, passing too quickly through the hallways, alarming the pages, who duck behind tapestries and into doorways at our approach.

At the door to the tower I lift my skirts and run, sheer terror propelling me up the stairs. The sanctuary of my door is in sight. I reach for it but his hand is there first. Habit makes me shrink away from his skin, his closeness pinning me against the wall of the tower, as he puts one hand on my door, keeping it shut, and extends his other arm so I can't move past him.

"What have I done?" he demands, his eyes blazing like marsh lights.

"Step back," I say, cowering against the wall as he looms over me.

"Twylla, don't do this. Talk to me."

"Step back, for the sake of the Gods, Lief. You're too close."

"Not until you tell me what's wrong. What have I done to deserve this?"

"Nothing."

"Don't be so cruel then." He steps closer. "Don't treat me as though I'm one of the others."

"Lief, please. You have to move away. If you touch me then. . ."

"Then what?"

"You die. You'll be poisoned and you'll die."

"Will I?"

"You know you will. The Telling—"

"The Telling is a lie."

I stare at him, shaking my head. "The Telling—"

"Is a lie," he repeats. "All of it."

There is a pause and then, my voice like ice, I say, "What do you mean?"

"You can't really believe it. Think about it, Twylla. How could you carry a special poison inside your skin that won't kill you because you have the right hair colour and the blessing of the Gods? How is that possible?"

"You know nothing of the Gods or their ways – you don't even believe in them." I can hear myself babbling, terrified by his closeness and his words.

"Do you think if there were Gods they'd allow the queen to do as she does?"

"I'm Daunen Embodied. I was anointed, I dedicated my life to the Gods—"

"You're not Daunen Embodied. There's no such person. They've given you a title and spread a nasty rumour to scare people into obedience. She's using you."

"How dare you?" I hiss at him. "You don't understand . . . how could you? You're from Tregellan. Things in Lormere are different."

"There is no difference, Twylla, and it's because I'm from Tregellan that I know. We used to have Gods too. And now we don't and yet the country doesn't falter; it thrives without them. Don't you see that? It's all made up. You're not beloved by the Gods – there are no Gods. There is no poison that you can take that won't kill you too. It's lies; it's all filthy lies, and you're too clever to believe it." He pauses and runs his hands through his hair. "Morningsbane isn't a real poison. Believe me, I could tell you about real poisons – my sister is an apothecary, remember? It's all a lie to keep you obedient, to make you do what they want you to. Don't you see that?"

"Stop saying that!" I scream at him.

"Not until you listen! If the Gods are real why haven't they struck me down for saying otherwise? Why am I not punished?"

"I don't know—"

"Because they're not real," he bellows. "They're made up to keep people like the queen above people like me, to make us all obedient. It's all lies. Do you see the foxes worrying about the Gods? Do you see the cows in the fields worrying about pleasing them? If the Gods were real, everything and everyone would worship them; everything would feel their impact. But it's only Lormere that does. No Gods in Tregellan. No Gods in Tallith. Doesn't that tell you anything? It's about power and control, to keep you all in

183

line. People like the queen tell us if we don't do as the Gods want – as she wants – then our souls are damned. Think of the amount of murder she's committed and tell me whose soul is more likely to be damned, hers or yours?"

"I'm the murderer," I shout back at him. "I am the executioner for treason. Of course I'm damned."

"You've never killed anyone," he says harshly. "It's not real."

"You're wrong."

He makes a sound of pure frustration, slamming his hands against the wall by my head and making me flinch. "What do I need to do to prove it to you?"

"You can't prove it to me."

"Yes, I can," he says slowly. "Yes, I can."

He leans forward, pressing his mouth to mine.

Chapter 14

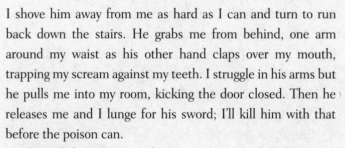

I shove him away from me as hard as I can and turn to run back down the stairs. He grabs me from behind, one arm around my waist as his other hand claps over my mouth, trapping my scream against my teeth. I struggle in his arms but he pulls me into my room, kicking the door closed. Then he releases me and I lunge for his sword; I'll kill him with that before the poison can.

"Wait!" he cries, catching me again and holding me against his chest. "Just wait."

"You stupid, foolish. . ." I sob. "Let me go, you're making it worse."

But he refuses, holding me firmly, and even though I know my kicks are landing hard against his shins he doesn't let go. I keep waiting for him to cough, collapse, to spill hot, sticky drops of blood on me but it doesn't come. I stand locked in his arms and he doesn't die.

After a few moments he releases me and I step back, staring at him.

"I'm not dead," he says quietly. "I feel fine."

I shake my head. "No, you're young, and strong. It must take longer. You're dying."

"I'm not dying. You're not poisonous."

"This is madness. You are mad."

"It's a lie, Twylla," he says. "It's not real. Look at me." He spreads his arms wide and stares at me.

But still it doesn't sink in. I keep waiting, deciding that as soon as he coughs, or his breathing changes, I'll do it; I'll draw his sword and kill him with it. Better that than the other way. The wait is agony. "What have you done?" I chant, over and over, under my breath. Skin on my skin. His mouth on mine. I tasted him and he tasted me. "You touched me. I'm Daunen Embodied and you touched me. What have you done?"

"You're not Daunen Embodied."

"Yes, I am."

"For the sake of your Gods, Twylla, it's a lie!" he roars. "You're just a girl."

I launch myself at him, my nails bared, my teeth snapping for his skin, forgetting that he's already dying from my touch. I hit and kick and scratch as much as I can, sobbing as I do. He tries his best to fend me off but I cling to him, beating him with my fists. I don't know when my mouth meets his, when my attack changes, but then my nails grip the sides of his face, keeping his lips against mine. Our kisses are hot, wet and messy; our teeth clash as he stumbles back against my bureau, I taste blood on his lips where I have bitten him. When I tear myself off him, he stares back at me, his eyes both bright and dark, the green of his irises close to being eclipsed by his pupils. He breathes as hard as I do and we both stand, watching, waiting. He doesn't fall to the floor. His nose doesn't bleed. I've never seen anyone look more alive.

He moves first, pulling me against him and wrapping his arms around me, kissing the top of my head fiercely as I give myself over to his embrace.

He must have held me for a long time, because when I pull my face out of the folds of his tunic the shadows in the room have moved, lying long across the totem. We are sat on the floor, I'm in his lap like a child, his arms around me, under my cloak, and he kisses my head intermittently. He's still alive. It's been hours, surely, and he's still alive. He strokes my arms, my back, his fingers never leaving me, touching bare skin where he can. I'm still trembling, but I don't know what I'm afraid of.

"Twylla," he says softly, moving a hand to tilt my face up towards him.

My eyes widen when I look at him. His lower lip is swollen, a cut visible on it. His hair is wild, standing out around his head like a halo. When I move my gaze from his, I can see scratches on his neck where I raked at him.

He moves my face gently back to his. "Are you all right?"

"Are you?"

"I'm well." He smiles softly. "Very, very well and very, very alive."

"I'm—" I don't know what I am. I don't understand this. There is only one thing I know for sure. "I betrayed the prince. I'm his betrothed. What can I do?"

"It will be all right," he says. "I promise. It will all become clear tomorrow. Trust me for a little longer."

I shake my head, knowing he is wrong, wishing he could be right. Betrayal is fenugreek seeds, unroasted and bitter. My coffin will be covered in them now.

"Say something, Twylla," he says. "Speak to me, please?"

I pull myself from his arms and get to my feet, my mind reeling. The feeling of flesh on my flesh, the warmth of his skin against mine is heady. I'd forgotten the comfort that comes from another person's touch. Memories wash over me: my hand in the king's as he led me back to my mother, the smell of my little sister's neck when I used to press my face into it during storms, the heat of my brother's palms as they slapped at me to share elderberries and cherries with them. Skin on skin, on my skin. I didn't know how starved of it I was.

But the moment we're not touching I remember what I am.

I turn away and walk to my looking glass. At first I don't recognize the girl who looks back at me with her kiss-swollen lips and her tangled hair. She doesn't look like the vessel for a Gods-given gift or a girl set to inherit a kingdom. She doesn't look like a killer. In the fading light of day my hair is a sunset of its own – red and gold and chaos – and confusion consumes me. Daunen's hair. Betrothed of a prince. Traitor.

"Talk to me." Lief says from behind me and I move before he can touch me, because I can't trust myself if he does and I am all I have to trust in at this moment. "Don't push me away, Twylla. Please. Don't shut yourself away from me and pretend I'm nothing."

"I'm not."

"Yes, you are. I've spent a moon in your company. This is how you were when I met you. And then you changed and you were better for it. You're better than them; don't be like them."

"You shouldn't say such things."

"Twylla, you can't deny—"

"No, I can't deny, Lief." I turn to him. "I don't know what this is."

A shadow passes over his face. "I know it's a lot—"

"You don't know! How could you? People die because I am Daunen Embodied. Did they die for a lie? And what of Merek? I'm going to be his wife, Lief. I'm betrothed to marry him next spring. This is treason, what we've done. We've committed treason. And I am the punishment for treason." I can't help it, I laugh, but it's a splintered laugh, without humour or joy. "How will I execute you when you are immune to me?"

He stays silent, gazing at me with his large eyes, his hands held in front of him to placate or beseech me.

"Please." I hold my own hands out to stop him stepping forward. "I need time. I have to think."

189

He looks at me before saying softly, "We could leave here."

"Did you not hear me? I'm marrying the prince. I can't leave."

"Don't. Marry me instead. We can run away."

"No, Lief. For a thousand reasons, no. Leave Lormere, now. I'll deal with the rest of it. I'll call for a bath. I'll only call for the guards once I'm done. That will give you enough time. Make sure you're far away by then."

He stares at me and then nods. I turn away. I can't watch him leave.

"I'll call for water for you."

Then he's gone, the door clicking shut behind him. The sound of the latch dropping is like a reproach.

My breath comes in pants, wave after wave of feeling washing over me. Every time I close my eyes it's as if he's kissing me again and the dizziness, the lurch of my stomach, makes them fly back open. I'm halfway to the door when someone knocks and I'm filled with the terrifying hope that it's him. But it's not; the maids have brought the water. I wait silently, skulking against the wall until they've all paraded through, more than a dozen maids, carrying ewers full of steaming water. What would happen if I touched one of them? Would they fall? I know they'd scream, but would it kill them? What if it did? What if it didn't?

When they are gone I strip and climb into my bath. The water is so hot that I shiver, feeling cold inside before the heat consumes me. Good, let me blame the water for the redness of my skin.

I stare at the ceiling, resting my head against the lip of the bath barrel, my thoughts crowding and pushing one another aside like women in the market. Why doesn't it work on him? Why am I not poisonous to him? All of those men at the Telling, alive until my skin touched theirs and then dead within moments.

I think of the Telling tomorrow. I'll fail. I've broken the Gods' faith in me. I've kissed a man who isn't my betrothed and I've doubted the powers they've given me. I'll be punished; the poison will finally kill me. And then Lief will be punished, the Gods will see to it.

Won't they?

I climb out of my bath, pulling my robe around me and settling in front of the totem that still hangs on my wall. *Are you there?* I ask them. They don't answer; they never have, but normally I feel a peace when I talk to them. This time I feel nothing.

I try to push my fear aside; it's always been harder to talk to them outside the temple. I'll spend the night there, asking for their help, begging for their forgiveness. Once I have the incense and Næht's Well behind me I'll be able to feel them.

But you should be able to feel them wherever you are, a sly voice says in my head and it takes me a moment to realize it's not Lief's but my mother's.

I try to recall what she'd said of the Gods. She spoke about serving Næht, but it was always in abstract terms. We never went to the temple to pray to her – before I came to the castle I'd never even been inside a temple – and my mother never invoked the Goddess, merely saying that she worked in her name. It was always Næht's will, the reason for everything. But when did she ever pray to her?

"Twylla, as you are Daunen Embodied, so the king and I are the worldly representatives of Næht and Dæg. That is how the villagers know they are blessed, because we exist," she had said.

And Lief.

"They're made up to keep people like the queen above people like me, to make us all obedient. It's all lies."

Oh, Gods. I wrap my arms around myself, mimicking how Lief held me. Is he right? Neither my mother nor the queen have ever said they believe in the Gods. My mother needs them because if there are no Gods then there is no Eternal Kingdom and that makes the Sin Eater nothing more than a prop for mourning. The queen needs them because the fear of death is what makes people obedient, and kind, and good, and sorry.

What kind of Gods would allow my mother and the queen to behave as they do, to make decisions and toy with people the way they do? And if the Gods aren't real then who am I, if not Daunen Embodied? If I'm not killing on behalf of the Gods, then I am a murderer killing in cold blood. Plate after plate of crow will sit atop my coffin. There will be no room for anything else.

Yet Lief said it was *all* lies. What did he mean?

When there is a knock at the door my heart feels as

though it's trying to leap out of my chest

"Yes," I call, trying to sound calm.

To my horror it's Lief, holding a food-laden tray.

"Your supper is here." He nods at the tray in his hand. "I don't suppose you want it?"

"What are you doing here? I told you to go."

"I'm going nowhere. I know I'm right, and tomorrow at the Telling you'll see it."

"Lief, if you care about me at all then you'll go."

"And if I go I won't get to see the look on your face when you realize you're wrong."

"You're impossible," I seethe at him.

"But I am right."

I sigh, turning away from him, both despairing at and thrilled by his bravado.

"There's no point in arguing, Twylla. I'm staying. I will be here tomorrow and I will walk you to the Telling. And I will accept your apology afterwards with grace." He smiles. "But I need you to do something for me."

"What?"

He holds out a small empty vial to me. "Don't take the Morningsbane tomorrow. I'll distract them and you hide the potion in your gown. Put this empty one down as though you've drunk it."

"Why?"

"I swear it's not what you think it is. I'll prove it to you. Trust me."

"You keep asking me to do that."

"And I haven't failed you so far," he says pointedly. "I'll be outside if you need me." He bows and saunters from the room and I shake my head at his departing back. He's a fool.

I look at my supper tray and then back at the totem. I want to go to my temple.

I dress and throw my cloak on before I open the door.

"If you're going to insist on staying then walk me to my temple," I say stiffly.

To his credit, he nods, with only the hint of a raised eyebrow. "Yes, my lady."

I ask Lief to wait outside the temple and I close the doors. I light the incense and all of the candles so the room blazes with light. Then I turn to the altar. The whitewash is bright where the totem used to hang, the wall around it obviously faded by comparison. I kneel in front of it and close my eyes, breathing in the frangipani as I wait. *Where are you?* I ask. *I need you, because I'm lost and I don't know the path I should be on. I need you to guide me.*

But there is nothing, no sense of peace, or rightness, of anything. The Gods, if they do exist, aren't here now.

Again I am awake and ready before dawn. Lief knocks while it's still dark and I stand, filled with a curious calmness. I slept well, to my surprise. Nothing disturbed me, nothing haunted me. No dreams of death or limbs entwined, or banishment and haunting green eyes. No dream-messages from the Gods. It's as if I'm watching myself, removed from the entire affair. There I am, walking ahead of Lief and the additional guard the queen has assigned to escort me to the Telling, my dress sliding across the stony floor outside the barracks, descending the narrow stairs into the bowels of the castle.

The castle reeks of the hunt and the acrid smell of the dogs lingers in the air. Can it only have been yesterday when I was so worried the queen was going to take my guard from me? I'd forgotten in the midst of Lief's revelations. How wrong I was. And how amused she'll be when she finds out that Lief and I have trapped ourselves and saved her the job, if she was ever planning it at all.

I should be afraid. . . I should be shaking, but I'm numb, waiting for Lief to knock on the door to announce my presence to Rulf.

I sit on the stool, staring steadily at the wall, ignoring all three men, ignoring the ghost of Tyrek laughing. I am serene, sure of what will happen. Perhaps the Gods will reject my blood as soon as Rulf adds it to the Morningsbane. Maybe the mixture will turn black and Rulf will know that I've betrayed the kingdom. Or the skies will turn black and everyone will know I've betrayed them. I only hope that whatever happens I have time to put myself between Lief and the other guard so he can run. I flex my fingers in my lap, stopping when Rulf tuts at me as he presses the knife against the crook of my elbow. In the other hand I hold the vial Lief told me to bring. I feel the tingling on my skin that I know means Lief's eyes are on me. I watch dispassionately as Rulf carefully cuts a small nick, as I turn my arm so a drop of blood falls into the bowl set below to gather it.

The other guard moves to stand beside Rulf as he adds my blood to the poison and Lief's eyes leave me to watch them both. I take the opportunity to study him. He's pale, his skin tight across the high bones of his cheeks, his knuckles clenching and unclenching against the hilt of his sword. So he is not as confident as he said that it's all a lie made up to cow the masses. What will he do when we're discovered? Will he try to cut Rulf and the other guard down to make his escape? Will he try to take me with him?

Rulf drops the vial into my lap. As I stare at it there is a crash and my heart stops; this is it, we are discovered. Rulf moves across the room and I see a broken glass on the floor and Lief apologizing, bending to scoop up the jars he's knocked down. Without stopping to think I push the vial of Morningsbane into my sleeve and take the stopper off the empty vial. I place it on the table and turn back to watch the men.

"I'm so sorry," Lief says, picking at the largest pieces of glass as Rulf waves him away, his lips moving angrily.

And then we are leaving.

Lief waits until we are alone in the stairwell of my tower before he holds his hand out.

"Give it to me."

I hand him the vial, still secreted in my sleeve, my fingers brushing his. And before I can stop him he opens it, sniffing it before he empties it into his mouth and swallows.

Immediately he winces and I grab desperately at his

tunic until he stops me, taking my hands in his.

"It's rowan," he coughs, pulling a face that would be funny under other circumstances. "Rowan in some kind of liquor. My mother used to make me drink it when she caught me cursing." He shoves the vial into the small chest pocket of his tunic. "It tastes bitter, but it's nothing. Certainly not poison."

I pull my hands from his and turn away. I have taken no Morningsbane, and no one knows any different. The herbalist who is so learned in the art of the Telling didn't notice and the Gods who govern my every move had done nothing to punish me. Yesterday I touched a man, I *kissed* a man and he lived. He lived when no one save the royal family should survive my touch. The same man has swallowed the poison I have been taking for four harvests and tells me that it's nothing more than a mother's penance for bad language.

None of what I believed – none of what I was told – has come to pass.

Lief was telling the truth. Everyone else has lied to me.

The Gods have not blessed me. I'm not Daunen Embodied. I don't know who I am.

I move past Lief and climb the remaining stairs until I'm back in my room.

"Write to Merek," I say, before he can speak, his arms already raised to pull me against him. "Tell him to come to my temple now."

Chapter 15

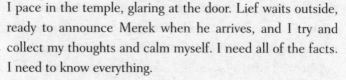

I pace in the temple, glaring at the door. Lief waits outside, ready to announce Merek when he arrives, and I try and collect my thoughts and calm myself. I need all of the facts. I need to know everything.

"His Highness, Prince Merek," Lief says and I turn to see Merek striding towards me, his face a mask of concern. At once the thin shell of composure I'd sought to create begins to crack. But before I can say a word Merek speaks.

"Twylla? You've heard then. I assure you it's nothing to worry about." At first his words stun me; how could he know what I have learned? Then I take in the rest of them. "It's a light fever, likely caught on the hunt."

"What are you talking about?" I ask him.

"The king. Isn't that why you've asked for me?"

I shake my head. "What's wrong with the king?"

"As I said, a fever. He will be well. Of course it means you won't have your audience with him tomorrow; Mother has ordered it postponed until we're sure it is innocent but I feel confident that he'll be demanding it before long."

I stare at him, frowning, my desire to rage at him gone.

"It's not like your guard." He misunderstands my expression. "It's not like that. You need not worry. It might amuse you to know that my mother plans to remain in the castle tomorrow to nurse my stepfather." His mouth curves into that faint ghost of a smile that he allows himself, but it quickly fades when I continue to stand there, mute. "What's wrong? Why did you summon me? Is it the Telling? Did something happen at the Telling?"

And that is all the comment I need for my rage to reawaken.

"What plant does Morningsbane come from?" I ask in a brittle voice.

"I don't understand."

"What plant does Morningsbane come from?" I repeat. "Because try as I might I can't remember ever hearing about a plant with that name. It does come from a plant, does it not?"

"I'm – I'm not sure. I believe so," he says firmly but not firmly enough, because in that small hesitation I saw his eyes widen slightly. "What is this?"

"It struck me this morning, as a man slit open my arm and then fed me poison, that I didn't truly know what it was I was taking. I know what it does but not what it is. And I would like to. I should have some of the flowers brought in

199

here to adorn the altar – that would be fitting, wouldn't it?" Every word I speak is clipped and precise. I sound like the queen at her most dangerous and it pleases me, even as I see him realize it too and blanch.

"I don't think that would be appropriate," Merek says, half turning to the door.

"I suppose it would be hard to adorn an altar with a flower that does not exist," I say calmly and he almost misses it.

Almost.

"To whom have you been speaking?" he asks and I should be delighted because it means Lief is right and I am not a killer. But instead I'm crushed; a pain shoots through my skull so strongly it feels as though it's pushing me into the ground. "Twylla, where did you hear such things?"

I shake my head. "I didn't need to hear it, Merek. I'm merely not as stupid as you all seem to think."

"Twylla, no one thinks—"

"You lied to me!" I shout at the heir to the throne. "You have all lied to me."

"I have never—"

"Is any of it real? Any of it at all? The Telling? How do the traitors die if it's not real, Merek?"

He covers his face with his hands as I talk. "Please let me explain." He moves them from his face and holds them out to placate me. "Please."

It's the fact that he said please, more than his face or reaching hands, that makes me stop. It reminds me whom I'm talking to because the pleading tone sounds so wrong coming

200

from those lips. I give a stiff nod and he nods in return before he begins to pace and I stand, rigid, in front of him.

"We – the kingdom was in crisis. The people were becoming nervous, restless. It wouldn't have taken much for real trouble to start. We had to give them back their faith. It was one of my mother's ideas."

"Of course," I choke. "But how did you pull it off? Because until today I believed I had taken the lives of thirteen men. If not by my hand then how?"

"Poisoned before you went into the room," he says slowly and I can see him weighing up his words against my reactions. I try to keep my face blank and calm. "In their last meal. They were given drafts of oleander. All of them."

"Did they know it?"

He shakes his head.

"So they all died thinking it was me? Tyrek died thinking I killed him?"

Merek hesitates and then shakes his head.

"What does that mean?"

"He alone knew it wasn't you."

I have to lean against the altar to keep myself upright as my mind scrambles to put things together. "That's why he had to die, isn't it? Because he would have told me the truth of it if he thought it was hurting me."

Merek looks at the floor. "He knew. He planned to tell you."

"So he was killed."

"He fancied himself in love with you," Merek says weakly.

"Is it treason to fall in love with me?"

"Please, Twylla. Lormere was heading for disaster. You have to understand," he begs and I step back, repulsed by it. "The kingdom was threatened and the people needed . . . they needed hope, Twylla. People need something to believe in. And the legends say that Daunen comes to bring hope. . ."

Though I knew it already, hearing the confirmation is as bad as standing in the temple and not feeling the Gods. It's real now.

"So I am a symbol? All of this, all of my life here, I've merely been an emblem to a realm? Why?"

Merek looks wretched, his mouth drawn down in misery. "My father had died. Alianor had died. Years had passed since my mother and stepfather had married and yet they still didn't have a daughter. The people . . . they were scared of what would happen to Lormere when my mother died if I had no queen to take the throne with me. She recalled being told the old legends of Daunen, stories of the daughter of a Goddess who came to Lormere in times of trouble to be hope and justice. And then my stepfather remembered you. Red-haired, with that voice. . . There hadn't been a Daunen for a century; no one alive could remember the last time. We were at war when last there was one; people were dying – but once Daunen was amongst us Lormere rallied and won. Because she gave them back their faith. So if we had a Daunen it would pacify the country, give them the sign they needed that things were well. And I needed a bride. The royal family has always been of the blood; if I were to marry someone not of the blood she'd have to be nothing short of a miracle."

He looks at the floor. "But we had to make it real, don't you see that? We couldn't bring in a commoner, call her the daughter of the Gods and then give her the throne; the people would never accept it. We had to make them believe it was divine; we had to make it watertight."

"So you added a little footnote to the legend? The new Daunen has powers from the Gods so she can kill with one touch?" I scoff. "It's neat, I'll grant you that. Who would want to argue with it, given what might happen to them?"

"Twylla—"

"I was kept in a tower, guarded from all, whilst you pretended that I was a tribute to the Gods? You gave me a pretty temple and told the world I was a killer and because we're ignorant peasants, we believed in it. Do I have the right of it?"

He sighs. "Twylla, I wanted to tell you. But then I went on progress and. . ." He trails off. "I'm sorry. But it had to be done. We weren't trying to be cruel—" He pauses, swallowing before he continues. "You were the daughter of a commoner. We couldn't announce you as my betrothed without making it indisputable. My mother invented the idea of the Morningsbane as proof of it. The records of the last time we had a Daunen were vague about how she meted out punishment; it wasn't hard for my mother to add in the elements needed to make it convincing. If we said you could drink poison it would provide the proof we needed that you were like us: chosen by divine right . . . and the obvious choice for my bride."

"But Rulf knew? And Tyrek?"

Merek turns away. "Rulf had to know, but my mother cut out his tongue so he could never tell. The boy wasn't supposed to know at all. I don't know how he found out. When my mother discovered that he knew. . ."

My stomach lurches and I have to clamp my teeth together to stop myself from retching. Because of me, all because of me. A man had his tongue removed and his son was murdered, all to make me into an icon.

"I thought I was blessed by the Gods. You let me sing in their name and worship them in a temple. Did you ever believe in the Gods, Merek?"

After a long moment he shakes his head. "Does it matter?"

"It did to me," I say quietly and turn away, walking past him.

"Where are you going?" He follows me.

"Back to my tower. I need to think."

"What is there to think about?" He stops me with a touch to my arm and I turn to him.

"Why it was that the man I am to marry allowed me to think I was a killer. That is what I need to think about."

"It is part of Daunen's role. It always has been."

"But I'm the only one who thought she herself was the axe, am I not?"

Merek clasps his hands together, pleading. "The little we could find in the legends said that Daunen sent those who would destroy Lormere – traitors – to their deaths. My mother made it literal, so that no one would make an attempt on your life. If it was thought you were immune to poison, who would poison you? If it was thought your skin could kill them, who would dare get close to you? Times have changed; the Gods didn't have the power they used to. We had to give it back to them."

I stare at him before I turn my back on him.

"Don't go, Twylla, please. Please try to understand. We couldn't tell you; if we wanted the kingdom to believe then you had to believe too. You were a child when you came here; you couldn't have concealed it."

"I have been keeping secrets since birth," I spit at him. "I was to be the Sin Eater of Lormere, remember?"

"If I'd been here. . . It will be different now, I swear. It will all be different. No more secrets."

I cover my face with my hands, desperate to put something between me and him. I stay like that, my fingers as a shield, until I'm calm enough to be able to speak to him without screaming. "It's a lot to understand, Merek. It's going to take time. I can't reconcile to this so fast."

After a long moment he nods. "You may ask me anything, at any time. I will answer all of your questions and with truth."

"Thank you," I say softly and then I leave him there in the empty temple.

Lief trails behind me, silent as we walk back through the castle to my solar. And as soon as we have crossed the threshold it is me pressing him to the door, kissing him as though my life depends on it.

*

We sit hand in hand on my floor, kneeling and facing each other. My body hums with pleasure that we're touching, that it means nothing, and yet means everything. I can't keep my fingers still, rubbing the tips of them over his knuckles and across his palm and he does the same, tracing around my nails and tangling his fingers between mine and we're both smiling, so much so that my cheeks ache from it but I can't stop.

"You have to explain," I say.

"You owe me an apology," he teases.

"Please, Lief. Tell me how you knew. Tell me how you could see it for a lie when I couldn't."

He sits back, looking at me with his head tilted. "Twylla, you Lormerians might have a formidable army, but you don't have better science than Tregellan. Nowhere does. Our medicine, our apothecary knowledge is far more advanced than yours. We'd know if there was a poison that could be transmitted through the skin – believe me, we'd have used it. Lormere has survived a century without Daunen, to the point where it's become a myth, a fairy tale, like the Sleeping Prince or the songs you sing. And then there is one again. Why? Why would the so-called Gods have suddenly sent their daughter back? Unless it wasn't the Gods at all, but someone else – for some other, less divine reason?"

I stare at him as I think. The Daunen before me saved Lormere during the war. Tregellan had invaded and Merek told me his grandmother was ill and not expected to survive childhood. Was the last Daunen like me, a girl being primed for the throne in case the true heir died? Is that how Daunen came to be? Was she invented as a puppet to masquerade as a child of the Gods to appease the realm?

"Why didn't they tell me when I came?" I said. "I would have understood it was for the good of the realm – I loved the queen. Why not trust me?"

Lief draws circles on the back of my hand. "I suspect because of Sin Eating. Even now, the way you talk about it, you hold it so close to you. It's such a big part of you that they had to give you something bigger. They had to give you a duty that would be bigger; they had to make it a destiny. You of all people wouldn't question a destiny, because you were born and bred with one," he says softly. "And who wouldn't prefer a destiny that involved living in a castle, instead of Sin Eating?"

"Sin Eating. . ." I repeat. I'd forgotten, or I'd not let myself remember, but now I do.

I was small, so small that Maryl was a baby. I'd spent hours rocking her, hushing her, anything to stop that horrid high-pitched crying where her face turned red and she drew her tiny knees to her chest. My mother had stayed in her room, only coming out once to put her to the breast. Finally Maryl was asleep and I was exhausted, nodding off in my chair.

"Come." My mother's door had opened and I'd dragged myself into the perfumed fug.

"What we do," she'd said, as though we were midway through a conversation, "is ancient. It's timeless. It has always been and must always be."

My eyelids had drooped as she'd spoken, the warmth from the room lulling me.

"Before Gods, before kings, there was us," she'd said. "They took us when they took the kingdom, piece by piece, and told us why we did what we do. But we don't do it for them, my girl. We do it because someone must, and before Gods and kings there were sins. There have always been sins. Do you understand what I'm telling you?"

I'd nodded, the nod of someone jerking awake, not a nod of understanding.

"We are ancient," she'd said. "We make them safe."

I look away from Lief, releasing his hand. It makes sense, but I don't want it to. I don't want it to be so simple. I've spent four years dedicating my life to this and moving steadily to becoming Merek's wife. To find it's nothing to do with my destiny at all, that it's a life based on the colour of my hair and my singing and a madwoman's delusions of grandeur is harrowing. And so many people have died because of it.

"Do you have Sin Eating in Tregellan?" I ask Lief. He nods. "Tell me how it works."

He looks nonplussed. "The same as here, I suppose. The Sin Eater eats from the coffin while the family says goodbye. Then the funeral. It's the same custom, a part of the ceremony."

"No, Lief, that's not how it works here," I say softly. "It's not a part of the ceremony here."

He shrugs. "I suppose Sin Eating is one of those things that was left over after belief in the Gods died out. Maybe it would have been too much change to drop it from the funeral ceremony so they kept it."

A token gesture. It seems all of my destinies are like cobwebs, easily dusted away in the sunlight. "What does Tregellan believe in?"

"Nothing, really. People had faith in the Gods before the monarchy fell. But it died out during the revolution. People didn't have time, I suppose. There are those in the smaller hamlets that still believe in some Gods."

"Our Gods?"

"No. They believe in the Oak and the Holly."

"*Your Gods?*" I say. "You weren't mocking me? Tregellan has different Gods?"

He nods. "I wasn't mocking."

"How could there be different Gods, Lief?"

"I don't believe there are any at all," he says quietly. "But I believe there are men and women whose lives are made easier by believing someone is watching over them."

My stomach swoops again. That's what my mother meant. "I felt nothing in my temple," I say jaggedly. "Nothing. Even then, I wanted to."

He pulls me against him, holding me as I try to understand what it is I've always known but never understood before.

"I'm sorry," he says finally.

I shake my head.

"What are you going to do?" he asks.

"I don't know. But I don't think I can stay here and pretend to represent the daughter of a Goddess."

"What about the prince?" he asks me.

"I . . . I can't marry him. Not now. I can't stand beside him and give myself to him and this family."

"Not after the lies."

"And not when I'm in love with someone else," I say without thinking.

"What?" He sits up.

The realization stuns me and my ears ring, blood rushing to my head and my skin as I realize what I have said. And how true it is. Suddenly it is the truest, surest thing in the world. I am in love. That's what's been wrong with me. I have been falling in love. For someone who sings of love I didn't recognize it at all.

"I'm in love with you," I whisper.

He devours the words right out of my mouth, pressing his own against mine and swallowing my worries. I let him, willing to sacrifice my questions temporarily for the taste of him, for his hands on my waist.

As soon as he pulls away I miss him, moving closer, desperate to gorge myself on contact after being starved for so long. He obliges, putting his arms around me and I turn to rest my back against his chest, pulling his arms around me. It feels right. This is where I am supposed to be.

"What are we going to do?" I say finally.

"What do you mean?" he murmurs against my ear.

"What do we do now? What happens next?"

"That's down to you," Lief says slowly. "What do you want to do?"

"I don't know." I shake my head. "I want to leave here but I can't. I'd never get away, not even with your help. But how can I stay?"

"Would . . . would you come away with me, if there was a way?"

In answer I twist and pull his face to mine, holding his jaw as I kiss him.

"So. . ." He pulls away, looking at me intently. "Was that a yes? Are you saying that you would be with me?" He tries to mask his hope but it's so open on his face.

"I want to be with you." I think of the queen. She tried so hard to make me into her puppet, and yet she threw someone into my path who wouldn't allow it. In little over a moon Lief has undone four harvests' worth of her work. I imagine her fury when she learns we defied her and it makes me smile. I lean against him again, relishing the contact.

"So what happens next?" he asks.

"We ask the Gods for a miracle." I smile weakly.

I feel his grin against my temple and he reaches around me to take my hands in his. "I might know of a way out. I'll have to check, but I'm sure Dimia mentioned a passage the servants use to sneak in and out of the castle and visit the village. Tomorrow during your audience with the king I'll sneak off and see whether it proves true."

"You can't." I remember what Merek told me in the temple. "My audience with the king is postponed. He caught

211

a fever during the hunt so there is no audience while he recovers. Oh!" I say realizing what it means. "We could go tonight, while all eyes are on the king."

"I doubt Merek's eyes are on the king," Lief says dryly. "I suspect his thoughts are all for you. Besides, I don't know where this passageway is, or where it comes out. And we'll need horses if we're to get out of Lormere. We can't afford to get caught in the act of trying to leave; we have to be well away before they realize we're gone. Far enough away to be unreachable. She'll come after you, you know. She won't let you go." He squeezes my fingers gently between his.

"Luckily for you, neither will I," he continues, planting a kiss on my ear as if sealing a vow. "We'll go via my mother's. She lives beyond the West Woods; I'll send a message on ahead and we can change our horses there, collect whatever provisions we need and then go further into Tregellan. We'll head north, towards Tallith. We'll be well beyond their reach there."

I nod, happier. "It's a good plan."

"If I'm honest, Twylla, it's not the first time I've thought about it." He smiles.

"Oh," I say softly, my face once again splitting into a grin. I'm not the Sin Eater's daughter. I'm not Daunen Embodied. I'm something else, something new. Not a monster in a castle, not a nightingale trapped on a thorn. "When can we go?"

"A few days," he says. "That's all I'll need to get everything ready. You must pack what you want to take and keep it ready."

"I don't want anything from here," I say swiftly.

"All the better for our flight." His voice is all smiles, his breath stirring my hair.

"We'll have to be careful," I say, more to myself than to him, my eyes fluttering closed as he strokes the backs of my hands and my wrists with his long fingers. "We must give them no reason to suspect anything. We must allow Merek to think I'm reconciled to the truth of Daunen. That I'm part of the secret and happy to be."

"But I can still kiss you?" he says. "When we're alone?"

"Are you so hungry for my kisses?"

"Starving. Ravenous," he smiles wolfishly. "You don't how lovely you are, do you?"

I squirm in his arms. "Enough, Lief."

"What if I refuse to stay quiet?"

"I'll find a way to silence you."

"Go ahead," he challenges me.

I twist in his arms to face him, my lips parted. Slowly, my heart thudding beneath my skin, I lean forward and kiss him. When my eyes flutter closed I open them to find him looking back at me. Our mouths move gently, brushing together, our lips opening and closing against the other's, our eyes locked. It makes me dizzy and I allow mine to flutter shut, concentrating on the feel of him touching me, his tongue dancing gently with mine.

This time he pulls away, cupping my cheek in his hand.

"A few more days and we'll be in our own cottage, somewhere safe, where no one can hurt us." He pulls my hand to his lips and kisses it, then places it over his heart.

Beneath the material I feel the outline of the vial and I trace it. "Here's your vial back." He pulls it out and hands it to me. "Keep it as a reminder."

I take it, something inside me hardening as I do. I unwind myself from his hold and stand, looking down at the thing that has controlled my life for the past four harvests. Then I fling it, as hard as I can, through the open window before I turn back to him. Our kiss is inevitable, like the sun setting over the West Woods.

Chapter 16

I used to take such pains to make sure I never touched anyone and now I have to clasp my hands together to stop myself from twining my fingers with Lief's. I barely slept at all last night. It ached to send him from my room and it ached to know he was on the other side of the door. It's painful to have him so close and yet so far from my reach. It feels wrong to not be touching him, and I'm impatient to be in a place where I might trace a finger across his forearm, or have him circle my wrist with his beautiful hands. I never knew it was possible to feel so many things at once – anger, hope, fear, desire, joy, and worry – my feelings are alive inside me and I'm terrified that we will come upon someone who will see it all in me and tell the queen. Though I want her to know eventually, I want to be sure we're far beyond her reach when she does.

I feel drunk on possibility. Everything seems brighter,

clearer and better for it. I know without looking at him what Lief's expression is, where his eyes are looking, especially when they are on me. I feel that as keenly as I felt his arms around me earlier. When the breeze blows I catch the scent of woodsmoke and limes and I smile. It's his smell. When I lift my hand to my face to push back a strand of hair, I smell it again on my skin.

There is terror too. His footsteps on the stone sound out my name with each step. For every Twylla he walks, I step out two Liefs and I'm afraid that we're announcing our deception for the whole castle to hear if they pay close enough attention to our footsteps. I must live a double life until we can run, like the spies and traitors I thought I'd killed. I am no spy; I feel I must wear my thoughts as openly as my red cloak. I'm bubbling away inside, like the water at the mere, with both hope and fear.

I can't stay in my room – despite my lack of sleep I'm still restless – so I ask Lief to come to the gardens with me, hoping the chill in the air will mean we're alone outside and able to continue making our plans. But as we enter the walled garden I see Merek on a bench, staring blankly at the walls, his guards loitering along the opposite wall. Panic clutches at my stomach and I turn sharply to lead Lief away when he calls my name.

"Twylla."

"Your Highness." I dip into a curtsy to hide my face, praying my fear isn't written upon it.

"You may leave us," Merek says to Lief.

Lief barely hesitates before he drops into a bow and turns on his heel. He hovers a distance away in the archway to the garden, standing sentry in it, and I admire him his composure.

"I – I was hoping to see you. I hoped you'd come here today. I know I said I would give you leave to think but . . . I don't want this to come between us."

"How fares the king?"

"Better. I'm told he's much better. His appetite has returned and he's demanded everyone stop fussing over him. By which I believe he means he wishes my mother would stop hovering over him. She's not a natural nurse."

I can't look at him and not only because I'm angry. "Please pass on my best wishes," I say. "I did not mean to disturb you here. I'll leave you to your solitude."

"Don't, Twylla," he says quietly. "I'd rather you be angry at me if it will set things right between us. I said I would be truthful and I will. Please don't walk away from me again."

We both stand awkwardly, him waiting for me to speak, me unable to think of anything to say that isn't vindictive or incriminating. A chance look at Lief shows him studiously ignoring us, though something in his stance suggests he's listening hard. "I missed you at the hunt," Merek says finally.

"I'm not fond of hunting," I say evenly.

He sighs, running a hand though his dark curls. "Well, there we are in agreement as I am not fond of it either."

"Are you not? But you said to the queen it was a pleasant distraction. Surely you weren't lying?" I can't help myself. I have to poke at the wound.

Merek nods to himself, as though accepting the reprove. "That wasn't a lie. To be out of the castle and riding free in the woods, yes, that was pleasing. But the hunt itself. . . I have no love for those beasts the king calls his hounds. And I can think of better things to do than chase down poor creatures in the woods." He pauses. "Especially people. I do not agree with that. It won't happen under our rule."

He looks at me but I can't look at him, not when he talks like that, not now. After a few moments of watching me stare at the flowers he continues.

"When we rule, hunting will not be part of the court. Not like that. I'd like to reintroduce falconry. There is more elegance there and both the ladies and gentlemen can hunt with birds. You could have your own merlin."

I remain silent, keeping my eyes fixed on the flowers, aching to look back and see what Lief is doing, whether he is watching the prince and me.

"Do you look forward to your next concert? When the king is recovered?"

"Of course. Will you join the king again for it?"

"Yes, I shall, if you permit it."

"We're to be married. Does it matter if I permit it?"

"To me it does, yes," says Merek. "And I imagine you, like me, appreciate the illusion of having a choice, even when illusion is all it is."

Again I keep my silence, glancing towards the sky. "I should return," I say flatly. "It looks like rain."

"Allow me to call on you later," he says hurriedly. "I will bring wine and we can talk, properly. I want to mend this, Twylla. May I call on you?"

"If you so wish." At least if he comes tonight I can pretend to make my peace with him, and Lief and I won't have to worry about him waiting for me around every corner.

"Thank you."

We begin the short walk back along the other side of the gardens. I can watch Lief from here, his shoulders straight and stiff, his back to us as he gives us the appearance of privacy.

"Until this evening then," Merek says as we reach Lief. I dip my head and he bows his before sweeping past my guard, who follows his path with furious eyes.

I walk quickly, as if to take another turn around the garden and he moves to my side.

"Does he plan to come and see you tonight?" he speaks through almost-closed lips.

"Yes. He wants to make it right between us."

"What will you do?"

"I'll tell him I understand that he was doing the right thing, but that I'm hurt and confused and I'd like to keep to myself for a while to better understand it all. I'll ask him if I may send word to him when I have reconciled it. I'm sure he'll agree."

Lief nods. "And then we'll go and he'll bother us no longer."

On the way back I call into the temple. Today I can see how dirty the walls are, how dusty the floor is. The benches are too

219

clean by contrast, no grooves or smooth wood where the grain has been worn away by people. It's an empty room. It means nothing now.

I had hoped Merek would come early that night. But the knock does not come. Lief enters and lights my candles, walking as close to me as he can, filling the air around me with his own scent of limes and leather and making my stomach leap. We dare not even talk, not when the prince and his guard are expected at any moment.

When the candles have burned low and my eyelids are heavy, I cross to the door and open it. Lief looks up at once, smiling at me, and I return it with ease.

"I'm going to prepare for bed," I say loudly. "Please tell the prince, should he come, that I have retired and am sorry to disappoint him." Then I lower my voice and whisper, "And you can also tell him that he's the worst kind of swine."

"Certainly," he says, then whispers, "That's why I've decided I'm going to steal his horse when we go."

As I laugh softly, he raises his voice to a normal pitch. "Do you need anything else from me tonight, my lady?"

I nod my head slowly as I speak, contradicting my words. "That will be all. You may also retire." I tilt my face towards his and he silently leans forward to kiss me. It's not enough and I step out of the doorway, catching his hands in my own, kissing him open-mouthed.

I pull away reluctantly, closing the door softly, our fingertips touching to the last.

When I am in bed, with my candles blown out, I wrap my arms around the bolster tightly. *Soon*, I think to myself. *I have managed four harvests here, another few days is nothing.*

There is a light knock at the door and it opens a fraction.

"Twylla," Lief whispers and I sit up.

"Yes?"

"I thought I might leave your door open a little, to be sure you are safe. It wouldn't do to leave you at the mercy of vagabonds who might try to get into your room. I would hate to be caught in dereliction of my sworn duty to protect you."

I smile widely and lie back down. "I admire your dedication to your duty."

"I admire your admiration of me."

I laugh as I hear him put down the bedroll and then the rustling of him climbing inside it. When he is settled I roll on to my side, facing the door. I cannot see him – the new moon is a thin crescent not bright enough to show me his face – but I can hear him breathing, the fabric shifting as he moves.

"Tell me a story," he says, his voice low and strange in the dark, different from his daylight voice.

"I don't know any; my mother wasn't the sort to tell bedtime stories." I rack my brains for a tale but come up with little. "Do you know about the Sleeping Prince?" I ask Lief.

"Of course I do. You can't tell me that one." I hear him smile. "Every child in Tregellan is told that story." When I don't say anything he continues. "Do you know any others?"

"I don't know that one," I admit. "Not well, at least. One of my brothers told it to me an age ago, before Maryl was even born. It's everywhere these days, even you mentioned it yesterday. All I can remember is that a prince became sick and fell asleep and a kingdom was lost because of it."

I hear him move on his pallet and then his voice sounds more like his own; he must be sitting up. "I can tell you the version I know, but it's not a nice story. Not the 'happily ever after' story I'd hoped for."

"Tell me," I say.

He takes a deep breath. "All right. Five hundred harvests ago, Tallith thrived. They say it was beautiful, a golden kingdom, walled all the way around, seven towers dedicated to love and beauty and grace and chivalry and. . . I forget the others." I hear the sheepish smile in his voice. "Anyway, Tallith was untouchable. They had medicine and alchemy that's lost to us now. People were healthy and wealthy; there were no beggars, little illness. It was paradise, bordered by the mountains and the sea. In the end, it was the sea that brought about their downfall."

"Yes," I whisper, beginning to remember.

"The king of Tallith commissioned ships to sail out to sea and explore and when they returned they brought tales of strange Eastern kingdoms and customs. They brought back spices and fabrics, things that had never been seen before. But they also brought rats. There were no rats here before, but they came on the ships and then they came ashore. And Tallith, with its abundance of food, quickly became overrun. So the king sent the ships back to sea and told them to return with a rat catcher, and in due course they did.

"The rat catcher arrived with his son and daughter and they were immediately taken to the castle. The king offered his daughter, the princess, to the rat catcher's son in exchange for ridding Tallith of the rats but the rat catcher refused. He said he would rid Tallith of rats and take the prince for his daughter. The king refused, for that would make the rat catcher's daughter the queen and mother to the heirs and he couldn't allow it. But the rat catcher refused all of the other riches and titles the king offered. He would only accept the hand of the prince for his daughter.

"Finally, with his people in outrage, for the rats were stealing food and dirtying the water and biting babies, the king relented and said he would give his son to the rat catcher's daughter. And so the rat catcher took a pipe from his pocket and began to play. Soon all of the rats were scurrying out of their holes, following the rat catcher as he wandered the streets of Tallith. When he had lured them all, he led them into the sea where they drowned and Tallith was free of them."

He stops and I sit up. "That isn't all of it," I say. "I know that the prince becomes ill and falls into a sleep." The words give me pause as I recall Lief telling me Dorin had fallen into a sleep. I see Dorin in my mind, wasted and parched, prone on a raised pallet. For a horrible moment he becomes Merek, and then Lief, and goosebumps erupt across my body.

Lief hasn't noticed my new horror. "He doesn't become ill, Twylla. He's cursed. He falls asleep because he's cursed."

"Cursed? Who says he was cursed?"

"It says so in the books. When Errin and I were little, my mother always ended the story when the rats drowned. We always thought it ended happily. Not so much for the rats, I suppose," he muses before continuing. "I was ill one winter, and bored, and my mother gave me her book of old myths and legends to keep me occupied. I think she forgot the full version of 'The Sleeping Prince' was in there and I read it. Do you want to know it?"

"Yes," I say, though I'm not sure if I mean it.

"All right. Well, after the rat catcher had got rid of the rats, he went back to the castle to see his daughter married. But the king refused to fulfil his side of the bargain and tried to buy the rat catcher off. In a fury, the rat catcher left and hid himself away. In his lair he conjured a spirit and asked her to curse the king, and his son, and his son's sons, for their treachery. And the spirit did as she was bid. What the rat catcher didn't know was that his daughter, who'd been anticipating a marriage, had allowed herself to be seduced by the prince. She was carrying his son when the curse struck, striking her down too. The king and the prince and the rat catcher's daughter all fell into a deep sleep and could be woken by no one. The king wasted away and died within a few weeks, but the prince and the rat catcher's daughter slept on. Every day the rat catcher would go and tend to his daughter, dribbling honey and water into her mouth to keep her and the baby alive.

"But it wasn't enough. After the rat catcher's daughter gave birth to her son, whilst still asleep, she died too and the

224

rat catcher buried her, before taking his seemingly unscathed grandson away. The prince carried on sleeping, though no one cared for him. He remained as he was on the day he fell asleep, perhaps a little paler, but he didn't waste away. He slept and as he slept Tallith fell."

I pull my quilt closer around me, suddenly cold. "I don't blame your mother for keeping the rest from you."

"It's not over," Lief says. "Around a hundred harvests later, a girl went missing from Tregellan. She'd been collecting mushrooms with friends and had become separated from them. A search was launched but they had no luck finding her. She was thought to have been eaten by wolves until a wandering minstrel claimed to have seen her following a man with a pipe. They were heading towards Tallith."

"The rat catcher," I whisper.

"His grandson," Lief replies and I shudder, transfixed at this new part of the story. "The rat catcher was long since dead, but the child he cursed without knowing what he was doing still lived. A cursed life, never to die. The girl's family raced to Tallith but arrived too late. Beside the abandoned bier where the Sleeping Prince lay was the body of the girl, her heart torn out, the remains clutched in the blood-smeared hands of the Sleeping Prince."

I raise my hands to my face, covering it.

"And every hundred harvests since," Lief continues, "the Bringer, for that is what they call the cursed piper boy, emerges and travels the land looking for a victim for his father. And they say if he brings a girl whilst the solaris ride the skies, then the Sleeping Prince will awaken for ever and devour the hearts of all the girls in the realm."

"I wish you hadn't told me," I say. "I wish I hadn't asked. There was no baby in my brother's version, no Bringer. I'll never sleep again now."

Lief laughs gently. "It's become mixed up over the years, I bet there's as many version as there are villages. That's the problem with fairy tales, they change with the telling. Some people say the Bringer can be summoned if you have his totem, but no one knows what the totem is or how to summon him or what he will do if you manage it. Some say the Sleeping Prince can be cured by love, and that if the Bringer brings him his true love he won't take her heart but he'll kiss her and Tallith will be remade, as good as new. Others say it's a load of old women's chatter and Tallith fell because a blood plague wiped most of the people out. Don't take it to heart, my love."

I pull the covers to my chin. "It would be horrible, to sleep for so long. Everyone he'd ever loved and known would be gone. I wouldn't want to wake up if it were me, it would be too sad."

"I'd be angry, not sad. If I'd been cursed to sleep for five hundred years because my father broke a promise I'd want to raze the world to the ground. Imagine it – waking up and finding that over the mountains a bunch of inbred peasants had founded their own kingdom while you were stuck in a ruin with only the clothes on your back."

"I'm one of those peasants," I remind him shortly.

"They're not my thoughts; you know what I think of you."
I blush in the darkness and he continues speaking. "I meant
that that's what I imagine a prince's perspective to be. Falling
asleep the heir to a kingdom and waking up a pauper in a new
world. It wouldn't be pleasing. It doesn't matter anyway; it's
just a story. A children's tale."

"It makes me glad my mother wasn't the storytelling type.
I think she would have enjoyed telling that one a little too
much. Did your mother ever find out you'd read it all?"

"She realized when she found me standing guard over
Errin one night." I can hear the smile in his voice. "I was
terrified the Bringer would come for her."

"Was she angry?"

"No. I think she was rather pleased I'd actually sat still
and read for once. Her father had been a bookbinder and we
had shelves of old tomes and scripts. But I was more of an
outdoors child. Errin is the scholarly one; she always has her
nose in some text or other."

I'm silent, my mind filled with images of a young Lief
standing in the moonlight, watching over a little girl who
resembled him. "I wish I could read," I say eventually.

"You could learn. I could teach you."

"Would you?" I ask. "And to write? Could you teach me
that too?"

"I can start now, if you want?"

"But it's dark."

"You're right." I hear the sound of his forehead being
slapped. "If only we had some way of lighting the room.

227

Something like a candle."

I pull the bolster from under my head and throw it in his direction, grinning when I hear an "ooof" from him. The next thing I hear is his bed roll shifting and footsteps coming towards me.

"Are you all right?" I ask.

"Yes. . ." I feel the bed dip as he leans on it, using it as a guide as he makes his way around it. When he reaches the other side I hear him fumble for the flint, catching his profile in the sparks before the candle splutters to life. He raises it under his face and I shiver as the light and shadows change him.

"May I get your quill and parchment?"

"You may."

He collects them and lights a few more of my candles, filling the room with a soft warm glow before he approaches the bed.

"Move along."

"What?"

"Move along. I won't fit if you don't."

"Here? In my bed?"

"Why not?"

"Because –" I feel my skin tingle and burn "– it's a bed."

"And more comfortable than the floor. I promise not to compromise your virtue . . . any more than I already have." He grins and I swat at him.

"Very well," I huff, moving along and pulling the covers around me.

He sits next to me, atop the covers, which reassures me

somewhat, and places the parchment on his knees. Carefully balancing the inkpot on mine, he dips the nib and makes a few quick strokes across the paper.

"Do you recognize any of them?" he asks, holding it up to me and taking the inkpot away.

I peer at the letters.

"No. . . Wait . . . that one's in my name." I point to a long stroke. "And that one too." I tap the first letter of the last word.

"The first one is an 'L'. You have two in your name. And a 'Y'."

"L, Y," I repeat.

"Any others?"

I look again and frown in concentration. "I know I've seen them before but I don't know what they are," I say, embarrassed.

"Soon you will," he says. He points to the first letter. "That's an 'I'."

"I," I repeat. "But you said it was an 'L'."

"No, that's different."

"But they look the same. How can they be different?"

"Here. . ." He lifts the nib and adds two small strokes across the top and bottom of the "I". "Now do you see the difference?"

"Yes," I say, though I don't understand how those two small strokes changed it. "So it says 'I L'."

"The next letter is an 'O'," he says, peering at me.

"Well, I can see another of those in that one." I point to the third word he's written.

229

"Good." He beams at me. "The next one is a 'V'."

"I L O V," I say and then pause, sounding the letters out. "I L O V. . . I love you!"

Lief's grin becomes the widest I've seen it. "How did you know?"

"It sounds like it when you say it quickly. I L O V. . . So that is 'I', that is 'love', and that is 'you'?" I point to the words and he nods.

"That's right. Do you want to try writing it?"

I nod, and he hands me the quill and inkpot. I lean over the parchment, carefully copying the marks on the paper. It's hard to move the quill; though I can draw, it's different trying to form such uniform shapes, and my version is much less pretty to look at than his.

That doesn't stop him beaming at me, his eyes soft in the candlelight. When I'm done, he takes the quill and ink away before returning and pulling the paper gently from me. He blows on it, drying the ink before he rips the paper in half. Silently he hands me the piece he's written and takes the piece I wrote in my beginner's hand.

"Oh. . ." I say softly, before twisting and rummaging under my pillow for the first note. When I pull it out, he looks at me in wonder.

"You kept it?"

"Of course I did."

"Twy—" he begins and then we both freeze.

The door at the entrance to my tower had clicked open.

230

Chapter 17

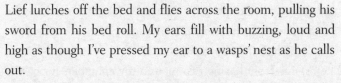

Lief lurches off the bed and flies across the room, pulling his sword from his bed roll. My ears fill with buzzing, loud and high as though I've pressed my ear to a wasps' nest as he calls out.

"Who is there? I warn you I'm armed and will cheerfully kill you if you take another step towards my lady's chamber."

"I'd rather you didn't," a voice drawls and my eyes widen.

"Merek?" I call, dread flooding my body.

"Who else?" He rounds the stairs and stands in the doorway beside Lief. "Forgive the lateness of my calling . . . though it seems you were not asleep." He nods at the candles.

"Not yet," I say shakily, looking at Lief.

Merek turns and looks at Lief, who sheathes his sword with a bored expression and kicks his bed roll from the door so Merek can enter.

"Why was the door open?" Merek asks him and my mouth dries.

"So the lady could escape if need be," Lief says without pause. "I opened it as soon as I heard someone outside the tower. My lady suggested it when I undertook sole guard duty. I will detain an intruder and she will escape to the guards' quarters and lock herself in."

Merek frowns. "Why in there?"

"Because I keep my spare swords and my knives in there. And it's lower to the ground; she could escape from the window if need be."

I'm amazed at how smoothly he lies, how reasonable he makes it sound. "It seemed the most practical way of assuring my safety," I add, though my voice doesn't have half the composure of Lief's and Merek notices.

"Is everything all right?"

"Aside from having two men in my chamber during the night, I'm quite well."

Both men look down, though I'm sure Lief is suppressing a smile.

"I apologize," Merek says. "Forgive me. I didn't want you to think I had forgotten. My mother kept me busy with a report on Tallith. I will return tomorrow."

"As you like," I say.

"One thing –" he turns back and looks at us both "– I notice there is a bolt on the tower door. Might it be more practical to use that, instead of trying to run from here to barricade yourself in the guard's room?"

The bolt. I'd forgotten there was a bolt. How could I be so stupid? "You're quite right. Lief, please do so once the prince has left."

Both men bow to me and leave. Moments later I hear the bolt clicking into place and Lief returns.

We stare at each other, my heart pounding at how close we were to being caught.

"Forgive me, my love."

"Why? It was not your fault. Had you not acted so quickly—"

"Not that. I forgot to tell him he was the worst kind of swine."

Despite myself I laugh.

"We'll have to take more care," he says.

"How could we forget there was a bolt?" I say.

"Perhaps it's good that we did. Now we can say it's kept bolted on the prince's orders."

"Yes, that is good," I say. "Less suspicious."

Lief looks at me and then down at the floor, unusually coy. "If the door is bolted, we could spend every night like this, until we go. Together. If you wanted. Only if you wanted."

I can't reply, my blood thundering through me. Him with me at night. In my bed, beside me.

"Yes," I say quietly.

He crosses back to the bed and his steps fall in time with my rapid heart. Then he is beside me, lying next to me, and I lie back, staring at the canopy. After a moment his arm moves, his fingers sliding between mine and he squeezes them lightly.

"Is this too much?" he asks and his voice is thick.

I don't trust myself to speak, so I shake my head.

In response he leans and kisses my cheek and I feel as though I'm going to cave in.

"I'll ask Dimia about the passageway tomorrow while Merek is here with you. You could dismiss me and I'll go and examine it. And the stables."

I nod, moving only my head. I'm hardly breathing, overwhelmed by how domestic, how adult it feels to lie beside him and hear him talk of our plans.

"Goodnight, Twylla," he whispers in my ear, turning on to his side. After a long, fraught moment I turn my back on him and he moves to curl his body around mine. I can feel his heart pounding as violently as my own against my back and I close my eyes. It's his regular breaths on the back of my neck that eventually lull me to sleep.

In the morning there is a delicious moment before I'm all the way awake when I remember his body against mine and I smile to myself, my eyes closed against the soft morning light.

"What's so funny?"

My eyes fly open and there he is, sitting on the chair beside me, his hair loose around his shoulders. I cannot speak, too struck by how handsome he looks, his head tilted to the side and his eyebrows raised in question.

"Are you going to tell me?" he asks.

"Merek," I say urgently.

"Merek *is* funny." He grins at me.

"No, you fool. Merek is coming here today. He might be on his way now."

Lief shakes his head. "The door is still bolted. I was going to kiss you awake, like a prince in a tale, until you started smiling like a madwoman." He leans forward and brushes his lips against mine, his fingers slipping into my hair as he deepens the kiss. "Now tell me, what amused you?" he murmurs against my mouth.

"I woke up happy," I say. "That's all."

"Any particular reason?"

"Nothing special," I say, grinning when he catches my lip briefly between his teeth. "Very well, there may have been a reason."

"Are you going to share it with me?"

"That would be terribly indiscreet. A lady never tells her secrets."

"Then a lady had better not expect her breakfast brought to her."

"You wouldn't dare."

His answering smile is wicked. "Would I not?"

I smile at him, as sweetly as I can. Again he leans forward and takes my lower lip between his teeth, sucking it before moving away, leaving my stomach aching.

"Be thankful you're beautiful," he says and grins. "I won't be long."

"Don't be," I call after him, sliding under the sheets and hunching myself together in happiness, before I stretch luxuriously and beam at the canopy of my bed.

It's not long before he's back, carrying my tray, which he deposits on my lap before bending to kiss me.

"Dimia's gone," he says as I pull a bread roll apart.

"What do you mean 'gone'?"

"Another maid brought your tray, grumpy little thing. I asked her where Dimia was and she said she'd upped and left."

"I'm not surprised," I say. "You heard what she said about her brother and the queen. She and her other brother may have decided it wasn't worth the risk of remaining here. She was on her way to see him on the day we – I. . ." I pause. "Perhaps they chose to go then, while the queen was away."

"Unless it was the queen who got rid of her," Lief says darkly.

"I doubt the queen even knows Dimia exists. Thankfully," I say. "But what will we do? How can we find out about the passageway?"

"We'll keep to the plan. If you give me leave to go while the prince is here I'll see what I can find out."

His words make me blush, the memory of him whispering in the dark filling me with heat.

He grins as if he knows what I'm thinking. "Promise me you won't fall in love with Merek while I'm gone." I throw the remains of the roll at him.

I have too much energy; my stomach is in knots as I sit at my screen. Lief is at my feet, winding my silks and untangling

236

them as I sing softly, for want of something to do until Merek arrives. I'm trying to act normally but I cannot remember what it is to be normal. I'm scared I'll give us away by smiling too much when I'm supposed to be both in mourning for Dorin and furious with Merek, or by looking at Lief too often.

The booming knock at my tower door comes much sooner, but also later, than I would have liked.

"Ready?" Lief asks and I nod, smoothing my hair back.

He leaves me, and I focus on steadying my breathing, unsure why I suddenly feel panicked.

"His Highness the Prince," Lief says and I stand, lowering my head respectfully.

"Twylla." Merek sweeps into the room. "I hope you had a good night's rest."

Without thinking I look at Lief, hovering in the doorway, and Merek turns to follow my gaze.

"Wait outside," he dismisses him with a wave of his hand before I can speak to give him leave. "It is coming along well," Merek says, studying the screen, as the door clicks closed behind us. "I'm glad in this at least that I have been of use to you. I wondered if I might ask you to leave your work though. The Hall of Glass is complete and I hoped that you would join me in exploring it. We can talk there."

"Can we not talk here?"

"We can." He frowns. "But I hoped you might want to come with me. I've not seen it yet and I would like to share it with you."

"I'm not sure what it is."

His lip curls. "It is a gift, for me, from my mother. As soon as she found out I planned to see Tallith she had my escort send her every Tallithi text that had ended up in Tregellan after Tallith fell. And in one of them she must have found the plans for the original Hall of Glass and decided to construct a copy here as a 'welcome home' gift for me. Something to tempt me back." His mouth twists cruelly. "It is a hall of looking glasses, simply put. They are arranged to distort the truth, so you may stand before one glass but appear in many others. Some you may stand before and see yourself from behind and from the side, all at the same time. Would you care to see it? With me?"

"Of course." I smooth down my skirts and smile at him. "It sounds intriguing."

He crosses to the door and I allow my face to fall a fraction when his back is turned.

"I'm taking my lady Twylla to the Hall of Glass," he informs Lief. "You are not needed. We will return later."

"When, Your Highness?" Lief asks and both Merek and I freeze.

"Pardon?" Merek's voice is cold, disbelieving, and I glare at Lief, who ignores me, his own eyes fixed on Merek.

"When will the lady return, Your Highness?"

"Is that your concern?"

"The lady's safety is always my concern, Your Highness. My only concern," Lief says smoothly.

"I assure you she is safe with me," Merek says, his voice as silky as Lief's. "You've fought me and I don't believe I

238

flatter myself when I say I held my own. I may not have beaten you, but I feel confident I can defend my lady. She is going to be my wife, after all. Twylla –" he gestures for me to leave "– after you."

I hesitate before I do as he asks, but when I don't hear his footsteps on the stairs behind me I turn to see him and Lief, locked in a silent battle of wills. Neither moves, nor speaks; instead they stand, facing each other down. The tension between them is hard and dangerous; I can feel barbs jutting from it, as though it's pressing into my skin. When Lief's fist flexes towards his belt I inhale sharply and it breaks the spell. Merek turns from Lief with terrible calmness, dismissing him as he walks towards me. Over his shoulder I can see Lief's hand shaking. Merek smiles; despite the heat from their silent conflict, his face is placid.

"Come, Twylla," he says and I can do nothing but turn and walk away, leaving my tower without my guard, once again alone with the prince.

As before, we are unguarded and the other courtiers bow and smile. It's amazing, the difference being seen with Merek makes. I stop being a monster when they see me with him and I start to own the role of their future queen. Inside I am reeling, but outwardly I return their smiles, dipping my head as graciously as I can, all the while wondering if Merek will mention Lief's behaviour . . . and how I will explain it. What was Lief thinking, goading Merek when he'd given him the perfect opportunity to do as we'd planned? But Merek says nothing, about Lief or otherwise, as we walk towards the Great Hall. Before we reach the large wooden doors that would take us there, Merek turns to the left, leading me down a corridor and towards the east tower. It was here that the royal nursery used to be – the whole of the east tower dedicated to princes and princesses and their legions of servants.

On the door of the tower, a taller, grander version of mine, two guards salute the prince and bow to us. In silence they open the doors and Merek nods at me to enter.

There is a small antechamber, barely big enough to contain us and I'm too aware of how close Merek stands once the doors are closed behind us.

"Step back," he says, and I do so, pressing into the stone wall as he moves towards a sheet of black fabric hung from the ceiling. He fumbles with it before pulling it aside, revealing another room beyond this one. "After you." He moves to allow me to pass and I do, entering the Hall of Glass.

As I step into the room I see myself reflected. I raise a hand to test it and am distracted by a movement to my right. It is me again, set in profile and as I turn to look more closely another flash of movement catches my eye and there I am again, my back visible in another glass. I turn this way and that, stepping backwards and forwards to see where I'll appear next and which side of me I can see. I can't help it; it makes me laugh to see myself everywhere I look.

"There is more than this." I am surrounded by Mereks. For every Twylla I see reflected there is a Merek behind her and I turn to look at him, watching as every me does the same. "Walk forwards. Keep your fingers before you so you don't walk into the glasses. It is supposed to be built as a maze." He demonstrates what he means, stepping past me with his fingers outstretched.

I am sure he is going to walk into the glass walls but he doesn't, disappearing instead as if he's entered the looking glass. I follow him and then we are in another chamber, all the walls reflecting us.

"Stop," he says and I do, my fingers still before me. "Look," he turns to the side and I copy him, but it looks the same; there we are again, in every surface, seen from every angle. "Come here. Stand where I am."

Nonplussed, I obey him and he walks to where I was and I gasp. From this spot I can't see my own reflection at all but his is reflected in all of the glasses and it seems that he has formed a circle around me. I look at what I think is him and he smiles, stepping forward, and the circle closes in.

"Stop," I say, a chill climbing up my spine and all of the Mereks shake their heads.

"Can you not tell which one is the real me?"

I twist around as he steps closer again and begin to point, but each time I choose the man I think is the real him he shakes his head again.

"Merek, please," I say, turning and turning and I'm no longer sure from which direction I entered the chamber. "I don't like this."

"One more guess," he says.

I turn slowly, looking at all of the Mereks, looking for the entrance so I can make my choice. I take a small step to the left and there it is, a gap between two glasses, the corner of his shoulder cutting across it.

"There," I point at him, but as I do I see a movement behind him, brown hair pulled back at the nape, a muted green jerkin and leather breeches. I gasp, and Merek turns, giving himself away, and proving me right but I can't feel satisfied by it.

Lief is in the maze. He's followed us here and there is no chance of hiding, not when every surface tells the truth.

"Well done," Merek says but he frowns, his eyes trained on the glass. "What is it?"

"As I moved I caught sight of myself. It startled me," I say, not meeting his eye.

"It is disorienting in here," he agrees. "Come, there is more. I won't trick you again. At least not on purpose," he adds and I follow his lead, walking forward slowly with my arms extended.

As we wander through the glass, mirrored by ourselves, I try to convince myself that it is impossible for Lief to be here, that he would have had to come past the guards, that we would have heard him enter.

Merek walks with confidence. Despite his words he does not seem disoriented at all, and I scurry to keep up with him as we roam the hall, corners and crevices hidden everywhere, my eyes darting over all of them. The glass makes the room feel so much bigger, though I know it can't be so large, and when I catch a snatched glimpse of my own dress, or Merek's hand, I startle, wheeling around to look at it. Each time I am met with my own scared face.

"Do you like it?" Merek comes to a halt in a room that seems to split into three different paths.

"No," I say honestly. "I don't think so."

"I do," he says. "There could be no deception in a place like this, where everything is displayed. I wish that all of life could be like this."

"As do I," I say sharply and then bite my lip as his face falls. "Forgive me, I know it was not your fault. Your mother will be glad you like it."

He snorts. "Yes, she'll be able to congratulate herself on this, I'll give her that."

As he speaks Lief materializes like a spectre behind him and I start, stretching my fingers.

"My talk of my mother shocks you, doesn't it?" Merek misreads my gesture. "But I feel after your recent discoveries, I can be honest with you. You know what she is."

I nod mutely, making pretence of turning to look at myself in the glass, trying to see where Lief is standing, and which glasses he can be seen in. I can only see him ahead of me, behind Merek, but I know that it must be a reflection as I can see myself and Merek in the glass too. A glance to the left and the right reveals nothing and when Merek follows my eyes it is apparent he cannot see him at all.

"Twylla?"

"Yes, forgive me. It's the glass. . ."

243

"We are so alike, you and I." Merek steps forward, and behind him I see Lief's face tighten, his fingers inching towards his hip where his sword sits. "Both of us with our mothers and our prisons and our roles. I have never had someone I could confide in before. . . Well, that's not true." He smiles. "I used to confide in my tutors and my nurses but they all went away. I'm lonely too, Twylla," he says softly.

Movement to the right makes me turn involuntarily and I see Lief, Lief proper, standing at an angle so the only glass reflecting him is the one behind Merek. Merek's eyes again follow mine but from where he stands I'm sure he can see only me.

I take a step forward to stop Merek from doing so and seeing Lief.

"I brought you here for a reason," he says. Behind him Lief's face echoes all of the reflections of my own: wary, frightened.

"Oh?"

"My mother. . . She is not a good queen."

"Merek, you mustn't—"

"We can speak freely in here; we are alone. And I know you agree – I've been watching you since I returned. I saw you trying to save Lord Bennel. You know she is not a good queen; whether you say it or merely think it, it's still treason and it's still true. She hungers for glory at the expense of the kingdom; she berates and belittles my stepfather. She kills her friends. She is cruel and vindictive and she is not good for Lormere. It cannot continue, do you understand my meaning? I have seen much since I returned and cannot, in good conscience, allow it to continue, for the sake of the court or Lormere or you. My mother is too much the product of her breeding. I fear she is mad; she talks about purity and legacy and. . ." He hesitates. "Can I truly trust you?"

He gazes at me searchingly and I hold my breath, nodding.

"I've asked to bring our wedding forward. My mother is weakened, for the first time I can ever recall. She allowed my stepfather to defy her publicly and she has not questioned my granting you your freedom without her consent. If we all stand together we might be able to do this amicably. The time to strike is now. I mean for us to be married and then to take the kingdom. I can't do anything until I'm married. And I must do something."

I stare at him, and Lief stares at me, and I can do nothing.

"But . . . your harvest day. . ."

"What does it matter?" he says, stepping towards me. "We're both adults and we've always known it would be this way. What are we waiting for? You know the truth about Daunen now and there is no need to keep up the pretence of it any longer. I want to marry you now." He seals his announcement with a kiss.

Chapter 18

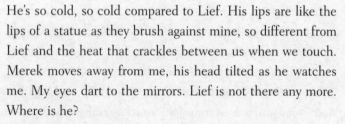

He's so cold, so cold compared to Lief. His lips are like the lips of a statue as they brush against mine, so different from Lief and the heat that crackles between us when we touch. Merek moves away from me, his head tilted as he watches me. My eyes dart to the mirrors. Lief is not there any more. Where is he?

"Forgive me, Twylla."

I look away. "Do I have any say in this at all, Merek?"

"What do you mean? We're betrothed, as good as married now. You were there; you gave yourself to me. The wedding is a formality."

When I don't speak, his eyes narrow. "Do I repulse you so much, Twylla? Am I that revolting to you?"

I open my mouth to protest but he does not allow me to speak.

"Do not lie to me," he continues. "Do you think I don't notice that you show more concern, more regard, for your guards than you do for your prince? You are not the only one who has been manipulated and used. I have never had a choice about my fate."

A year ago, even a moon ago, I might have felt differently. But not now.

"This is not how I would have us begin," he continues. "I knew it would be hard to tell you the truth but I thought you'd be happy to know that you're not what you thought you were – a killer."

"Can't you say you won't have me?" I say desperately. "Can't you refuse me?"

He reaches for my arm, pulling me around to face him. "I prayed for you," he spits at me. "I don't believe in the Gods but it didn't stop me praying for you. Every night for eleven years, I have lain in my bed and begged the Gods to bring you to me, to let me keep you. I dreamt of you. I heard you sing and I was glad it would be you. If I am to have a wife – and believe me, Twylla, I have no choice about it – then I will not have one related to me. I would end my life before I did. I have spent two years waiting to come back here so I could finally be with you. You will be my wife and I am glad of it. I want it to be you. I have always wanted it to be you."

He releases me and turns back to the looking glass before he speaks, calm again. "You are clearly overwhelmed and that is my fault. You have dealt with much lately. I'll have you escorted back to your solar so you can rest before tonight."

"Before tonight? What is happening tonight?"

"I've called for a feast, in honour of our wedding being brought forward. I want it announcing now, while my mother is weakened. I want it announcing formally. Then you can move to the royal solar and prepare to become my bride."

He stalks through the Hall of Glass, taking my arm and pulling me with him, guiding us back through the curtain.

"I am sorry it's been presented to you like this." He pauses before the door as I stare at him. "I will be a good husband to you, Twylla. I will try hard to make it as easy as it can be." He raises my hand and kisses the back of it, before holding it against his cheek, his fingers as cool as his lips. "Now is the right time. We need to strike now while her sting is drawn. The kingdom needs us to. I shall see you later."

He throws open the door and entrusts me to two severe-looking guards, who bow to Merek. I forget to bow to him, as we walk away. I don't suppose it matters now.

I don't know where Lief is, whether he is still in the Hall of Glass or whether he left. If he stayed then he would have heard it all.

When the door of my tower opens, Lief is there.

There is no fire in his eyes, nothing that I recognize about him. Those dull eyes are ringed in red; his hair is askew. The guards leave and I walk slowly towards him. He watches me impassively, gesturing for me to pass him as he closes the door. I climb the stairs, listening to his tread behind me, slow, steady, and in complete contrast with my heartbeat.

"Lief. . ." I say as soon as we are in my room.

248

"I suppose I should start calling you 'Your Majesty'." He sweeps into a mocking bow as my face crumples and I finally cry.

I would give anything for his comfort but he offers none. He stands over me, watching me dispassionately as I weep.

When there are no more tears and he has still not moved, there is nothing left for me to do but turn from him. I move to the basin to wash my face and then his arms are around me, his face buried in my neck. We stand like that, my back pressing against his chest, his arms iron-tight around me until I feel dampness on my skin. When I turn, his face is shining under the weight of his tears and my heart breaks at how wretched, how broken, he looks.

"I was going to marry you." His voice is ragged.

My heart soars at his words and then clenches at the tone, joy and horror warring inside me. "You still can," I whisper, my hands reaching towards him. "We can still go – we'll go now."

He shakes his head. "There isn't enough time, Twylla. We'd have hours, at most."

"And after tonight we have no time at all. We have to go tonight. I can't marry him. I can't be with him."

"He kissed you," he says slowly.

"I never wanted him to."

"I wanted to kill him."

"We'll go, Lief. It won't matter then."

"Twylla, he is a prince. I can't beat that."

"You already have!"

At this he pulls me into his arms. When our mouths meet I taste salt on his lips; no matter how many times I kiss them clean the salt returns and I don't know whether it's from; his tears or mine.

"There has to be a way," I say. "You and I, we're clever. We're not from the castle. We know how to live outside of here. Did you find the passageway? That's all we need. We can go. We can make it."

He nods, releasing me and turning his back. I watch as he straightens his shoulders, holds his shuddering breath until it is under his control. When he is himself again, he turns back to me and there, in his eyes, is the spark of the man I love.

"Tomorrow night. We'll go then. I'll send word to my sister to be ready."

My face falls as I shake my head. "We can't. After the feast he plans to move me to the royal solar to prepare for the wedding. It must be tonight."

He whitens. "Can we risk it? With everyone preparing for a feast?"

"Can we risk staying and losing this chance?"

At that he pulls me back into his arms, folding me against him, safe in his grip. "He can't have you," he murmurs against my lips. "You're mine, my Twylla, my love. I won't give you up, no matter who tells me to. No queen, no prince, no one."

"I don't want to marry him," I say.

"And you won't. I promise. If I have to give my life for it, you won't."

"Don't say that," I plead. "Don't say things like that."

"If they knew of us, you could not marry him."

"And you would be dead."

"They might not kill you."

"I'd want them to! I cannot go back now; there's nothing to go back to."

He makes no protest as I pull him towards the bed.

Afterwards we lie with our legs and arms twined, breathing softly, his breaths becoming my breaths. Our skin is damp and we stick together, as though nothing could separate us. My limbs are heavy and liquid, the dying light of the afternoon making me want to curl around him and sleep. He rubs his lips across my forehead and I smile, tilting my head back so my eyes meet his.

"That wasn't quite the escape I had in mind," he says softly. "Not that I'm complaining. Are you well?"

"Very," I smile, my skin heating as he grins back at me. "As for escaping, I think we'll be able to go after the feast."

"You thought about it?" He props himself on his elbow, looking down at me with his eyebrows raised. "When did you think about it?" A smile plays around his mouth.

I redden again at the implication, ducking away from him. "Not then. A moment ago, while we were lying here. If I plead a headache during the feast, I can ask to retire. We'll go while they celebrate. By the morning we'll be miles away and they'll be none the wiser. Once they realize it'll be too late to stop us. At least I hope so."

I watch as he works through my words in his head.

"Come." He untangles his legs from mine and pulls me from the bed, throwing a fur over my shoulders. I feel self-conscious, drawing the fur around to cover myself, but one look at his face, at the hope and joy there, makes me forget and it's easy to follow him.

He leads me to the window, standing behind me with his arms around my waist, resting his chin on my shoulder as he points to the sun setting over the trees.

"Look, those are the West Woods. Beyond that forest is our new home, somewhere far over there."

I nod, leaning against him.

"And we'll go tonight. It ends tonight."

"It begins tonight," I say.

"It begins tonight," he agrees. "But in the meantime, we have to get ready for this feast. Shall I call for water for you?"

"No, thank you." I don't want to bathe; I want to keep the smell of him on my skin.

"Shall I leave you to dress?"

I'm tempted to ask him to stay and help me, but in the end I nod. "I won't be long."

"I'll be outside when you want me." He turns me around so he can kiss me and I'm more than willing to let him. When I open my eyes the room is noticeably dimmer.

"Go," I say. "I'll be ready soon."

He bows to me at the door, his eyes blazing into mine, and I try to ignore the ache I feel when he closes the door softly behind him.

*

Tonight my red dress suits me. My cheeks are still flushed and the dress complements them; instead of being swamped by the colour I command it. I'm glowing with excitement, my eyes bright and my skin clear. It seems to me that what we've done is written all over me but I couldn't care less. Let the court believe I'm happy to be marrying Merek. Let them think that is the reason I cannot stop myself from smiling, why I'm lit up from inside. After tonight we'll be away from here.

When Lief enters to escort me to the Great Hall his jaw drops comically as he looks at me and I cannot help but laugh in delight. I twirl delicately for him, watching as the dress flares around me. When I step into his arms and kiss him, his hands rise to cradle my face. He holds me so carefully, so gently, that it scares me and I press myself against him, wanting the reassurance of his body. Too soon he releases me, his eyes dark again, a promise held within them that makes my stomach tighten.

"Let's stay here a little longer," I say.

"Why?" He grins and I bat at him with my hand.

"Because as soon as we leave this room you have to be my guard and I have to be Daunen Embodied. I want to be Twylla and Lief for a few more moments."

"After tonight, we'll be Twylla and Lief no matter where we are."

"I know." I beam at him. "So let me have a little more practice?"

He tilts his head to the side, chewing his lip briefly. "Do

they dance, at these feasts of yours?"

"Sometimes."

"Better sing us a song then, else how will we dance?"

The world bursts into colour as he takes me in his arms, my soul ringing with joy. I start to sing softly, "Fair and Far", and he twirls me around the room. One hand at my waist, the other at my shoulder and I rest my hands on his arms. For the duration of the song the world is perfect, as it should be, and I could not be happier. I laugh midway through as my skirts fly behind me, and he smiles, picking up where I left off in his funny off-key voice. We finish the song together and when it is over he leans his forehead against mine and we breathe each other in and out as our hearts calm themselves.

The feeling of joy remains as we walk to the Great Hall, following the lords and ladies and other courtiers as we enter the heart of the castle. Everyone is in their finery, the jewels on the rich silk gowns reflecting in the candlelight, the men walking stiffly in breeches that are rarely worn. Everyone is chattering, buzzing with excitement, hands fluttering in the air like moths as they talk, the corridors filled with the spicy taste of anticipation. Everything seems lovelier to me, even the sharp face of Lady Shasta seems friendlier now. After tonight, I'll never have to look at her again.

As we approach the door they all fall back as though I've already been crowned. Courtier after courtier murmurs my name, bowing to me as I walk past.

Merek is waiting at the door, a gold circlet woven through

254

his dark curls, his ceremonial sash in purple and bronze proud across a velvet doublet. He offers his arm to me triumphantly, and the joy seeps away. Merek and I walk to the high table, past the tables of courtiers who rise and bow. He pulls out a chair at the king's right and I allow the prince a small smile.

I turn and bow to the king and queen before I sit. All of the royal family are arrayed in their regalia, king and queen with their crowns atop their heads and furs at their throats, the king's staff leaning against his chair. To my surprise it's the queen who looks happy; the king looks pale, still recovering from his fever. I had expected it would be the other way round but it's the queen who beams at me, proud as any mother, as I take my seat beside the king. Merek rests a hand briefly on my shoulder before he takes his seat next to the queen, who leans across and kisses his cheek. He stiffens before smiling tightly and the queen turns to me again and smiles.

I take my seat, scanning the room subtly for Lief. The threads that I feel between us draw me to him and I see him standing by the corridor that leads to the royal solar. He meets my gaze for a second before he looks away, casting his eye calmly over the room, as I revel in the warmth from his glance. I allow the server to pour me some wine and take a sip, nodding at the courtiers who smile at me. They all know why we're here, that much is clear. Their faces are filled with happiness; everyone looks expectant and ready to raise their glasses to us – so different from the last time we all assembled here. Out of the corner of my eye I see the king reach to touch the queen's hand and she allows it, turning to smile at him. She truly is weaker then, or at least reconciled to what's happened.

We eat and drink, the room merry as lute players and harpists walk the aisles between the tables, playing the songs of the realm, songs I would normally sing. The king and queen talk softly as we feast, too softly for me to hear, but it touches me that they are being so warm. Perhaps things in Lormere are changing for the better, perhaps they don't need me at all. When the queen offers the king some capon from her own plate, I smile, imagining myself doing the same for Lief someday soon. It's only when I see Merek watching me, smiling at me, that I turn back to my own plate and eat.

When I risk a glance at Lief, his gaze is fixed on Merek; he stares at him with narrowed, flinty eyes, apparently not caring that he might be seen.

As some signal, the musicians stop playing and everyone turns to the high table. With a glance at each other, the king and queen rise and the room falls silent. I see Lief gazing at me and I gaze back, my eyes blazing, trying to tell him how much I long to be away from here, and with him.

"We thank you for joining us tonight," the king begins. "As you all know, Lormere has been built on the proudest of traditions, traditions which have kept us strong and true throughout our glorious history. We have fought off many threats, both distant and recent –" at this I glance at Lief again, suppressing a smile, knowing we are both thinking of Tregellan "– and we have endured."

"And we will continue to endure, and not only endure,

but to thrive," the queen picks up seamlessly from where her husband left off. "Today, we look to the future." She smiles and the court smiles with her.

"As you know, the Gods were good enough to give me both a son and a daughter, but they saw fit to take our beloved Alianor away. We despaired at first, not understanding what we had done to fail them. But the Gods have plans that we mortals can rarely understand and when they take with one hand, they give back with the other. And they gave us Twylla, our Daunen Embodied, as close to our hearts as any daughter could be. For years she has lived here with us, longing, with us all, for the day when she would marry Merek and become our daughter in truth."

At this Merek rises and makes his way to me, and I stand, allowing him to place his hand atop mine as we did so long ago at our betrothal.

"So it is our greatest pleasure to tell you that time will come before the year is out." The queen smiles at us. "On the final day of the harvest this year, my son Merek will make her his bride and a new Golden Age shall begin."

The room erupts in cheers and jubilant shouts; goblets are raised and drinks consumed with vigour. Merek leads me in front of the table, nodding at the court and smiling down at me. Behind us the king and queen stand proud and beaming and I look at Lief.

But he is looking past me, staring at the king with a frown, and one by one the rest of the court are doing the same. I turn to see what they look at.

The king is frozen beside the queen, his smile contorted into a wide-mouthed grimace and even as Merek and I begin to move he is falling, falling into the table with a terrible crash, his hands scrabbling and knocking his goblet to the floor as he collapses next to it.

Then the screaming starts.

Chapter 19

The screams fall away as abruptly as they began. The guards rush to the dais, swords drawn as though the king has been attacked and they will defend him. But even as they begin to surround him, the king is trying to sit up, waving his hands at them. Habit makes me move away as the guards crowd around us and Merek grips my arm, pulling me back behind the table and keeping himself as a shield between me and the room. I try to look over his shoulder for Lief but can't see him. The queen kneels next to the king, her hand pressed to his forehead. He says something to her, too low for me to hear, and Merek's fingers tighten on my arm, enough to make me gasp. Below us the rest of the court is watching, their mouths dark holes in pale faces, hands clasped over their hearts as they all stare at the dais, frozen like a tableau.

Two of the Kingsguard try to help him to his feet, but

he still cannot stand and they have to lift him, their arms tucked under his legs. He looks shamed as they carry him from the room. The queen stares after them, a hand held to her mouth, before she lowers it. She casts one searing glance at Merek and follows the king. Merek looks down at me, his eyes narrowed, before he releases my arm.

"Stay here," he says. "Don't eat or drink anything but stay here as long as the others do. Don't let on anything serious is amiss, let them think it's nothing and that they should carry on with the feast. Only leave when the rest of the court does and then go straight to your tower. Do you understand me?"

When I nod dumbly he walks swiftly from the room, leaving me standing on the dais, surrounded by guards, with all eyes on me. I stay frozen, looking back at the court.

"The king has taken ill," I say in a quavering voice. "It's nothing serious, praise be to the Gods, and His Highness, Prince Merek, insists we remain here and continue to celebrate."

Everyone eyes me with suspicion and takes their seats, but no one eats or drinks. They whisper amongst themselves, casting dark glances at me, and I sit down, painfully aware of my isolation on the dais now the guards have faded away. I look down at the remains of the feast, at the servants hovering near the doors as if they would run, and I know the rest of the room wants to do the same, myself included. It doesn't take long for the first of them to dissent. I am not the queen and they don't fear me half as much as they fear her.

"I am going to pray for the king's health, my lady," Lady

Shasta announces and rises and half of the court agrees, standing with her.

I look to the door and see Lief standing there, frowning at me.

"I shall do the same," I say, rising as swiftly as I can and stepping off the platform, moving so fast the court has to scatter to get out of my way as I make for the door. I hear someone murmur "poison". The whispers follow me from the room and I notice that despite their hurry to pray a moment ago no one leaves behind me. Lief's expression is fixed as he takes his place at my side.

"Now?" he says quietly and I shake my head, heading back to my tower in terrified silence.

"When?" Lief says as we round the last corner. "Twylla?"

"Merek told me to go straight to the tower," I say as he opens the door.

"What does it matter what he says? This could be our best chance," he says, following me up the stairs. "Everyone will be focused on the king and—" He turns as the tower door opens again behind us. "Who goes there?"

When there is no answer Lief pushes me up the last few steps and follows me into the room, drawing his sword and turning to the doorway. But it is Merek who strides through the door, moving past both Lief and me to lean against the window ledge, his back to the room.

"What is it?" I say. "Is it the king?"

"Stay on the door, outside the room," he orders Lief. "Let no one in."

Lief looks to me and I nod, watching as he bows stiffly, his eyes boring into mine as he closes the door behind him.

"It is important to me that you're happy, Twylla. And that you are safe," Merek begins as soon as the latch clicks, still keeping his back to me. The words sound rehearsed, reminding me eerily of his mother and her vows for my safety.

"I am, Merek. Both of those."

"No." He shakes his head before turning to me, and my breath catches in my throat. Aside from two red spots of colour on his cheeks, his face is as pale as a corpse's, and his hair is awry, as though he's been pulling at it. Fear clutches at me, scraping at my insides, making me feel hollow. He walks over to me, taking my hands in his, and I fight the urge to pull away. "You don't understand. I must ask you to do something for me. For us."

I shake my head in confusion and he tugs my hands again. "It's important. It will sound terrible but you must, because if you don't. . ." He trails off.

"Merek, will you please tell me what's going on? You promised me the truth. What is this? What is happening here?"

Merek looks at me, licking his lips before he speaks. "I think my mother poisoned the king. In fact, I'm sure of it."

I blink rapidly, trying to find the sense in his words. "I don't understand."

"It seems my stepfather's plea for clemency for Lady Lorelle was the final straw. Theirs was never a love match but she cannot have him diminishing her power. And now

262

this. . . I doubt very much he will make it through the night. You were there; you saw him."

"But surely it's the fever, surely it's a relapse. Rest, time. . ."

"I don't think he ever had a fever. I think she misjudged the dose the first time and tried again tonight. He won't see dawn, Twylla."

"What kind of poison? Not oleander?" I ask, the hair on the back of my neck rising, but he shakes his head.

"I've no idea, but I will write to my Tregellian contacts, tell them the symptoms, see if they know of anything that causes it."

"Merek," I say softly, "where does this come from?"

"Because she's grown tired of him not being the husband and king she needs him to be. I believe she plans to marry again."

"Whom?"

"Me."

I stare at him as revulsion washes over me. "What do you mean? How can you say this?"

"Because she said it." He covers his mouth after he's spoken, as though he could take the words back and trap them inside, as though saying them aloud had taken something away from him.

In all my life, at every Eating, every execution, never have I seen anyone look so lost.

"I heard her say it." He lowers his hand and continues. "I followed her to the room where my stepfather was taken and

263

waited outside to hear what she would say. And she told him. It would be over by dawn, she said, and when he was gone only she and I left would be left. And that she knew what that meant, knew what she had to do. And that it would be no worse than marrying her brother."

I freeze, staring at him. "Merek, that's . . . . madness."

"I am not the mad one here!" he shouts and I step back, wincing at the sudden loudness. "She said it, Twylla. She said it. She's the mad one, Twylla. Not me. She wants two children of the blood to take the throne. It's all she's ever wanted. To remake the Golden Age of Lormere: sister and brother, king and queen. But my father died, and Alianor died, and there were no more children. Don't you see, she hates him for that? She could never have loved him fully – he was merely a cousin – but the fact that he couldn't even give her a half-sister for me means he's failed her. So she will get rid of him and clear the way to marry me. She cannot keep her throne without a king by her side and I am the last of my bloodline. She will marry me."

I back away from him, leaning against my bureau. "But I'm still here. What does she plan to do with me? Does she plan to kill me too? Is that how she will clear the way?"

Merek's eyes become wilder. "I didn't wait to hear her announce your murder. As soon as she confirmed what I'd suspected about her plans for me I came straight to you."

"Confirmed it? So you have thought this before?"

"I've suspected, for some time. . . She would say things about the future of Lormere without our blood ruling it, about whether you had the stomach to be a queen, about whether she was right to force me into a marriage with someone so different from us. . . I tried to tell you in the Hall of Glass but it seemed so melodramatic at the time. Yet now my stepfather is dying and I'm sure it is at her hand. She's made her move, Twylla."

"You have to tell someone." I pull away from him, heading towards the door. "She cannot do this; she cannot kill the king – it's treason."

"Whom do I tell?" he says as he pulls me back. "Who has more power than she does? Who can stop her?"

I stare at Merek and I wonder for the first time whether he is a little mad too. "So what can we do? Does she mean to poison me or –" a thought dawns on me, a small spark of something like hope "– will she make you put me aside in her favour? Is that what you must ask of me?" If he puts me aside, I'll be free to be with Lief.

Merek's face tightens, the skin stretching over his cheekbones as his mouth gapes in a silent moan, his face hollow and gaunt.

"If I were to put you aside she might not kill you," he says raggedly. "You might, at least, be safe. But it would kill me." He looks at me, his eyes wide. "I would throw myself from this tower. To marry my own mother? Marry *her*?" He shudders. "So I must ask for your help. Because I have nothing and no one else."

I look at him, into his pleading, desperate face.

"I've no right to ask anything of you. I know that," he says.

"I know what a thing it is to ask you to ally with me, and to trust me after what I have kept from you, and in this way too. But I will show you my gratitude every day for as long as we both live if you will help me. Anything you want, you need only name it and you shall have it."

"What do you need me to do?" I ask.

"Once my stepfather is dead, we must marry. If I have a queen I can take my crown and give you yours and we can put my mother somewhere she can hurt no one."

"But she'll kill me," I say. "She'll kill me before we can arrange the wedding."

"Not if we move quickly." He fumbles for my hand again, pressing it to his chest. "If we act before she realizes what we're planning. We can even pretend that we want to delay the wedding out of respect for my stepfather; that will throw her off the scent. She won't need to hurt you as long as she believes her plan is still progressing; too many deaths would look suspicious. We won't have to keep it up for long."

The walls of the room close in around me. "When?" I say.

"Tomorrow night. I must send for a priest we can trust but I know of a man. There will be no ceremony to it. Just you and me and witnesses." He looks at me with hope-filled eyes. "I know I am asking you to commit treason," he says. "And believe me, I know I have no right to ask you for anything. But this is our only chance, Twylla. We must end this now. Because if we delay, we'll both be dead. It must be tomorrow."

Tomorrow. I won't ever be free if I agree to this. But if I don't then what? The queen will marry Merek and she'll kill me to do so. I don't believe there's anything she wouldn't do to keep her crown. If I stay, then I will lose Lief; I will lose myself, but if I go . . . Merek will take his own life. I know it. I can see the truth of it in his eyes and if I refuse to ally with him then he might even do it tonight, before anything else can happen. I would be his killer, an executioner absolutely. I would have walked away knowing that doing so was his death sentence. He would die so Lief and I could be together. His life for ours.

He crosses the room and takes my hands, before sinking to his knees, his arms wrapping around my waist and his cheek resting on my stomach. When I look down at him he stares back at me, his dark eyes filled with dread. He looks so much like his mother.

"Please, Twylla," he says softly. "I cannot do this without you."

"Merek—" Before I can continue my door is thrown open and a huge red-faced guard struggles into the room, trying to push Lief from him. Merek rises to his feet, his face wholly pale now.

"Forgive me, Sire," he says as he kneels and Merek looks at me, his eyes so wide I can see the whites of them all around his dark irises.

"What did you call me?" he asks the guard, his voice strained, and Lief stops pulling at the guard as the meaning of the greeting sinks in.

"I had to come. Her Majesty the Queen insisted," the

guard pants. "The king is dead." He looks up expectantly as his words assault me over and over, beating against my ears. "The king is dead," he repeats when we do nothing but stare dumbly at him. "The king is dead."

Merek looks again at me, his face etched with misery, haggard and desperate, his fingers wringing the collar of his tunic, pulling it tight like a noose.

Duty or choice. His life or mine.

As if in a trance, I kneel before Merek, completing the proclamation: "Long live the king."

Then I nod at him, once, and his face clears, the lines fading as he breathes out. He lifts me into his arms, whispering "Thank you" in my ear as my heart breaks.

I look away, unable to speak, and Merek takes my hand and kisses it.

"Thank you," he says again and turns to the guard. "We'll leave the lady to pray," he says and the guard dips his head at me before following Merek from the room.

Lief looks back and forth between the door and me.

"We're not leaving, are we?" he says flatly.

"Lief—"

"You promised me. You said you would never marry him. You chose me."

Gods help me. "Lief. . ." My voice cracks and I can't force the words that will break my promise to him from my lips. I can't abandon Merek. If I do then he'll kill himself. His death would be our curse. And not just ours, but all of Lormere's. Leaving would damn every soul that lives here. Lormere would become Tallith, a lost kingdom. But Lief would never understand that.

Lief nods and turns.

"Please!" I say. "You can't leave me."

"Don't ask me to stay here and watch you marry him," he says. "You can't have it all, Twylla."

"I don't want it all, I want you!"

"Then come with me." It is his voice that cracks now and I feel my heart shudder, as if it means to leap from my chest and into his hands.

"I can't."

"Why? What's changed, Twylla? What did he say to you?"

I shake my head, trying to find a way to explain to him what Merek has asked of me and why I can't refuse. But again the words clog in my throat and I stare at him, mute.

He looks at me for a long moment. "This is goodbye then."

He turns and leaves me.

An hour later, when the door opens again, I expect it to be him, full of fire and demanding an explanation. But it is Merek, his eyes still bright.

"Twylla?" He rushes to my side. I have not moved since Lief walked out on me. Gently he guides me to the bed and sits me down. He leaves, returning a moment later with a goblet, which I drain without question. Brandy, from the burn in my throat. I should have known it would be alcohol of some sort.

"Are you well?" he asks and I turn to look at him. My

face feels slack, my whole body is limp and numb as though it's no longer mine to control. I am empty; there is nothing inside me at all.

"Speak, my dear."

His dear. I cave in on myself, collapse into grief, and his arms snake around me. The wrong arms, the wrong smell, the wrong man.

"My mother has gone to pray at the mere." His mouth twists and I shudder as we both realize what she has gone to pray for, why she'd choose a fertility mere to pray at. "I've told her we wish to delay the wedding in light of what has happened. She consented. She says we may take as long as we need, that Lormere will understand."

I nod, trying to sit up.

He pushes my hair back from my face in a gesture so tender it brings new tears to my eyes. "I know I scared you earlier, with what I said, but it will be well, I promise you that. Everything will be fine, as we've planned. I must marry you, Twylla. And then we will have our coronation and we'll both be safe."

I close my eyes, opening them immediately when Lief's stricken face appears behind my lids.

"Your mother has been sent for," Merek continues. "Once she has Eaten, and he is cremated, we can marry. As soon as it is done you have nothing to fear. We will be free."

My sob is loud and takes him by surprise. I shake my head, turning away to collect myself.

"Will I fetch something to calm you?" he asks.

Again I shake my head, taking a deep breath. I made my choice and allowed Lief to leave without me. I did this to myself. "Forgive me."

"There is nothing to forgive. I know I have done nothing but heap devastation on you these last few days, but in a few more we shall be safe. As soon as I am crowned, I can control my mother."

As he talks, his other words sink in. "My mother is coming?"

"She is the Sin Eater and it must be done. Would you like to see her?"

There is no hesitation. "No, I think not. There is no use in it. My life is here now."

"With me," he says, making no effort to disguise his triumph.

Chapter 20

Every window in the castle will be covered; every looking glass will be draped with black fabric. In the Great Hall the silver plate that normally sits on the tables will be put away, replaced with tin; any surface that might give reflection will be dulled or covered. The servants and handmaids will work through the night to bring out the black robes, gowns and tunics, and hastily adjust them for us to wear in the morning.

And as the castle prepares to mourn its king, Merek stays in my room, talking again of what he wants to do, what we together could achieve. After hours, I finally beg him to let me rest and he takes my face in his hands.

"Forgive me, my love, of course you must rest. Have your guard lock the tower door behind me, tell him to open it for no one but me."

"He's gone," I say dully. "He had to return to his home."

"Then I will be your guard until we take the throne." Merek kisses my head. "Come down with me now and lock the door. I will come for you in the morning."

I do as he says, trying not to shudder when his cold hand cups my cheek in farewell. I pause with my fingers on the bolt; if I lock it Lief won't be able to return. Then I recall his face before he left. He won't return. I slide the bolt into place and slowly climb the stairs back to my room.

Sleep does not come. Instead I spend the night recalling every word Lief said to me, wondering if he hates me now. They say when a limb is amputated you can still feel its ghost, and that is the sensation I experience now. The soul-deep knowledge that he is gone not for a moment, but for ever, leaves me haunted. I have failed him, and myself, and even knowing it was the right thing to do is no comfort at all. I sit in the window with my face pressed against the curtain until the sun rises, when I can bathe and put on my mourning gown. I wait for Merek to come, to be my guard as he said he would, but no one comes. No maid brings my breakfast, no one arrives to protect me, or tell me where I should be. I wait by the window, watching the sun rise higher and higher and still no one comes. I toy with the idea of staying here, imagining someone finding me years from now, just bones heaped beneath the window.

But then I grow angry with myself, at this maudlin sentimentality. I *chose* this, and so I force myself to stand, to smooth the creases from the black mourning gown and to leave my tower, unescorted for the first time since I came here.

I'm braced for fear and suspicion from my fellow courtiers, perhaps even cruelty, given that I am unprotected and my reputation precedes me. Part of me even wonders if I'd welcome it as a balm for the agony of knowing *he* is gone; it would at least give me some new pain to cling to. But the corridors are empty, they feel vast to me, as wide as the ocean my brothers used to speak of. I float through them like flotsam, far from land and home and anchor. Nothing to bind me. Nothing to keep me. When I walk to the royal solar, announced by the guards on the door there, Merek is waiting with the queen, his promise forgotten.

"Your mother is here," she says, turning her gaze on me.

"Twylla does not wish to see her." Merek speaks for me. "She won't be attending the Eating."

The queen looks at me. "I'm afraid you must. This is the price of marrying into the royal family, Twylla. Sometimes we must do things that are painful. We put our own needs aside for the greater good."

Something hard and rocklike settles in my chest as I think of what I have put aside for the greater good, and all because of her. "I understand, Your Majesty," I say flatly.

She nods. "I must change, better to begin early. The kitchens have prepared the feast. After it is done, we will find whoever did this and execute them."

"Do you have any idea who it could have been?" Merek asks, his voice level, though his eyes are hard.

"A Tregellian," the queen says and my heart stutters.

"Who else would want to kill the king of Lormere? I've suspected for some time that they're not as peaceable as they claim to be, and now I am convinced of it. You said yourself, Merek, that their knowledge of medicines and science far exceeds our own. And now we know why they've always been unwilling to share it. It seems they plan to use their knowledge for ill, as far as Lormere is concerned. It's an act of war, Merek. They've sent someone in to try to kill us all and it will not be borne. If it is a war they want then they will have one."

I recall Lief telling me how he knew the Morningsbane was a lie because Tregellians knew so much about poisons and my fingers clench into my palms. It's common knowledge. Blaming a Tregellian is plausible.

"Mother, we cannot afford a war," Merek says. "And there is no evidence it was a Tregellian."

"The poison itself is evidence," the queen spits. "Tregellians know all about poisons; it's a coward's weapon."

Merek looks at me and frowns. "Perhaps best to talk of this later," he says and the queen smiles grimly.

"I plan to talk of nothing else until I've set everything in Lormere to rights."

With that she sweeps from the room, the sway of her gown punctuating her threat.

I catch Merek watching me as I stare after her. "You did well," he says softly. "She has no idea."

"She's not even pretending to grieve, is she?"

Merek smiles, and then laughs, the sound absorbed into

the drapes. "Why would she? She believes she's on the cusp of her own Golden Age. She cares for nothing but the crown and glory."

"Will people believe it was a Tregellian who killed the king?"

"I expect so. Would you question her if I had not told you what I heard?" Merek says, and my mind slides to Lief, causing a pain my chest. "Besides, it's better for us if she thinks she's fooled us all. Let her believe her plan is working. We can avenge my stepfather later."

I stare at him, still not fully able to believe that the queen killed her husband, and plans to marry her own son to keep the throne.

"We'll send her away, once this is done," he says softly. "There's a closed order of women at the base of the East Mountains. She can spend her days there. Away from us."

He stands and pours himself a glass of wine and we both remain silent, lost in our thoughts until the queen returns, her face covered in a mantilla of black lace that does little to hide the spark in her eyes. Merek stands and makes as if to offer me his arm, only turning to his mother when I shake my head. The queen nods at me and I fall in behind them.

I haven't been to this part of the castle since I was here as a child for the last king's Eating. It is down beyond the barracks, in an undercroft near the north tower. It is peaceful, sepulchral and completely at odds with the churning inside me. I cannot settle; I lurch from heartache to fear, from loss to dread, and none of it is to do with the poor dead king.

My mother waits, vast and serene, in front of the coffin. She has always been able to fill a room, and not only because of her size. There is something in her bearing that commands you to pay attention to her and even in this room, with a prince and a queen, she is the ruler. She stands wide-legged, her arms crossed across her chest, draped in the black she always wears. I had forgotten how tall she is. I study her face, trying to find some sign of my own in it. But there is nothing. She doesn't look at me as we enter, staring instead at the coffin. The lid has been covered with the royal coat of arms and atop it is a small selection of food, much less than there had been for the previous king, or Alianor. My mother will not like it.

We file along the wall and take our seats on the stools placed there for us. Then the Eating begins. My mother works as she always has: slowly, methodically. Three bites of bread and then a sip of ale, a mouthful of ham and then more ale. She is a stalwart Sin Eater, ploughing her way through the meal with the quiet dignity of a shire horse in a field. I watch the flesh on her upper arm ripple as she reaches across the coffin for an apple. The crunch as she bites into it is agonizing but she is mindless of it, her eyes moving from one morsel to the next as she charts her course.

She always starts with the smallest sins – lies, deceptions, angry words – spiralling in slowly to the largest ones. I used to worry at extravagant Eatings that she might fill herself before she reached the worst sins, but she never did. It's as though the taste for the smaller sins whet her appetite for the terrible ones. The king has no terrible sins, merely the usual ones. My mother prefers a more wide-ranging sinner.

As I watch her work a kind of calm falls over me, the routine of the Eating still familiar and comforting, despite the years, because this is something I know, something that cannot and will not change. On my far right the queen is fidgeting; her hands are restless in her lap, her fingers writhing in between each other like eels. In contrast my mother seems to almost move slower, and then it hits me; that's precisely what she's doing. As the queen uses her body to try and hurry the Eating, my mother uses hers to slow it. She won't let the queen be the ruler of this; death is her realm and the Eating will proceed at her pace. It stuns me to see it; though I knew my mother was powerful I never understood she was this powerful; that in the queen's own castle she can make time her servant, and the only wishes she obeys are those of the Eating. Whatever battle rages on, my mother will be the victor as long as she plays her part, and she will, because my mother lives to be her part. Through my despair, a tiny slice of hope cuts, because whether I like it or not I am my mother's daughter, and if she can hold her own here then so can I. I will take a leaf from her book and be as she is. I will hold true, despite the cost, to my role. And that way I shall win.

Merek looks at me, his face unreadable, and then turns back to observe my mother at work. Time has altered her appearance little, a strand or two of grey hair, lines visible around her eyes as she squints to see how much ale is left.

I'm wondering what my sister looks like now when I realize with a start that she is not here. As the Sin Eater in training, she ought to be here with my mother, observing the rights as solemnly as I used to. I look sharply to Merek but he keeps his gaze fixed on the coffin.

Despite what I'm sure is deliberate slowness, it doesn't take her long to finish the meal; the Eating is complete within the hour. As soon as it is done, the queen rises and leaves, without a word to any of us.

My mother looks at Merek and me and then completes the ritual. "I give easement and rest now to thee, dear man. Come not down the lanes or in our meadows. And for thy peace I pawn my own soul."

I shudder as I always have at the words and on cue Merek removes a silver coin from his purse and offers it to my mother. She takes it, tucking it away inside the folds of her gown, before bowing to Merek and turning to leave.

"Will you not greet your daughter?" His voice startles me, echoing painfully off the marble walls of the crypt.

My mother turns to me, looking me up and down slowly. "She's no daughter of mine, Your Majesty. Your mother saw to that the day she took her. What is it they call her now? 'Daunen Embodied'?" A faint smirk plays at my mother's lips.

"Where's Maryl?" I blurt out.

My mother appraises me, as if she could see my sins, the mark of Lief's hands on me, then purses her lips. "She's

279

dead. She took ill with the fever and passed over." There's no sadness in her eyes as she tells me.

"When was this?"

"Two harvests ago," she says, turning to Merek. "If that's all, Your Majesty?"

I know I haven't imagined the sneer in her voice when Merek grips my hand tightly. "Go," he says and she does.

Two harvests ago. Maryl has been dead for two years. And no one has told me.

As soon as my mother is gone, I turn on Merek.

"Did you know?" I demand.

"No, of course not," he says. "I've been away on progress, Twylla, you know that."

"But your mother did, didn't she?" I hiss.

He looks at me and nods slowly. "She must have done. Please, Twylla," he says as I open my mouth. "Not today. I've lost the only father I can remember and we cannot do anything to anger her now. We're so close, my dear. We'll have time enough to punish her for all her sins." He takes my hand tentatively and squeezes it, before dropping it and walking away.

I stare at him, floored by his callousness. How can he be so dismissive of my loss, especially in the face of his own? I try and recall my sister's face and realize I can't; she is so long lost to me. For half of the time I've been here she has been dead. I have slaved and obeyed and resigned myself to all manner of things because I thought I was making her life better and she was not alive to feel the benefit of it at all. No one told me. No one thought I would care to know.

But of course they didn't, because when have I ever made it clear that I care?

I never truly fought for her. I could have fought harder to see her, asked Merek, asked the king. How many times have I asked how she is, asked anyone to find out, bribed or threatened someone to do it? I managed to use my reputation to secure extra helpings of cakes but not to find out how my little sister was. I have never tried to send word to her. I have sat and felt sorry for myself and pined over her loss but I've never done a single thing about it.

I wanted so much to leave my mother's house, to not be the Sin Eater. I walked away knowing my seven-year-old sister would have to pick up that mantle as I lived in a castle. I sentenced her to all of the horror I'd hated, and I'd told myself it was all right because I was at least ensuring money was sent home for her. I lied to myself and pretended my actions were for the greater good and all the while I lamented the loss of her and drowned in self-pity. Even today, I forgot to expect to see her until the last.

I sacrificed my sister for a chance to be a princess. I was greedy, and I was selfish, and I hid it behind a mask of pious duty and resignation to the job I had to do. A job I chose over her.

I am more my mother's child – I am more the queen's child – than I ever knew before now.

And for the first time I find myself feeling something more than merely resigned to marrying Merek. I deserve this.

I deserve to have to stay here and see it through. That is my destiny. Finally I understand. It's time I stopped wishing for what I cannot have and do what I'm here for. I'll marry Merek and become the queen. It is no less than I deserve.

As the king's body is burned, Merek drinks, the queen sits and makes endless lists and notations in a leather-bound book and I stare at her, itching to scream at her, to strike her. She must have been laughing herself sick watching me mope around, with my long face and my limpid eyes, melting into the shadows like a ghost and hiding behind the skirts of the Gods, longing for something that didn't exist. She knew me for the coward I was. She encouraged it. And for this I hate her more than ever.

So I imagine her face as Merek places the crown on my head. Her crown. My sister is dead and Lief is gone. She has taken everything from me and now I will do the same to her. I will take the one thing she values and she will know what it is to suffer.

When the bell tolls to say the cremation is complete, the queen shrugs as if shaking off a heavy cloak, before she rises and pours herself some wine. She drinks it slowly and then stands.

"I have some writs I must send," she says, looking at Merek. "You will have to add your seal to them, alongside my own. I've demanded the arrest of every Tregellian in the land."

I'm so shocked that I lurch forwards and Merek looks up

from his wine glass. Lief. But no, he left last night. He'll be across the border now, far from her reach.

"I will root out the murderer and avenge the king," the queen continues, apparently not noticing my horror. "Twylla, I'm afraid this means you'll have work to do in the near future."

I look at the queen, confused, until I realize she means work as Daunen. Merek hasn't told her I know that the Morningsbane is false. She wants me to touch men she's already poisoned; innocent men. "I'd be happy to punish the person who killed the king," I say coldly. "I will take great pleasure in it."

The queen looks at me curiously before nodding. "I'm only sorry it took the death of my husband to make you see how valued you are," she says and I don't know whether it's paranoia or some sixth sense that makes me hear the threat in her words. "Excuse me, both of you. I have much to arrange." She rises and steps towards the door, before turning. "Your guard, Twylla. He is Tregellian, is he not? Where is he now?"

Merek answers for me. "He had to return to his home. I will make sure Twylla is safe. Given we have a poisoner on the loose I trust no one but myself to do it.'

"He left? How odd," the queen says. "How odd the only Tregellian in the castle would leave so soon after the king dies." She leaves without another backwards glance and my jaw aches from the effort I put into not screaming at her as she goes. Once again I silently thank whoever is listening that Lief is long gone.

"I'm grateful," Merek says, turning to look at me with his head tilted.

"For?"

"Doing as I asked. I know what it must have cost you."

"As you said, there will be time."

"After tonight, we have a lifetime." He smiles.

Though I've eaten nothing, I feel my stomach lurch. "I might rest for a while," I say carefully. "Last night was long, and I need time to prepare for tonight."

"You should," he agrees. "I'll walk you to your room. I think it's best for now if you stay there, away from my mother. I've sent word to a priest I know from Haga. I'll look for him by the Water Gate tonight. Then I'll send word to you. We're almost there, Twylla."

He takes my hand in his and escorts me to the west tower, accepting the condolences of the few courtiers we see on the way, but otherwise saying nothing, occasionally squeezing my fingers gently.

He follows me into the room, checking beneath the bed and behind the curtains before he's satisfied the queen isn't hiding there with a knife.

"Bolt the door," he reminds me as he leaves and I do. But when his footsteps have faded I pull the bolt open. Let the queen come and attack me if she wishes; I'll be ready for her. On my way back to my room I call into Dorin and Lief's room. Dorin's things are still on the chest beside his bed: a small tin soldier and a knife. I pick up the knife. Yes, let her come. I owe her for Maryl. And myself.

*

But all my courage leaves me when I enter my room and a hand claps over my mouth. My assailant drags me inside and slams the door behind me and I swing wildly with the knife, screaming into the palm that tries to silence me. Then the hands release me and there, before me, is my lost guard, his eyes burning, chewing his lips as he watches me. I drop the knife to the floor, every single noble thought of accepting my fate flying out of my head.

We stare at each other, both warily trying to read the other's intentions.

Then in a crash of bodies we meet, not knowing who moved first, who pulled whose face to theirs, only aware of the need inside us both, of the rightness of our being together, even as the king's soul goes to wherever souls go, the Eternal Kingdom or nowhere at all.

Chapter 21

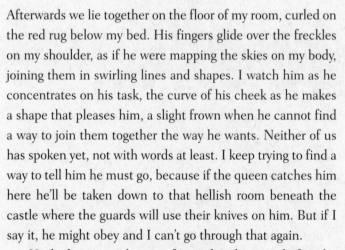

Afterwards we lie together on the floor of my room, curled on the red rug below my bed. His fingers glide over the freckles on my shoulder, as if he were mapping the skies on my body, joining them in swirling lines and shapes. I watch him as he concentrates on his task, the curve of his cheek as he makes a shape that pleases him, a slight frown when he cannot find a way to join them together the way he wants. Neither of us has spoken yet, not with words at least. I keep trying to find a way to tell him he must go, because if the queen catches him here he'll be taken down to that hellish room beneath the castle where the guards will use their knives on him. But if I say it, he might obey and I can't go through that again.

He looks at me, leaning forward to kiss me before he sits up.

"We need to decide what we're going to do," he says. "I

can't leave you, that much is clear, and I can't keep from you if I stay, which means you'll be cuckolding the king."

"You have to leave," I say quietly, finally finding my voice. "The queen is telling everyone a Tregellian poisoned the king. If you stay you'll be arrested and they'll question you."

"Then come with me. Take your life into your own hands and come with me. I thought that was what you wanted?" His mouth twists as he tries to find the words he needs. "I cannot stay here, regardless of what madness the queen is spouting. I cannot stay and watch you become another man's wife. Yes, he will be wounded, and yes, they will come after us." He talks rapidly. "But surely it's worth it, for the chance to be together? I believe in us; I believe I am supposed to be with you and you are with me. I would rather die than live without you. And if you don't feel the same, if—" He gently places a finger against my lips as I try to interrupt. "If you don't feel the same, I will understand and I will go. I'll never bother you again. But think, please. Can you stay here with him when I'll be taking your heart away with me?"

I try to duck my head away from his gaze but he doesn't allow it, tilting my chin upwards so I have to meet his eyes.

"It's time for you to make a choice," he says softly. "No more doing what he wants, or what I want, or what the queen wants. You have to choose what *you* want. Either him or me. Whatever you decide, I won't fight you. I won't make you feel guilty for the decision. I promise. Your choice . . . as long as it's me." His smile is heartbreaking: tender and hopeful and scared.

"I knew it."

The hard voice of the queen rips us apart. She is framed by the doorway, her face pale save for two blood-red spots staining her cheeks.

Lief scrambles to cover my body with his own to spare me the shame of being seen by the guards who stand behind her, their swords drawn and pointed at us, held in gloved hands. I can do nothing except lie beneath him, naked and frozen. No. This cannot be.

The queen glowers at us, both rage and triumph illuminating her face. "Get up. Cover yourselves," she orders.

"At least give us the privacy to clad ourselves," Lief says, his arm extended as if it alone could ward them away.

"What right do you have to ask me for consideration?" the queen says. "You poison my husband and then sleep with my son's betrothed and you ask me for goodwill?"

"I didn't kill—" Lief begins but the queen raises her voice, drowning him out.

"We have all seen your shame; no amount of cloth will disguise the crimes you have committed here. You are both under arrest for treason, for conspiring against the throne of Lormere. Either dress quickly, or be taken as you are."

Lief opens his mouth to protest but as he does the guards move forward and I whimper, terrified the queen will drag me through the castle naked. Lief turns his attention to me but I cannot move and he turns his back on them to lift me, still mindful to shield me as much as he can. My hands shake and he has to put my gown on me, dressing me as though he were my maid. Over his shoulder I notice the guards have all looked away. But the queen watches it all, a smile playing at her lips as she revels in my humiliation.

"I love you," he whispers as he pulls the ties on my dress together.

When I am covered, Lief dresses himself, turning defiantly towards the queen as he does. He moves slowly, deliberately, pulling his garments on in the reverse of a seduction. As he bends to reach for his sword belt, she makes a gesture and two of the guards move forward. Before either of us can cry out, one has clubbed Lief on the back of the neck with the hilt of his sword and I watch in horror as he falls to the floor. As soon as he is down, two of them begin to kick him, bringing their boots back and swinging them into his ribs and spine.

"No, stop!" I find my voice and my feet and fly towards them but it is the queen who grabs me by the arms and forces me to watch as the guards beat Lief in front of me. Each grunt makes me scream and writhe but she holds me with a strength that surprises me. One of the guards grins at me from the doorway and I bare my teeth at him, still struggling in the queen's grip.

"Enough," she says in a bored tone when Lief has stopped moaning and grunting, finally unconscious. "Take the murderer away." They seize Lief by his arms and drag him from the room.

"Wait outside," she says to the two remaining guards, who bow and withdraw, closing the door behind them. When we are alone she flings me from her and I stumble, landing in a pool of blood. Panting, I look at her, filling my gaze with as much hatred as I can muster. She stands and assesses me, her eyes sweeping up and down my form.

"How stupid you are," she says finally. "To have the chance to marry a prince and to throw it away for a farmer's boy. For the best, though. You'd make a terrible queen; you make such poor choices."

"I've never had a choice about anything," I spit at her.

"You are a fool, Twylla. You've always had choices," she seethes. "You chose to come here, to give up your home and family. You chose to befriend the son of a servant and make him and yourself a liability to my rule. And you chose to lie with your guard, the man who killed my husband. Did you aid him? Did he teach you his Tregellian ways? Is that how you are able to touch him without killing him?"

"He didn't! It was you, I know it was you. And I know about Daunen; I know about the Mornings—" My cries are cut off as she backhands me across the face, making my ears ring.

"How much more treason do you plan to commit today?" she hisses at me, glancing towards the door and I realize she's putting on a show, for the guards who must be able to hear us, trying to keep her story alive to the last.

"You—" I begin but she raises a hand to silence me.

"There will be a trial," she continues. "In front of the whole court I will see you confront what you have done and what you have said. You have broken the kingdom's faith in

290

you. You will die for your crimes and your sins will not be Eaten. And that still won't be punishment enough for opening your legs to another man while my son planned to wed you. While my son loved you."

My anger ebbs at those words and I have to look away, the fire in her eyes is too much to bear, her judgement washing over me and damning me.

"I had hoped, for a time, that you would be good enough for both of my sons," she says, her head to one side as she watches me. "I have two sons, you see" she continues. "My son by birth and my son by inheritance, for Lormere is as much my child as Merek is. I have nurtured this land as I have cosseted my son and you have failed them both. It is your fault it has come to this. And one day Merek will see that. Guards!" she calls but it is Merek who opens the door and dread fills every part of me.

"What is the meaning of this?" He glares at his mother, his eyes darting to me, concern clouding his expression before he turns back to his mother.

"Ask her." The queen thrusts me forward and I collapse at Merek's feet.

"Twylla?" he says softly.

"Tell him!" the queen cries. "Confess what you have done."

I cannot bear to tell the man who stands over me what I have done to him, had planned to do.

"Mother, enough. I command you to explain this."

"She –" the queen's raised finger is a malediction "– was

with her guard. In here. On the day we said goodbye to your stepfather. I found them naked here. She has betrayed you."

I look at Merek, witnessing the anger on his face give way to anguish.

"No, it's not true. Twylla, it isn't true, is it? You wouldn't do that, not after all we said? All I told you?"

"I'm sorry," is all I can say. It is enough.

He covers his face with his hands, a gesture of defeat that damns me. "I knew," he says. "Of course I knew he had feelings for you. A blind man could have seen it. But you – I thought you understood. Gods, I am a fool! I thought you were with me."

"Merek, please—" My plea is cut off by the queen, flying at me with her hand raised again. The second slap echoes across the room and I reel from the force of it, my own hand rising to clasp my cheek, the skin burning under my palm.

"Don't you dare address my son by his name, you little slut," she hisses at me. "You dare take your lover in my castle and then beg my son for his aid?"

Merek places a hand on his mother's arm, restraining her. He looks at me coldly, his face returning to the same inscrutable plane it was when he first came back to Lormere.

"The smoke from my stepfather's funeral still hangs in the air. This morning you attended his Eating at our sides. This afternoon, you lie with your guard in the castle where I grieve," he says quietly. "You are charged with treason against the throne of Lormere." He repeats his mother's words. "There can be no mercy. That is the price of what you've done to me."

He turns on his heel and leaves the room, not fast enough to prevent me seeing the shaking of his shoulders as he goes.

"Do you know what astounds me the most, Twylla?" the queen says. She lowers her voice to a whisper, her tone intimate, almost maternal. I tear my eyes from the doorway to look at her. "It's that you did this to yourself. You've lost him and given me what I wanted all along and I barely had to do a thing. It couldn't be any neater. That calls for a celebration, don't you think?"

I say nothing, watching her.

"Ah, I have it," she says. "We won't hang you for your crimes. We'll hunt you. I'll take you to the forest myself."

"No—"

"Yes. I'll have the whole court follow." She nods to herself. "I have a mind to make you watch the dogs eat your lover first. Perhaps I'll put you both there and we'll see how much he loves you then. Do you think he'll try to shield you from their jaws when they tear your heart out?" She laughs as I shiver. "We should make a wager. Wouldn't that be amusing? How far will you get before they bring you down? How long before you're on your knees? Wait, I have an idea. . . Do you know what my father used to do? He used to slice across the ankles of the wretches we were hunting. He'd cut them and leave them in the trees. He'd give them an hour to try to escape. Rohese abolished it, saying it gave the dogs an unfair advantage but it might be time to bring it back."

She bends over, her Tallithi medallion falling into my face, the piper and the three stars above him all I can see as

293

she whispers her next threat in my ear.

"I look forward to watching you both crawl."

She stands and wheels from the room. "Take her down," she calls behind her.

I cry out, my voice strangled, as the guards step forward and lift me roughly to my feet, their thick gloves chafing my skin. My legs are too weak to hold me and they have to half carry, half drag me out of the room and down the stairs.

The hallways are lined with courtiers, lords and ladies and even pages and servants, all witness to my fall. They say nothing, no jeers or recriminations; no one spits at me. They simply watch like silent sentinels as I am taken down into the lower level, through the barracks, to the dungeons.

The guards push me inside a small dank cell and I fall against the rotten rushes that coat the ground. As the door clangs shut behind me and the key turns with finality in the lock, my mouth falls open and I scream silently; my breath leaves my body with force as I clutch at the straw and pound at the floor beneath it. There is nothing but fear and pain and loss as I fall apart in the darkness.

There is little light in the dungeon; the only source is the weak glare from a torch in the passageway. And it is silent, save for the occasional drip of water from the vaulted ceiling. There are no screams, not even my own; I sit with my fist in my mouth to stop myself from crying out.

I can't see a guard posted so I call softly through the iron bars of the door. "Lief? Lief, are you here?"

I smell it a second before it moves, the cell filling with the odour of the grave as instinct drives me back against the wall. Silhouetted between the bars, a shape appears: long, muscled legs, a flat head that turns towards me, too many teeth gleaming as a mouth opens. As I press against the cold stone, bathed in my own sweat, it lunges towards the bars and I can't help the harsh scream I make. A metallic clang resonates around the cell as the creature hits the door; it whimpers, straining briefly against the chain I can now see around its neck. It stares at me through the bars with those soulless and empty eyes, before it turns and slinks away. It can afford to be patient. I am captive prey. I listen over the sound of my blood rushing in my ears as it settles back down in some dank corner and I bunch my fist back into my mouth to stop from screaming again.

I stare into the darkness, my ears straining for movement. As quietly as I can I brush my other hand through the damp rushes, my skin crawling at the feeling of their putrid stickiness against my skin. When a piece breaks off and embeds itself under my thumbnail, I nearly cry out again; only a timely grunt from the hound silences me. I remain frozen for what feels like an age before I pull the piece out and begin to search again through handful after handful of rotten rushes, trying to find something I can use as a weapon. As panic threatens to overtake me again I force myself to be calm. It cannot get to me through the bars; though that doesn't quell the fear that someone could let it in, if they chose to.

Defeated, I lean against the wall and my thoughts turn back to Lief, held somewhere, my heart stuttering again when I realize he may be unconscious or dying from the blows the guards dealt him. I hope he is, if they do the things to prisoners that my guard told me they did. I couldn't bear to hear him make that sound. I don't want him to become a scream. He'd be better off dead.

Which he might already be, I realize. Because of me.

Choice. For years I've craved it, idealized it as a dream I can never have and, though it pains me to admit it, the queen is right. I have had choices, but because I didn't like them I didn't acknowledge them. I've been the agent of my own misery, time and again. And now I've dragged Lief down with me. I replay the queen leaning over me, the image of the piper on her medallion seared on my brain as she tells me she looks forward to watching us both crawl.

Left with my thoughts in the dark, a strange calm fills me, despite the musk of the hound. My tears dry and my heart slows to a steady pace. This time tomorrow I will be no more. All that I am and ever have been will be gone. Will Lief's wraith and mine meet in the West Woods and drift together through the trees? Will there be enough of us left to know each other? I wonder if my mother will be sad to hear I am gone. I wonder how much it will hurt to die. Lief's tale of the Sleeping Prince plays through my mind. The queen's dogs will tear out my heart like the Sleeping Prince supposedly does. I don't blame Lief's mother at all for not telling him the whole sorry tale. The Sleeping Prince. For some reason I keep

296

coming back to the tale, to the Bringer and his calling away of a girl for his father, and I think of the girls who have died so he might wake. Girls like me, called from their homes and taken to a ruined castle to feed a monster. I was called from my home to a beautiful castle to be a puppet for a monster. And even though I don't believe in the Gods any more, I find myself praying to them.

Slumped on the floor I begin to doze, my thoughts becoming muddled as Sleeping Princes and hounds and Gods all take turns to laugh at me in my dreams. I see a white-haired man wearing a crown bowing to a Goddess shrouded in black. I see a God with a pipe at his lips, playing as dogs snap at his heels and shooting stars fall above him. Then I am wide awake, sitting bolt upright and staring at the walls of my cell.

At the first hunt after Merek's return he asked his mother about the medallion she wore; the coin he'd brought her from Tallith. He said it had a piper on it and she told him she'd filed the image away to make it Lormerian. But I saw him on her medallion. Not filed away, but there in my face: a piper, with three shooting stars in the sky above him. What was it Lief said about the solaris in the sky? What are the solaris? I never thought to ask. Is it possible they're shooting stars?

Then my blood turns to ice.

Not shooting stars. Comets. I saw comets the night Dorin died, three of them burning in the dark skies. Three comets. Three stars on the medallion.

The next day, the day of the hunt, Dimia and I heard

music in the courtyard, music Lief couldn't hear. Music from a pipe.

The last time we saw Dimia before she left.

Did Dimia leave because of the music? Did she follow the Bringer?

Lief told me that one of the old versions of the story said the Sleeping Prince could be awoken for ever if the Bringer brought him a girl while the solaris were in the sky. And that the Bringer could be summoned by the totem, if someone had it and knew it for what it was. The queen has a pendant with a piper on it; a piper who wasn't there before but is most definitely there now, with his halo of comets.

The pendant is the totem; it has to be.

The queen summoned the Bringer.

Chapter 22

I rise, pacing the cell, my gown trailing through the dried rushes and making an eerie rustling. The hound strains at his chain when he hears the movement but I can't bring myself to care about it, not in the face of this.

Certainty settles in my stomach, the weight of it comforting, even as my skin prickles. She summoned the Bringer and he came. That is why she had the castle emptied; she thought I was still banished to my tower so I was out of the way. She summoned him when she knew the comets would be in the sky. She has people who track celestial events; people who track Næht and Dæg's paths across the skies. So she arranged a hunt to get the men away and took her ladies to safety, leaving only the servants at the Bringer's mercy.

My hand rises to my mouth to trap my moan inside. Dimia is dead. Poor, harmless Dimia. But worse than that, if the version that says the Sleeping Prince can be awakened when the solaris ride the skies is true, then the Sleeping Prince is awake for good. But why? Why would she want him? It's Merek she wants, not the heir to the Tallithi throne.

I cross the cell, ignoring the dog as he almost strangles himself in a bid to get at me. "Merek!" I scream, pounding the iron bars with my fists and, when that hurts too much to bear, the flat of my palms. "Merek! Fetch the prince – the king! Please! Hello? Merek?" I call and call until my throat is hoarse and my hands throb with pain. No one answers me. I don't know if anyone is even down here with me. The dog has long since abandoned his attempts at attack; instead he watches me with eyes that tell me it's too late. In despair I sink back to the floor, curling in on myself, shivering, though not from the cold.

I must have slept, because when I open my eyes, Merek stands before me, alone, watching me through the bars. The hound sits quietly by his side, its chain now held loosely in Merek's hand. I didn't hear either of them moving and that chills me more than Merek's blank gaze. We remain in silence, my mouth dry with terror that he might open the door and let the beast in. When he walks out of my sight my stomach drops, before he reappears without the dog.

"You were calling for me," he says flatly.

I stand, my limbs cramped and tight from the stone floor. "Merek – Your Majesty – the queen has summoned the Bringer." I'm surprised by how calm my voice sounds.

He raises one eyebrow. "Pardon?"

"The queen has summoned the Bringer, from Tallith. The son of the Sleeping Prince. She summoned him and he took one of the maids – Dimia – the maid you sent to find me the day Dorin died. She's been taken by the Bringer. It means the Sleeping Prince is awake."

"I never had you down as the type to make a plea of insanity," he says sadly.

"I'm not! You have to listen to me – the medallion you gave the queen, the Tallithi coin, it was blank at the hunt, you remember? You asked whether she'd filed the piper and the stars away and she said she had. But it's not blank any more; the image is there now. I saw it when she found me, and the piper is on it."

Merek looks away, his expression disgusted. "What is this, Twylla?"

"She summoned the piper! The night before the last hunt there were comets in the sky. The solaris. The story says that if the Bringer is summoned when they are in the sky then the heart the Sleeping Prince eats will awaken him. She summoned him, emptied all of the castle, and he came and took Dimia away. She's woken the prince."

"And you summoned me for that? To tell me a children's story is coming true? For the love of the Gods, Twylla, have you not done enough? Am I not suffering enough? I have lost my stepfather to poison and my bride-to-be has – was. . . I did not come down here for this."

"Then why did you come?" I say hotly.

"I thought you. . . I thought you had an explanation. I thought you wanted to help me understand."

Unexpectedly I feel my eyes sting with tears. When I look at him closely I can see how much older he looks, how tired. And I realize he came here because he wanted an explanation he could believe. He wants to forgive me, even now.

"Mer— Your Majesty, I am sorry. Of all the things I wanted, hurting you was never amongst them," I say softly.

He dips his head in acknowledgement. "I want to know when it started."

"The day before the last Telling," I say softly. "On the day of the hunt."

"Do you love him?"

"Yes," I whisper.

He blinks, his lips pursed. Slowly, he sinks to the floor, sitting in front of my cell, his legs crossed before him like a boy. For a moment I feel as though I am the one granting him forgiveness. I can feel the weight of my old life around me; the Sin Eater's daughter, the granter of peace and absolution.

"I would still marry you." He cannot look at me as he says it, staring instead at his ankles. "If we say that he forced you, that he made you—" He stops.

I sit down too and reach between the bars to take his hand, again feeling as though it is him atoning, not me. When he doesn't flinch or pull away, I begin to speak. "Merek, he didn't," I say as gently as I can.

"The court doesn't have to know that," he says quickly. "At the trial you could say he attacked you. If you say that, I can pardon you and we can marry and put this behind us."

"And if I refuse?"

"Then you will be tried for treason and sentenced to death."

"Marry you or die? How I am supposed to answer that?"

"Say you'll marry me." The ghost of a smile haunts the corner of his mouth.

"Oh, Merek," I say, forgetting myself. "You don't deserve to live like that. You don't deserve a bride who married you to save her skin after she'd wronged you."

"I know I don't, but that is the bride I want. You're the bride I always wanted," he says, and he looks so sad that the "yes" has formed on my tongue before he's finished speaking.

But I can't and he sees it in my eyes.

"You'll be charged with adultery, for breaking the betrothal," he says, without looking at me. "It's treason, because I'm a prince. The guard is to be tried for high treason, regicide."

"Regicide? But he didn't kill the king; you know he didn't! It was her, you said—"

Merek shouts across me. "Do you think I care? Do you honestly think I care what the reason they give for his death is?"

"But she'll get away with it. And she'll marry you when she's killed Lief and me. And the treaty with Tregellan—"

And that's when the full extent of the queen's plan hits me.

"Merek, you have to listen to me. She summoned the Bringer and poisoned the king to get to the Sleeping Prince:

the last member of the Tallithi royal family. She wants her own alchemist. She means to bring him and force him to make gold for her so when she executes Lief and breaks the treaty with Tregellan, she'll have gold to finance a war. You heard her in the solar; she said a Tregellian killing the king was an act of war and you said Lormere could not afford one. But it can with an alchemist to finance it. Merek, she's planned it all! She's raised him to be her own pet alchemist. Ask Dimia's brother – she has a brother – Taul! His name is Taul! He'll tell you he doesn't know where she is! Would she leave the castle without telling her brother?" As I say it I know it's true; I feel the rightness of what I'm saying settling into my bones.

"Enough, Twylla." He rises and turns to leave.

"Merek, please! Listen to me!"

He looks back at me, his mouth tight with anger. "I've heard enough," he says. "Your trial is at dawn tomorrow. Make your peace with whatever it is you hold dear." He dips his head once and turns, leaving me kneeling on the floor. I wait until I'm sure he's gone before I allow my tears to fall.

Time moves on and without the sun I have no idea that dawn approaches until footsteps come towards my cell. I shake myself out of my daze and stand, gripping the bars. I take a sharp breath when two guards approach the cell in uniform step, one bearing a blazing torch and the other the keys. The cell door is thrown open and one of the guards motions for me to leave.

I do, stepping forward slowly. I've thought all night and I know what I must do. I have to tell the court what the queen's plan is. Even if it doesn't save me, I have to tell them. With luck someone will listen and maybe then she can be stopped. The guards draw my arms behind my back and secure them. And before I can stop them they gag me, tying a filthy piece of fabric over my mouth. I struggle and try to scream but the gag does its job and all I can manage are muffled shrieks that no one will be able to decipher. They pull me roughly by the elbow, though they make sure to keep their hands away from my bare skin and I wonder if the queen plans to keep up the deception about Daunen until the last

They lead me from the cell, out of the dungeons, towards the Great Hall. The light outside is dim, dawn light, and my heart thuds violently beneath my ribs. Everything is lost.

The doors to the Great Hall are thrown open as we approach and I'm pulled inside. As with Lady Lorelle's trial, the benches are arranged in rows, all facing the dais, where the queen and Merek sit. The queen is doing her best to look grim, but the sparkle in her eyes gives her away. Beside her Merek looks like a man with nothing left to live for, his ceremonial sash askew on his shoulder so it sits awkwardly on his chest, his hair a manic halo around his wretched face. I wonder what he will do once Lief and I are gone and the queen's plan is fully under way.

As I'm forced to stand before the dais I hear the sound of a struggle behind me and I turn to see Lief being dragged in. He is gagged too and above the gag his eyes are blackened and swollen. It seems as though he can barely stand after the beating he took and I move towards him. A guard pulls me back and I can only watch as Lief struggles to right himself when his guards release him.

"A sad day for Lormere," the queen says, looking anything but sad. "I am no stranger to sadness. In my life I have seen a daughter and now two husbands go to their eternal rest before me. And yet none of those losses compares with the devastation I felt when I discovered the girl we called Daunen Embodied in bed with her guard."

Lief looks at me, his eyes full of sorrow as the court explodes.

"How?" one voice calls as another screams "The Gods!" at us. "Daunen!" someone wails and it's echoed, "Daunen, Daunen, Daunen," until I can't bear it.

The queen shoots me a triumphant glance before raising her voice to speak over the outcry. "I know it wounds deeply to know we have been taken in by an imposter; I know it is hard to learn of such a diabolical betrayal but hear it we must. Bear witness we must. Because I found the pair of them, naked, in her room mere hours after the king's funeral. She is guilty of adultery; she has betrayed the prince and all of you. All of us. But there is worse than that. Because the man she was sleeping with is the man who killed the king!"

A low rumble fills the room like thunder as the courtiers begin to talk amongst themselves, and I shake my head, trying to knock the gag loose so I can tell them the truth.

"You saw the king collapse at the feast. He was poisoned. He died, in agony, hours later. Because that man, that Tregellian –" she points at Lief "– poisoned him. He is a spy sent from Tregellan and had I not discovered him in bed with Twylla, I've no doubts he would have poisoned me and the prince too. He must have used his wicked knowledge to find a way to use her without succumbing to the poison. They have those skills, the Tregellians. And though it pains me to say it, I cannot be sure the girl was not involved with his scheme. That she did not encourage him in his evils and offer herself as payment for it if he could achieve both antidote and murder."

Lief makes no sound, staring at the queen with undisguised hatred, and I know he's making it worse by not even attempting to struggle. So I do it for him, screaming into my gag, trying to pull away from the guards.

Merek, who until now has stared resolutely at the door, slams his hand down on the table, silencing both the still-buzzing court and me.

"Twylla, is now really the time for theatrics?" he says slowly, his eyes fixed on mine.

Theatrics.

What was it he said after I'd sung for his stepfather?

How nice to spend an afternoon without theatrics, don't you think?

I look at him and he pushes his sash aside, revealing a small golden flower at his breast. A dandelion. So that is why the sash hung strangely; he was trying to hide it. He

307

blinks at me, firmly, and then I know.

He believed me after all.

"This is a trial," Merek continues. "Not a performance. And as such we will conduct ourselves properly. Send in the first witness," he says and the queen's face falls.

"The what?"

"The first witness. I have summoned a Tregellian physician here to share his expertise. I will not have anyone say that my first trial as king was unjust. I can be merciful."

Behind my gag I smile.

"Absolutely not!" The queen stands. "He'll be bound to defend his countryman. They are all in league against Lormere. Merek, I will not have it."

Lief turns to look at me, a bewildered expression in his eyes. Behind me the court is fidgeting impatiently and the queen hears it too. She tries to cow them with a look but there's an undercurrent of doubt now and she knows it. She sighs loudly.

"Fine," she says. "Bring your witness. Bear in mind," she says to the court, "that the witness will not be unbiased."

The guards throw open the doors and usher in a small man, dark-skinned with short black hair. He bows to the queen and Merek and looks studiously away from Lief and me.

"Physician, I have no body for you to examine, but every soul in this room saw my stepfather collapse. He later died. I would tell you his symptoms and I want you to tell the court your diagnosis based on them. Can you do that?"

308

"Yes, Your Highness," the physician says.

"My stepfather had a sudden weakness in his legs. He lost control of his limbs and could not walk nor stand unaided. This weakness spread across his body, eventually leaving him unable to talk. He died not long afterwards."

The physician clears his throat and nods before speaking. "Your Highness, it sounds to me as though His late Majesty had an incident in his brain." The queen leans forward and the physician takes a step back. "The flow of blood to the brain can be interrupted and this interruption prevents a man from using his limbs. He may try but his body will not obey. Eventually he will die as his blood cannot flow where it is needed."

"And how does this malady occur?" Merek asks.

"Naturally," the physician says and the court all draw in their breath as one. "It can happen to anyone, at any time."

"Lies!" the queen shrieks. "It was poison!"

"I doubt he's mistaken, Mother. He is a physician. So you rule it was a natural death?" Merek turns back to the pale Tregellian man.

"I do, Your Majesty."

"Then I accept your expert diagnosis."

"This is absurd," the queen seethes. "The Tregellian poison musquash root causes paralysis of the nerves and then asphyxiation. A mere six to eight leaves is enough to fell a grown man. That Tregellian –" she points at Lief "– used it on the king, and that one –" she gestures to the physician "– is trying to cover it up."

"How do you know what musquash root is, Mother?" Merek says quietly. The hall stills. "Where did you learn so precisely that it causes paralysis and asphyxiation? Odd words to use, for someone with no vocation in medicine?"

He's trapped her.

The queen pauses for a beat too long before she answers. "The herbalist, Rulf, showed me a passage in one of his books. I consulted him on it, with my fears, and he confirmed them. That's where the language comes from, of course. I was quoting directly."

"Show me your pendant."

"What?"

"Show me, and the court, your pendant."

"Merek, now is not the time for—" Merek leans and snatches at the chain, forcing the pendant out from where it was tucked inside her bodice. The queen tries to pull away but Merek doesn't let go and she is forced to stand still, the chain digging into the white flesh of her neck as her son examines the round medallion.

"At the hunt, when I returned, you told me you'd filed this off to make it look more Lormerian." He holds it up and I can see the piper. "Then Lord Bennel asked if I'd found the Sleeping Prince. A short while later you had Lord Bennel killed, ostensibly for insulting Twylla. Was that it, Mother? Or was it his reminding us all of the Sleeping Prince that angered you?"

"What is this?" the queen hisses. "Have you taken leave of your senses?" She jerks away from him and Merek finally releases the medallion, watching coldly as it lands against her gown.

"I have dispatched a party to Tallith. They should be back within a ha'moon and they will tell me whether the body of a maid lies beside an abandoned bier in the remains of Tallith Castle. I have also alerted my own guard to seal my castle and to tell me if a bedraggled creature in ancient dress tries to gain access to seek out his mistress. The mute apothecary you keep under the castle has been taken for questioning and your rooms are being searched now. I call my second witness, the Lady Twylla." He turns to the court.

The courtiers don't bother to remain calm and I hear scrapes behind me as people knock the benches askew when they jump to their feet to look at me, the accused turned witness. The guard who holds me pulls the gag from my mouth. He has the same heart-shaped face that Dimia had. Taul.

I feel the weight of the gaze of everyone in the room.

"Twylla, if you'd be so good as to tell the court what it is you discovered," Merek says.

The queen looks close to amusement and I speak loudly and clearly, my singer's voice ringing through the room.

"You summoned the Bringer." I look at the queen, watching for the moment my words will wipe the smirk from her face. "The necklace you wear is his totem and on the night the solaris rode the skies you called him. The following day you drew everyone away from the castle so he could do his work. I heard the music. I saw a maid bespelled by it." Her jaw twitches and I continue, speaking slowly, pushing every word towards her like a knife. "On the night the prince announced he and I were to be wed you poisoned the king and tried to frame my guard in order to start a war with Tregellan. You want the Sleeping Prince to be your pet alchemist and make you the gold you need for your war. For the new Golden Age of Lormere." I leave out the part about her wanting to marry Merek and he shoots me a grateful look.

The court remains deadly silent once I've finished. It was better than singing.

Then the queen speaks. "Do you honestly expect the court to believe the childish stories of a whore? This is a fairy tale. The whole realm knows The Sleeping Prince is a fairy tale."

"And Daunen Embodied?" I counter. "Do they know that is a fairy tale?"

I sense the court sit even further upright, tensed.

"Blasphemy," the queen hisses.

"There is no Morningsbane. There is no Telling. I have killed no one," I say finally. "It was all invented by you. You know it; Merek knows it; Rulf knows it. Tyrek died for it. Lief made no antidote for the Morningsbane because it does not exist. I am not, and never have been, poisonous. It's all a lie and it always has been. Admit it."

The volume of the court's howls of anger and fury is astonishing, but even above it the queen's screams can be heard. "You are raving. You might have bewitched my son, but you can't fool them all. My people—" The queen is cut off as a guard – the same one who announced that the king had died – rushes into the hall with a small glass vial. The room falls silent, the atmosphere pregnant and treacherous.

"Forgive me, Sire." He ignores the queen and skids to a halt in front of Merek. "This was discovered in the queen's wardrobe, in her jewellery box." He holds a small glass vial, identical to the one I would drink from at the Telling.

Merek nods for him to hand it to the nervous physician, who takes one sniff and looks at Merek.

"Musquash root, Your Majesty. Suspended in grain liquor."

"It was planted!" The queen rises to her feet. "You are trying to depose me, you and the whore. Arrest the prince!" she screams. But the guards do not move.

"I do not need to depose you. Your husband is dead; you cannot hold the throne without a king. You should have thought of that before you killed him." Merek looks at his court. "I charge the former queen with treason against the throne of Lormere – my throne," Merek adds calmly. "Do any oppose the charges? Can anyone offer proof of her innocence?"

The queen is frozen beside Merek. She stares at us, her fists clenched, and there is a moment when I am sure she will try to run but then she straightens her fingers and smoothes her gown. Her eyes harden and she looks at Merek.

"And how will you rule without a queen? You cannot hold the throne alone either. Unless. . ." She shoots a sly, vicious look at me. "Unless you plan to pardon the harlot and marry her still?"

"She has committed no crime," Merek says, his voice only cracking slightly. "I am the regent of Lormere now, if nothing else, and I acknowledge no crime was committed against the throne."

The queen arches an eyebrow. "So you do still want her? Even though I saw her coiled around him like a snake as he—"

"Silence!" Merek screams.

The queen looks at him, her eyebrows raised. "You will apologize to me, Merek. For all of this, for your tantrum and your cruel words and your wicked plan."

"I won't," Merek says, his voice odd, distant.

The queen smiles at him fondly. "You need me, Merek," she says. "The Sleeping Prince is coming. You need me to control him. I have the totem. Without it who knows what he'll do?"

Merek looks at her – the whole court looks at her – and I see him falter.

"The totem summons the Bringer," I say, only half sure what I'm saying is true. "It has nothing to do with the Sleeping Prince other than that. It won't control him."

"Don't you dare talk to me." She spins around to look down at me, and I take a step back. But my words were enough to bring Merek back to himself and once again he reaches for the necklace, this time tugging it sharply so the chain snaps. They both watch the medallion dangling in

Merek's hand, both of them wide-eyed at Merek's actions.

"Now I have the totem," Merek says. "So if it has any effect on him, I will be the one to wield it. I will be the one who talks to him."

"He'll slaughter you!" The queen laughs manically. "Do you think you can negotiate with him? You think because you sat down for dinner with the council in Tregellan you'll be able to talk with the Sleeping Prince? He's been asleep for five hundred years. He's woken to nothing! Everything he knew is gone: his family, his kingdom. He won't sit down and share a cup of wine with you, you stupid boy! You haven't a clue how to run a kingdom, let alone defend it from a monster. You need me."

"No," Merek says, his voice dead. "All I need from you is for you to be gone from my presence. From my castle. From my life. I sentence you to hang by the neck until you are dead."

The words ring around and around the room.

The smile slides from the queen's face like hot butter from a knife. "What?"

"The penalty for treason is death. You know that." Merek does not look at her as he speaks.

"You can't hang me; I'm the queen."

"No. My wife will be the queen. And you will not be my wife. You are a traitor."

"I'm your mother."

The court sits in utter silence watching this exchange and Lief and I stand still, watching them. The guard who held me has let me go and when I turn my head I can see others have appeared at the doors. Waiting.

"You have until my men return with the body of the girl to make your peace with yourself. Once they return your time is over. Take her to the cells," he orders the guards. They step forward, all of them eager to be the one to secure her and I'm glad when it's Taul who pulls her hands behind her back. She is a statue again, putting up no resistance as they take her from the dais. She doesn't move her eyes from Merek's face, even as he resolutely turns away.

"Release the lady's hands and the guard's," Merek says.

"Wait!" the queen shouts as my wrists are unbound. We all turn to look at her, to see her planted in the doorway of the Great Hall, her eyes blazing. "I'm not the only villain of the piece, am I, Lief? Tell Twylla how you came to be here, why don't you?"

"Get her out of my sight," Merek commands and the guards drag the queen away, her deranged laughter ringing in my ears.

I turn to Lief in confusion and the bottom falls out of the world. He is so pale that his bruises shine against the pallor of his skin. He does not look like a man who has been reprieved. He looks like a man who has been forsaken and condemned.

"What does she mean?" I ask him.

He stares at the floor and inside my chest I feel a sharp pain that I know is the beginning of heartbreak.

Chapter 23

"Out!" Merek turns to the court. "All of you, leave us."

"What does she mean?" I ask Lief again but he won't look at me. I take a step forward and then Merek is moving, leaping from the dais to stop me from getting to Lief. He holds me until the room is emptied of all but us three, the doors closing us in.

Merek looks at Lief. "What did my mother mean, guard? What have you done? Did you help her summon the Bringer? Did you help her to poison my stepfather? Is there some truth in her claims a Tregellian did it?"

"No," he says quietly. "No, I swear I had nothing to do with that. With the king or the Sleeping Prince."

"Then what, Lief?" I say. "What does she mean?"

He shakes his head and Merek looks at him.

"Either you can tell us or I'll drag her back here to tell

us," he says harshly. "But one way or the other we will know."

Lief closes his eyes and it seems to me that all three of us hold our breath. "I was working for the queen."

"But I knew that – she hired you to guard me," I say stupidly.

"No, Twylla. I was hired, by her, to seduce you. So you couldn't marry the prince."

As when Tyrek died, all the sound and colour is gone, leaving only his words: "I was hired, by her, to seduce you." Over and over they run through my head, the sense of them jumbling, and then Merek's arms are around me and he's holding me as my knees give way beneath me. I right myself, keeping one hand on Merek's arm as I look back at Lief, the man I love.

"She hired you to seduce me?"

He nods, once. "To make sure the prince couldn't marry you."

"I don't understand," I say quietly.

Lief takes a deep breath and looks at me. "I told you I was a farmer's boy; that's true, I am, and my father is dead. But my great-grandfather wasn't from farming stock. He was the captain of the Tregellian army and my family lived at the castle as courtiers under our then king. Until the war. He was killed because of the Lormerian war."

My eyes widen as he speaks.

"After the war, the people revolted. They blamed the king and what was left of his army for their losses and they rioted. The mob captured the royal family and their supporters. Including my great-grandfather. They were beheaded, every last one of them, and my great-grandmother had to flee for her and her son's lives, lest they suffer the same fate. She had to lie about who she was in order to keep my grandfather safe. She married a farmer, well beneath her station as a lady of the court, but what choice did she have? They had no children so the farm went to my grandfather, then my father. All because of Lormere."

"I don't understand," I say slowly and Merek tightens his grip on me. Lief looks at a spot to my left, no longer able to meet my gaze.

"When my father died, we had nothing. My mother lives in a hovel at the end of the world and my sister can't leave the house because the people who live there. . ." He pauses and swallows. "It's Lormere's fault. Were it not for your queen and her family, I'd have been brought up in a court too. I would have been a scholar, instead of learning to read in secret. Had it not been for Lormere, there would have been no uprising. I'd be like him." He jerks his head at Merek. "So I came here to rob the castle. I planned to break in and take everything I could, then take it home and sell it. Put us back where we should be, at least part of the way."

His eyes flicker back to me briefly before dropping to the floor. His fingers fidget by his sides.

"I wanted the money. Enough to get the farm back, to get us back on our feet. But I got caught and thrown in the dungeon. I thought I was done for – a Tregellian caught stealing from the castle. But then your queen came to see

319

me. I suppose someone must have reported me to her. She offered to free me, and to pay me a lot of money if I could get rid of you. All I had to do was to get you to fall in love with me and convince you to leave with me. To leave him. And I agreed. The queen reassigned your other guard and then a trial was staged and I won." He shrugs arrogantly. "I'd have gold and revenge on Lormere, with the queen's own help."

I hold up my hand to stop him from continuing. "This can't be true."

Lief screws up his face. "I was supposed to convince you to leave and once you agreed I'd tell them when and where to catch us. You'd be disgraced and sent away and I'd be paid. But I saw the way the prince looked at you and I knew he'd forgive you, find a way to make you stay. He'd win; his kind always do. But he might not want you if . . . if you weren't a maid. If you weren't pure, if someone else had beaten him to it. If a commoner had had you first."

I run from the room, propelled by some instinct of self-preservation, sickened by what he has said. I race blindly down the hall, collapsing, helpless to prevent the churning inside me, shaking as I heave, spitting on to the floor.

A cool hand rests on the back of my neck and for the first time I appreciate Merek's cold skin, soothing the fire that rages inside me. Lief used me. He said he loved me and he shared my bed and all the while he was planning for this, to break the royal family and get his revenge.

I sit back, and Merek looks at me, gently wiping my

mouth with the sleeve of his tunic. My eyes stream from the force of my retching and he wipes the tears away too.

"I owe you a great debt of thanks," he says quietly. "All of Lormere does. I'm sorry I let you think I didn't believe you, but there were guards waiting for me around the corner in the dungeon. I didn't know where their loyalties lay so I had to make it appear that I thought you were lying. One of them was Taul and he confirmed what you'd said about his sister. At supper I saw my mother's necklace and it was as you said. So I sent for the physician I'd hoped would get here in time for Dorin. I knew she must have hidden the poison somewhere, so I arrested the mute – it must have been him who got the poison for her. As she prepared for the trial, my men went in to search her rooms. I'm sorry I couldn't tell you. But I needed her to trip herself up in front of everyone, where she couldn't deny it, or murder her way out of it."

"He lied to me," I say, ignoring everything that Merek has said.

"I had no idea about your guard. I'm so sorry."

"Dorin," I say. "If he had not been stung, it would never have come to pass. He would never have let Lief near me."

"Twylla . . . I'm not sure he did die of a bee sting."

"What do you mean?"

"I can't be sure, but I suspect strongly he was poisoned too. By her. To push you into Lief's arms. When I discovered he was dying, one of the healers said there had been a time when he was rallying and they felt sure he'd recover. And then he went downhill, rapidly. I didn't want to tell you at the time. It seemed pointless. But now I believe she had him poisoned."

Something inside me turns to ice, to iron. It's so clever.

"If she'd reassigned Dorin I would have been shaken," I say, my voice sounding as though it comes from far away. "I would have trusted no one. I would never have let my guard down. But if he were ill and Lief offered a shoulder to cry on . . . because I thought he trusted Lief, I also trusted Lief."

"What would you have me do?" Merek asks and I look at him. "What will make you happy?"

"Her body burning where I can watch it."

Merek's jaw drops.

"I mean it. She's raised the almost-dead to try to start a war. She's killed my guard and your stepfather and countless, countless others. She's insane."

Merek looks at me as though I'm a stranger. "But don't hang her," I continue. "Give her a dose of that musquash. I want her to know she's dying."

"You don't mean this?"

"Oh, Merek, I do. I really do."

And I do. For the first time in my life I want someone dead and I want her to suffer. But no matter how much she suffers she will never, ever suffer enough for what she has done to Dorin, to Merek. To me.

"Why?" I ask him. "Why would she go to such lengths? Why not give me to the Bringer and get rid of me that way?"

"How could she? She'd trapped herself. She'd spent years telling the kingdom you were its saviour and the emblem of faith, sent especially to be my bride – the hope of Lormere. If you'd been taken the people would have rioted, gone out to find you. I would have gone to find you. She made you too meaningful. She made you too important to kill."

I think of the poor king, not important enough despite his title and bloodline. "So she chose to discredit me? To ruin my reputation?"

Merek nods. "I told you the people need something to believe in. They have to put their faith somewhere and they put it in you. She had to take that faith away to eliminate you from her plans. If you'd died at any point, no matter the circumstance, then people would have thought Lormere cursed and forsaken and the country would have fallen apart. Using the Gods to control the population works both ways. But if it emerged you weren't truly Daunen, if it turned out the Gods had forsaken you, then she could get rid of you. She could have sweetened the blow with news of Lormere's new-found alchemy and thrown you to the wolves."

I nod, barely able to keep up with him.

Merek continues. "I told you that she asked me to bring back everything I could find from Tallith. I suspected she wanted alchemic knowledge. I thought she'd try to force scholars here to learn it. I didn't see the harm in it; I told you I wanted that knowledge too. But fool that I was, I brought her back everything I could find, including the totem. She must have been hoping for that; much better to summon an alchemist than try to decipher the ways of alchemy. Then all she needed to do was get rid of my stepfather, blame

323

Tregellan, marry me and secure the bloodline, and she could use the Sleeping Prince to make her gold."

I wrap my arms around myself, as though that's the only way I'll be able to keep myself from unravelling completely.

"What shall I do with the guard?" Merek says softly. "He's still committed treason. You're obviously the innocent party in all of this."

But that isn't true. I'd taken Lief to my bed after I'd been in the Hall of Glass with Merek. I tell him as such.

He swallows, but shakes his head. "You are not accountable for this. You have been a pawn in a game. But I will take your lead, and if you want to execute him too I will sanction it."

No. The thought is immediate and consuming. I can't see him dead. I know what he's done – he told me in his own words – but despite it all, I don't wish him dead and I don't hate him.

Because I still don't believe him. Try as I might, I can't. My heart is screaming at me that he's lying, that he couldn't. . .

"What good would executing him do?" I ask. "The damage is done."

Merek's jaw tightens. "It would be rightful punishment for his crimes. Unless . . . unless it were to emerge that he was not successful in his actions."

"What do you mean?"

"If it turns out he hasn't divided us. If we continue along the path we've been on these past four harvests. . ."

I smile sadly.

"I need you," he says. "The Sleeping Prince is coming. And she was right, I can't handle him alone. I needed you to help me stop my mother, I can't fight him without you."

"He might not want a war. He might want to understand what happened to him."

"Trust me when I tell you that no prince would rest if his castle were snatched from him. No man, even. Look to your guard, at what he did because he lost a farm. Imagine what he would have done if his whole kingdom was taken from him," he pauses. "We didn't exist when the Sleeping Prince was last awake; Lormere was a mere handful of hamlets in the mountains. Now look at us: towns, villages, a capital city and a castle. We thrive. We're everything Tallith once was. Can you honestly believe he won't try to take it? Won't think it's his right to take it? You heard my mother – I can only govern as regent without a queen. Lormere will need me to be a king. I need to be as he is. Be my queen, Twylla. Stay by my side and rule with me; help me keep Lormere safe."

"Merek, the people will accept you as the king, with or without me," I say, reaching for his hand. "What's happened here will be more than enough to convince them that the old ways have to change. The lords will stand behind you. The people will accept change if you're honest with them. Tell them the truth. Tell them he's coming and they must trust you to protect them."

"All of it? Even the truth about you, and Daunen?"

I think for a moment. "No. Let that die quietly. They don't deserve that." Colour spreads across his cheekbones and I squeeze his fingers briefly before I let go of his hand. "Be a good enough king that they won't need to pray to Gods. Don't fail them. Tell them you love them, and Lormere and you will always put them first. You don't need me for that."

"But I want you," he smiles at me. "Not just to make me a king. I've always wanted you. Despite it all, you are still the bride I would choose. I do choose you."

He is so earnest, so sincere. I would be good for him, to curb his temper and warm his coldness. He needs a queen he can talk to. He needs someone to love. I could be that woman and we could see what happens next for us. And if war does come then surely it would be better for us to face it together? Lormere is my home too.

I cup his cheek in my palm. "I would like," I say carefully, "to think on it. I would like to be able to come to you with a decision that is mine and mine alone, and not because I'm told what it will be, or because it allows me to take revenge on anyone, or prove them wrong. And not because of war. If I come to you, I want it to be because I am choosing you, for no reason other than that. I don't want for you to ever doubt it."

Though his face falls, he nods his agreement. "I have waited eleven years for you to save me," he says softly. "I can wait a little longer, I think."

Save him. He thought I would save him. The idea of being a heroine is so appealing that I'm about to tell him that I will marry him.

"So what shall we do with the guard?" he asks again, cutting across my thoughts.

"I'd like to talk to him. Then send him away. Banish him from Lormere. On pain of death should he ever return."

Merek takes my hand from his face and kisses the back of it. "You would make a good queen," he murmurs. "I'll be in the gardens when you have decided."

He helps me to my feet, checking my face and smoothing my hair before he allows me to go back into the Great Hall. I close the door behind me and turn to face Lief.

He still stands in front of the dais, his hands clasped before him, as though he's remained frozen since my flight from the room. I pause by the door and the two of us lock eyes across the room, assessing, competing for dominance. When I tire of the contest, I walk to a bench and sit down, waiting.

"I'm sorry," he says finally.

"What are you sorry for?"

"All of it."

I nod. "I didn't know she hated me that much."

He looks at the floor before speaking. "She didn't, at least not always. I think she hated herself."

Despite myself I look at him. "What do you mean?"

"She failed. She thought she was cursed, you know. First her daughter dying, then her husband. Then she couldn't have another child. All she wanted was to keep her throne and be the greatest queen Lormere had ever known. She hated herself for needing you."

I clench my teeth before I speak. "And did you know she planned to marry Merek in my stead? Did she tell you that when you hatched your scheme? Her own son? She planned to depose me to marry her son. And start a war with your country. With your people. Did she tell you that's what she'd do? Lief, she raised a monster from a story and now we're all at risk. What do we do when he comes? Did you think about that?"

"I didn't know about that. And I don't care what the mad royals of Lormere, or anywhere else, do," he says.

I stand and advance on him, my hands clawed at my sides. "What had I done to you to deserve it, Lief? What did I – me, Twylla – do to you to make you so determined to ruin me? Or was I to be a casualty of war?"

"I didn't know you when it started," he says.

"And now? Now you know me so intimately? By the Gods, Lief, I believed you!"

He looks at the floor, shaking his head.

"You've destroyed my world," I say to him. "Not the royal house of Lormere, but me. And you did it whilst pretending to love me."

"I didn't lie about that," he says hurriedly. "I didn't lie about loving you. Not in the end."

"You lie to me now!" I scream at him.

He starts towards me and I know that if he takes me in his arms, despite all of this, I will lose myself. I move swiftly and put a bench between us.

"I tried to tell you in the apothecary garden and couldn't. I have tried to tell you every day. If we'd got away I would have confessed then."

"How can you lie to my face?"

"I have come to love you," Lief pleads. "That much is

328

true now. If it wasn't always, it is now. I didn't start so well, but I didn't betray you in the end. I would have run with you. I wanted to. I came back for you, not for gold or for revenge, but for you."

"You dare—"

"It's true," he says swiftly. "I went back and forth with you. You would do something good and I would regret my deal with the queen and decide to break it. Then you would do something as you did to Dimia and I would find my resolve. But when I saw him kiss you in the Hall of Glass I realized that I loved you, truly loved you. And that all of the plans we'd made, I wanted them. With you."

"Oh, Gods." I clutch my stomach as it churns again at the memory. "That was all a lie. That was why you wouldn't run with me that first night! You needed to ruin me first. Ruin me and make sure she knew where to catch us."

"But I didn't because I fell in love with you! We were first together that afternoon and I said nothing! I could have betrayed you then and I did not. I would have run with you again when I returned. I was ready for that!"

"But you told her! She caught us! Oh, Gods!" I moan as I recall the guards that arrested us. They wore gloves, which meant they could touch me. They came there prepared to arrest me. Because of him. "You knew she was coming. You lay with me and you knew she would come and see us, find us naked like that. You shamed me."

"I did not do that! I had planned to leave you, leave the whole thing behind but I couldn't. I came back to take you away. I would have told you everything. I didn't know she would come. Please, Twylla, you must believe me."

"How can I believe anything you say? You lie; you have lied all along. The only thing you've not lied about is lying."

"But you love me, despite that. As I love you, despite everything. We could do this, Twylla. I know we haven't had the best start, but surely it's how we end that counts? Be with me?"

What big eyes he has, green like the starfire in the winter sky, and I turn away, unable to stand his gaze.

A noise in the corridor startles us both, and Lief takes his chance and darts around the table, reaching for me.

"Twylla, my Twylla. I will give you the rest of my life. It's yours, only yours. I will spend every hour of every day until the end of mine making up for the wrongs I have caused you. But I need you to let me. And if war is coming you won't be safe here; he can't keep you safe. I can and I will. Just forgive me. Let me prove myself to you."

No, he cannot do this to me. He cannot be sorry and ask for my forgiveness. Not now. For the first time in my life I am in a position to truly choose my fate. I have all the facts; nothing is concealed from me. I can control my destiny; I can choose what happens next. But what a choice, between the callous liar I foolishly love and the broken prince who thinks I can save him.

I look again into Lief's eyes.

Who will save me?

Epilogue

In the stories of old, a hero is the one who sweeps in with drawn sword and noble face, to kill the dragon and free the princess. In the stories of old it never seems to dawn on the princess that she should be careful not to put herself at the mercy of those who would do her ill in the first place.

I don't live in the stories of old.

When the fire burns low, and the light outside is not enough to read by, I add another log to the glowing embers in the small hearth. As the flames rise and lick greedily at the new fuel, I go to my small kitchen and prepare my supper, nothing fancy: bread and the creamy, salty Tregellian cheese they make here. I eat it slowly, smearing the cheese across the bread with one hand, using the other to hold my book open as I continue reading. When I've finished I move the crumb-laden platter distractedly to the hearth, only to pause as the light reflected in it catches my eye. I stare for a moment, watching the round metal plate turn from silver to gold in the firelight, reminding me of another time and sending a shiver down my spine. I move the platter away from the source and turn back to my story, shaking the past off. I've read all of the old stories now – "Red Blood and Dirty Gold", "The Winter Witch", "The Scarlet Varulv" – and I want more. Though I want fantasy – made-up, impossible things – I don't want stories that step out of the pages and into the world around me. I don't want anything like "The Sleeping Prince".

Merek said he'd write to me, and I promised I'd return if the Sleeping Prince ever arrived in Lormere, but months have passed and he hasn't sent word. Just in case, I pay close attention to news that occasionally trickles in to the village from Lormere, even though the tiny hamlet I now call home is as far from Lormere as you can be without being in Tallith. No one here knows who I am, or who I was, and that's how I want it to be. I'm a blank slate, tabula rasa.

I'm beginning to believe that the Sleeping Prince is finally dead; that the curse has been broken somehow and his story is finally over. I know it's wishful thinking, and a habit I should have abandoned, but each day that passes without news makes me a little looser, a little freer. A little happier.

Some of the other villagers have taken to inviting me to dine with them – they worry about me living here on my own – but for now it's too great a pleasure to stay in my own cottage, with my own books, and do exactly what I want to do. I've learned that being alone and being lonely are not the same thing. Once I was surrounded by people and lonely for it, but now I'm alone and I've never been so content. Lately I've noticed I'm humming all the time, a melody I've never heard before. A new song. One of my own. I must write down some of the words as they come to me.

I close the curtains on the outside world, smiling at my barren garden before it's gone from my sight. Come spring, there will be wild flowers.

I'm curled in my armchair, reading by the light of the fire and the few candles I've lit. My eyelids droop, from the heat and possibly even a little from the wine I've been sipping as I read. Finally I press my bookmark between the pages and put it down, deciding it's better to go to bed than wake in the morning with a stiff neck and a book jammed into my ribcage. I've taken a deep breath to blow out some of the candles when there's a knock at the door and I freeze.

I know that knock. For one bright, beautiful moon in another world I heard that sound every day. *Rap, tap-tap*. As familiar to me as the sound of my own voice.

I should feel dread, anger, hatred. That knock should be unwelcome.

But it's hope I feel as all thoughts of tiredness leave me and I open the door.

Acknowledgements

I hope you enjoyed reading this story. If you did, then you should know that all of the following people played a really large part in making it happen.

My agent, Claire Wilson, at Rogers, Coleridge and White. Thank you for everything. And I mean EVERYTHING. You are quite simply the best. I could use all the superlatives in the world and it still wouldn't come close to explaining how majestic you are. This wouldn't be happening without you. And you, Lexie Hamblin, you're pretty wonderful too. Thank you both.

Everyone at Scholastic UK, but especially my UK editor, Genevieve Herr. You championed this story (and me) from the start, so it's safe to say that none of this would have happened without you either. For that, and numerous other reasons, you're one of my favourites. As is Sam Selby Smith, for being so incredibly supportive, Emily Lamm, for such good editorial support, Jamie Gregory, for making me cry with the beautiful cover art, and Rachel Phillipps, my ever-patient publicist. Sorry and thanks.

Mallory Kass at Scholastic Inc. Having one editor who completely gets the story is brilliant; having two is an absolute dream. I don't know who sacrificed the goat to make this happen for me but thank you too. I am tremendously lucky. Thanks to everyone at Scholastic Inc. for your Team Lief/Team Merek debate. I long for T-shirts and badges. And maybe flags. Or bumper stickers.

Thanks to Robin Stevens, who told me that this story was worth telling when I thought it was the worst thing anyone had ever done. You were right. Again. I like being on this roller coaster with you.

Thanks to Liv Goldsmith, the very first person to have read this story and also the very first person to send me really harsh swear words about it. It made my Slappy Ham very happy.

Thanks to Jules Blewett-Grant, who has made room for me in her home, and her family, and her life, and who makes the best Yorkshire puddings ever.

Thanks to Emilie Lyons, my most dangerous friend and the James Potter to my Sirius Black. When I got my first proof copy of this book, Emilie came to Paris with me and we took it to the top of the Eiffel Tower and had champagne with it. She also dropped it in some Brie, but I've forgiven her for it.

Thanks to Jim Dean, for ruthlessly hunting down a proof

copy, loving it, and then raving about it. Often. I'm very glad I met you and even gladder than we're friends. Even though you're a Hufflepuff.

Thanks to all of my friends, you've all been wonderful, but particular thanks should go to Adam R., Alexia C., Alice O., Catherine D., Denise S., Emma G., Gary M., Lauren J., Nichole K., Pe M., Rainbow R., Sophie R., and Stine S., for your excitement, enthusiasm and encouragement, and for making me ugly laugh a lot. I'm fond of you. Shout out to Jeff Goldblum. Because he's Jeff Goldblum and that's reason enough.

If there is anyone I've forgotten, forgive me, I'll get you next time. That wasn't meant to sound like a threat.

If you didn't enjoy this story, feel free to blame all of these people. Mostly blame me, but that lot supported and encouraged me shamelessly.

A final note:

If you are familiar with the Victorian Language of Flowers, you might want to reread the parts of the book where flowers are mentioned and apply your knowledge.

Melinda Salisbury lives by the sea, somewhere in the south of England. As a child she genuinely thought Roald Dahl's *Matilda* was her biography, in part helped by her grandfather often mistakenly calling her Matilda, and the local library having a pretty cavalier attitude to the books she borrowed. Sadly she never manifested telekinetic powers. She likes to travel, and have adventures. She also likes medieval castles, non-medieval aquariums, Richard III, and all things Scandinavian. *The Sin Eater's Daughter* is her first novel.

She can be found on Twitter at **@AHintofMystery**, though be warned, she tweets often.